Praise for *Golfing with God*

"Amid the laughs and playful banter, *Golfing with God* is a serious story of self-examination and growth, the hardest games of all." —*The Washington Post Book World*

"Merullo weaves humor and humane theology into his engaging plot." —*The Boston Globe*

"Merullo writes such a graceful, compassionate and fluid prose that you cannot resist the characters' very real struggles and concerns. His prose is as wonderfully down-to-earth as his tale is heaven-sent." —*The Providence Sunday Journal*

"[A] delightful little book." —*The Cleveland Plain Dealer*

"*Golfing with God* salts its serious story of growth and self-examination with humor and telling insight. . . . Amid the lightness of this tale is the deeper story of a man, much like the rest of us, looking to shed his pride and dampen his urges." —*The Orlando Sentinel*

"A tender story and a clean slice of life, full of smart, clean prose." —*Milwaukee Journal Sentinel*

"Merullo's patient good humor makes the journey with Hank a surprisingly universal undertaking." —*The Sunday Seattle Post & Seattle Post-Intelligencer*

"Will appeal to fans of Alice Sebold and Mitch Albom. . . . Highly recommended."

—*Library Journal*, starred review

"An uplifting and humorous look at life and faith, a philosophical view of our role in this world and the next." —*The Southern Pines (NC) Pilot*

"Part spiritual, part philosophical and part sports drama. . . . An enjoyable and inspirational read for anyone, regardless of his or her handicap."

—*Macon Magazine*

"Great and memorable golf novels are the rarest of literary treats. In *Golfing with God,* Roland Merullo has pulled off a small miracle of economy and charm—a beautifully told tale that will have you in its otherworldly grasp from the opening page. . . . *Golfing with God* is the best golfing novel I've ever read."

—James Dodson, author of *Final Rounds*

"Merullo . . . writes with wit and subtlety rather than trying to pound inspiration into our heads with a titanium driver. And, best of all, he gets the golf right."

—*Booklist*

Golfing with God

Golfing
with
God

A NOVEL

by

Roland Merullo

ALGONQUIN BOOKS
OF CHAPEL HILL
2007

Published by
Algonquin Books of Chapel Hill
Post Office Box 2225
Chapel Hill, North Carolina 27515-2225

a division of
Workman Publishing
225 Varick Street
New York, New York 10014

This is a work of fiction. While, as in all fiction, the literary perceptions and insights are based on experience, all names, characters, places, and incidents are either products of the author's imagination or are used fictitiously.

Library of Congress Cataloging-in-Publication Data
Merullo, Roland.
    Golfing with God : a novel / by Roland Merullo.—1st ed.
      p. cm.
    ISBN-13: 978-1-56512-501-8 (HC)
    1. Golfers—Fiction. 2. Heaven—Fiction. 3. God—Fiction.
1. Title.
PS3563.E748G65 2005
813'.54—dc22   2005047844

ISBN-13: 978-1-56512-549-0 (PB)

For

Joe Merullo, A. J. Blasi, Ron Ferullo

And for Jeff and Lisa Forhan

excellent golfers and extraordinary friends

When I face the celestial tribunal, I shall not be asked why I was not an Abraham, Jacob, or Moses, but why I was not Rabbi Zusia.

—RABBI ZUSIA

Golf increases the blood pressure, ruins the disposition, spoils the digestion, induces neurasthenia, hurts the eyes, calluses the hands, ties knots in the nervous system, debauches the morals, drives men to drink or homicide, breaks up the family, turns the ductless glands into internal warts, corrodes the pneumogastric nerve, breaks off the edges of the vertebrae, induces spinal meningitis and progressive mendacity, and starts angina pectoris.

—A. S. LAMB

Waste no more time talking about great souls and how they should be. Become one yourself!

—MARCUS AURELIUS

I see people who talk about religion constantly quarreling with one another. Hindus, Mussulmans, Brahmos, Saktas, Vaishnavas, Saivas all quarrel with one another. They haven't the intelligence to understand that He who is called Krishna is also Siva and the Primal Shakti, and that it is He, again, who is called Jesus and Allah. "There is only one Rama and he has a thousand names."

—RAMAKRISHNA

ACKNOWLEDGMENTS

I would like to thank Marly Rusoff for finding the right home for this book; and Chuck Adams, Ina Stern, and everyone at Algonquin for their efforts on its behalf.

Golfing with God

PROLOGUE

This is the story of some time I spent in heaven, and then on earth, in the company of God. I know that the events described here will seem extraordinary, perhaps even, for some readers, impossible to believe. I know, too, that the ancient game of golf is not as fascinating to everyone as it always has been to me (and as it is to God). But, though golf runs through these pages like, say, the notes of the first violin through a symphony, this is mainly the story of the spiritual education of one soul. An ordinary enough soul, I have to confess, a soul riddled with quirks and urges, old failures and fresh embarrassments.

And yet, one of the lessons I learned during my time with God is that there is really no such thing as an ordinary soul, only souls who have not yet burned away the fog of confusion that surrounds them. That fog might be composed of fear, anger, bitterness, violence, regret, shame, greed, lust, or any combination of the above. It might spring from a pool of self-criticism and apparent unworthiness, cooking in the heat of life's troubles. Once the fog starts to lift, though—and this usually takes many many lifetimes—once the swirl of habitual thoughts begins to thin, a very different world comes into focus. This process can be compared to the gradual elimination of flaws from a golf swing, the slow improvement of a devoted player, accompanied, as it almost always is, by a growing sense of joy and peace.

So, this tale from my time in heaven is the description of one part of my own spiritual journey. There is still far to go. But at least the fog has lifted, the larger flaws in my game have been addressed, and my purpose on this planet—our purpose—is clearer to me now. It seems to me that ours is a world of mostly well-intentioned souls, and yet we boil in disappointment and pain and this foggy confusion. I was fortunate enough to escape all that for a while during my trip to paradise, and to have the guidance of some of the Great Ones—on the course and off, on earth and in heaven. If the story of this lucky adventure brings a bit of amusement or clarity to one other life, then I'll be pleased. In any case, the writing of it—such difficult work—is finished now. I've done what God asked me to do, part of it at least, and I'm free to get back to the game I love.

PART ONE

ONE

There are 8,187 golf courses in heaven, and new ones being built even as I write this. Given the fact that golf has been around for five hundred years, and tens of millions of people played the game while they were on earth, that might seem like a relatively small number. But the fact is—how can I say this politely—for one reason or another, a fair percentage of golfers never make it to paradise.

It is true, though, that some world-class course architects call that place home, and God keeps them busy designing and building new eighteen-hole layouts. This is one of the surprising things I want to tell you about heaven: People bring their skills up there with them. Which doesn't mean that if you were a secretary or a surgeon on earth—and hated it—God forces you to answer phones or cut out gall-bladders to earn your keep. That would be more like hell, if such a place actually existed . . . but I'll get into the structure of things more as I go on. For the purposes of this story, the point is that we carry our talents beyond the grave—and most of our quirks and flaws, as well. Heaven isn't nearly as static as I thought it would be. People change and grow there, too. Even God does, to a certain extent, which is something I still find difficult to understand.

There are 8,187 golf courses in heaven, and, as you'd probably guess, some exceptionally fine players. I'm not allowed to name names. I can tell you, though, that God is one of those players. I almost said "God Himself is one of those players," but something you often hear in heaven is that God isn't really a He. That is, according to those longtime residents who claim to know, sometimes He's a He, and other times He's a She, and many times God takes a form that cannot be described as either. Until my most recent visit, I had no experience of this myself. I had glimpsed God, once, just as I arrived, but it was a perfunctory greeting. Quick handshake at the gate type of arrangement. After that, I was left pretty much on my own, surrounded more by rumors of God than by any actual presence. But it turns out that rumors are quite accurate in heaven, and the self-proclaimed experts maintain that not only is God neither He nor She, but He can't be pinned down to any one race or ethnic group. Even His age is a matter of debate: the white-haired patriarch? Matriarch? Beautiful young thing? God likes to play with superficial details like that. After a while, people say, you learn to recognize Him or Her by something else, some aura of grace or sudden gust of power. But God is famous for His sense of humor. He likes to keep you off balance if She can.

So God golfs. That should come as no surprise to golfers. It isn't true, as some people in heaven like to suggest, that God also bowls, figure skates, and throws darts. God is busy. When He decides to cut Himself some slack He heads out to one of these 8,187 courses, often disguising Himself. He does not play Ping-Pong. He does not watch TV.

As I said, we carry our talents beyond the thin dark curtain of death. If we enjoyed the work we did, God gives us some of that work to do in paradise. For instance, I was a golf professional, a teacher of the game and a fairly good player in my best days. Never quite good enough to make it as a regular on the PGA tour, though I did climb up onto that exalted plateau for four seasons and I did have my moments even there. Nor was I ever famous as a teacher . . . outside my small home territory. None of my students went on to win major championships, though I like to think they played better after working with me, and enjoyed the game more.

I was devoted to my craft, and loved it, and over the years there were a few hundred people who claimed I had fixed their swing when it seemed beyond repair. In fact, that was sort of my specialty, if you will: rehabilitating golf swings that were once quite good but had been poisoned by some mysterious demon.

There are no secrets in heaven, and I suppose my earthly reputation, such as it was, got around. In any case, one perfect spring morning during my most recent residency in the higher realms, I was sitting out on my perfectly comfortable patio in front of my perfectly comfortable condominium, looking out at the thirteenth green of one of heaven's more modest layouts, the El Rancho Obispo Country Club, when a middle-aged man came striding across my lawn, walked up and sat opposite me. He had a worried look on his face, something you don't often see in heaven.

"You're Herman Fins-Winston, aren't you?" he said, by way of an introduction.

I had never liked my name during my previous incarnation on earth; in fact, I'd been embarrassed by it. Upon moving to the United States from Great Britain (another long story, that), I'd asked everyone to call me Hank Winston. And, once in heaven, I continued to introduce myself as Hank, so it had been a while since I'd heard the Herman or the Fins-Winston thing. In any case, I winced, nodded, asked my unexpected guest if he wanted a cup of cappuccino (things are rather informal in heaven; there we walk on other people's lawns; we couple and separate more easily than on earth, though certain relationships persist for very long periods of time indeed).

My guest shook his head impatiently. "Julian Ever," he said, as if I'd asked. "You've heard of me, I imagine."

"Everyone's heard of you, but no one seems to know what you actually look like."

This remark drew a small smile. On that day at least, Julian Ever was an odd-looking fellow, thin, tall, handsome in an offbeat way, with green eyes, a long, elfin nose, and powerful hands.

"'God's lieutenant' is what they call you around the pro shop," I added.

Julian blinked disingenuously, as if he'd never heard the phrase before, then leaned in a little closer, let the smile fall from his face, and said: "Listen, I don't have a lot of time."

I laughed. But Mr. Ever did not seem to be joking.

"You were a golf pro in your last life on earth, isn't that so?" he asked.

"It is."

"A famous teacher?"

"No, not famous. In local circles I had something of a reputation, you see, but—"

"Pennsylvania, wasn't it?"

"Yes, outside of Bethlehem."

"God wonders why you never moved south."

"Well, the move from Britain to America was traumatic enough, and, in good years, when my wife and I were still together and happy, we used to go to Miami for a month in winter."

"But . . . *permanently,* as they say. Why didn't you move there permanently, to a place where you could play more often?"

I shrugged. "British roots, you see. We're not used to the bright sun."

"You don't have some kind of a bias against the South?"

"What?" I said. "No. Not that I—"

"You're not biased, racially, are you?"

"What are you talking about? Of course not."

Julian seemed satisfied with this honest answer to his bizarre question, and I had the feeling he had been mainly checking to see if I had, in fact, been born in Great Britain. I'd known other prospective clients to do the same thing. Just being born in the place where the magnificent game of golf had been invented, it seemed, gave one a certain authority.

"Well, I have a teaching opportunity for you, if you're interested. Very special student."

I'd heard of other pros being asked to do small jobs now and then. It sometimes happened that a former PGA star would suddenly discover—even in heaven this happens, believe me—that he was pushing all his long irons to the right, or that his putting stroke had turned sour and he couldn't make an eight-footer to save his soul. What would happen then would be that his angel—yes, such spirits do exist—would go in search of just the right teacher, and the teacher would straighten things out, receive a token payment—some favor to be named later—and get that old satisfaction we remembered from the blue planet, where one had to work for one's keep. I'd never been approached in such a manner, but so many of my friends had that it wasn't a terrific surprise. The surprising part was that Julian Ever himself had come to ask me. God's lieutenant. He could have gotten any teaching pro in heaven to do him any favor he asked.

"Why me?" I couldn't keep from saying.

"Because you're the best."

Flattery, in case you haven't already noticed, is a big part of heavenly conversations. I dislike it, personally. I've always preferred British understatement and modesty. But longtime residents told me you get accustomed to it in time, even come to enjoy the forms it can take, the creative possibilities of exaggeration. It is the closest thing heaven has to outright lying, which, of course, does not exist there.

"Who is the client?"

"I can't say until I'm sure you'll commit."

"But there are no secrets in paradise. You have to say."

"At my level there are secrets. Are you interested in the job or not? The payment will be that you get to design a course of your own."

Against my own will I took in a sharp breath. I sat staring at him for a moment, looking for a wink, a quick smile, anything to signal that this was all some kind of a joke being played on me by my friends at the clubhouse. "I know nothing about designing," I said.

"Right, but it's been your secret dream for a long time, hasn't it?"

"It has. Forever."

Another wry grin. "That's the payment then, and it's not something we offer just anybody. Some new land is being created to the west of here—another ocean, with sandy rolling soil nearby. The climate will be rather like Wales—windy and never too hot—but without any rain during the day. So you'll make a links course there, along the sandy shore, if you want to. A yes or no answer if you'd be so kind, Mr. Fins-Winston."

I'd always been partial to links courses. I said: "Yes."

"Fine." He eyed my cappuccino. "Very good. I can now tell you who the client is."

"It must be someone very—"

"It's God," Julian Ever said, and if I live for a billion years I shall never forget the sound of that syllable echoing around my little patio in the heavenly light.

"God? But God plays perfectly. God invented the golf swing. He—"

"Change into your golf attire," Julian said. "We leave in four minutes."

TWO

You can imagine my state of mind. Those minutes had a dreamlike quality about them, a sense of unreality that is very unusual in heaven, where events tend to have clear, sharp edges. I changed into chinos and my best striped jersey, and when I went back out onto the patio, Julian had retreated toward the course and was sitting behind the wheel of a gold-trimmed golf cart, gesturing impatiently. I climbed in beside him and he took off as if he'd been a Grand Prix race-car driver in one of his past lives.

"I've never seen anyone hurry in heaven," I said nervously, holding onto the edge of the gilded roof with one hand.

"God is impatient."

"But that's impossible."

Julian turned his eyes to me for so long that he nearly drove off the gravel path. "Listen," he said, facing forward again and jerking once at the wheel to keep us from careening into a ditch. "If you're going to work with Him you're going to have to get rid of all these assumptions. The universes move incredibly slowly to His eye. The suns and planets twirl as if mired in honey. People learn their lessons over thousands of lives, when, in fact, those lessons seem to Him almost absurdly basic, ridiculously simple. In His frustration, He keeps sending saints, saviors, and various kinds of prophets down to speed up the process. People listen for a while, some of them, then keep forgetting what they've been taught and start reverting to old habits—hatred, greed, murder, war, and so on. Plus, on top of all that, He's been playing golf perfectly since the day He invented it. And when I use the word *perfectly* I mean exactly that. Now, suddenly, as of yesterday morning, something has gone terribly wrong."

"What?"

"I'll let Him describe it."

"So He *is* a man."

"Today, yes."

We rocketed down beside the eighteenth fairway at El Rancho Obispo, took a left past the clubhouse, and raced off along a path I had never seen there before that moment—and, in my seven years in paradise, I'd played at El Rancho thousands of times. The path led through some

gorgeous almond-colored hills with snow-topped mountains in the far western background. Newly created land,
it seemed to me, though I hadn't been in paradise long
enough to be able to know for sure what was new and
what wasn't. Rocking side to side in our souped-up golf
cart, we crested one of these hills and skidded to a stop
beside a helicopter, its blades already turning. The red-
headed woman in the pilot's seat was pleased as could be,
you could see it on her face. She was flying for God.

We crouched, sprinted, climbed up into the copter like
soldiers under fire, and lifted off. On earth, I'd always
been afraid of flying, but one of the nice things about
heaven is that, though you remember your fears, they no
longer have any power over you. There are people there
who indulge this freedom. Former agoraphobics who attend every festival, every sporting event, every crowded
theater they can find. Men who were afraid of any sort of
romantic commitment but now spend three or four hundred years with the same woman, just to see what it feels
like. Women who suffered for dozens of lifetimes from a
terrible fear of drowning, and now they're the ones you see
taking junkets to new oceans as soon as they're created, or
swimming laps in the various indoor and outdoor Olympic
pools. From what I understand, this infatuation with your
own fearlessness doesn't usually last very long—a few
centuries at most—and some souls don't experience it
at all.

I enjoyed the helicopter ride, though I was a bit nervous about my assignment, if that's what it could be called.

We flew a long distance, over the snow-topped mountains and into what seemed to me truly ancient land. It was green and gently rolling, fields of grain, orchards with fruit weighing down the limbs. Looking at it you had the sense that souls had been walking the paths and picking from the trees for a very long time indeed. Julian must have noticed my interest. He leaned in close, gestured down at the luxurious pastures with his long nose, and shouted in my ear, "Eden."

The pilot looked at me over her shoulder and smiled.

"You're joking," I said to Julian Ever.

"I don't joke."

Another few minutes and we touched down next to what turned out to be the first tee of what is undoubtedly still the most beautiful, and most difficult, golf course I have ever seen. The fairways were magnificent, glistening, perfectly groomed and shaped in gentle curves that moved right and left over hundreds of little valleys and mounds. Far far ahead I could make out the first green, tucked impossibly into a grove of white birches, with only the tiniest of openings in front, and deep pot bunkers all around.

"God's home course," Julian said. And then, pointing with his nose again: "There's the practice green. I'm leaving you now, have to be off on another errand, but I'll check back from time to time to see how things are progressing."

"But where is He?" I whispered.

"You'll find Him."

"But how?"

Julian and his beautiful pilot zoomed off without answering, leaving me standing in a whirlwind of fertile dust.

The practice green had something like four hundred holes to it—the flags in those holes were festooned with the colors and symbols of all the nations that had ever existed—and it must have covered a full acre. It didn't really surprise me to see that the sod was without blemish, that there were new balls and gleaming clubs lined up on the apron, in racks, for the taking. Three other people were knocking putts around, a husband-and-wife pair and a solitary man. I didn't pay them much attention at first. To make good use of my time and to show God that I wasn't in the least bit worried about meeting Him (these are the kinds of things you find yourself doing in His presence), I took one of the gleaming putters from its rack, picked out three balls (the brand I'd used when on earth, but, of course, I can't tell you the name; in heaven, for reasons I'm sure you'll understand, golfers are not allowed to endorse), and began practicing my four-footers. Plunk, the first one dropped in beneath the flag for ancient Greece. Plunk, plunk, the second and third. I moved over to the Soviet flag, just for fun, brought the ball back to six feet, and it was the same. Uphill, downhill, fast and slow putts, straight ones and big breakers—everything I touched went straight into the center of the cup like a frightened white animal racing for its burrow. I'd had days like that on earth. In fact, putting had always been the strong point of my game, so I knew this was something more than heavenly magic.

Still, a run like that doesn't happen every day, even in paradise. I became so absorbed in the natural fluid ease of my putting stroke that I failed to notice that the husband and wife had left the green. When I did finally miss a putt—a thirty-footer with a nasty sharp break at the end, aimed for a flag from one of the Atlantis colonies—I looked up and saw (strange that I hadn't noticed before) that the other person still on the green was an older fellow with wild white hair pushing out on all sides. "Einstein," was my first thought, because it seemed somehow proper that he should be up there, in a privileged section of the promised land. The fellow was sinking putts, too, most of them anyway, but muttering to himself in an unhappy tone. I stopped and watched. He had a beautiful stroke, though his attire left something to be desired. Shaggy, wrinkled old blue chinos and a threadbare jersey, no cap, no socks. Even the shoes were a bit unorthodox: plain white with blue stitching at the seams. I supposed it was Einstein after all, the eccentric genius. The muttering was likely some new theory he was working on.

He was putting with one ball. Four-footers, eight-footers, more four-footers. He was having a little trouble with some of the shorter putts, I noticed. After a few minutes, I decided to walk over and make conversation while waiting for God to show.

"Beautiful stroke," I said, and when he looked up the light in his eyes very nearly bowled me over. There was a clear force there, the kind of otherworldly gleam you might glimpse once in your life, for just a moment, at twilight, over the surface of a calm sea. But the voice that came out of his old mouth did not match that light at all. It was gritty and coarse, a smoker's voice, a drinker's.

"Worthless," he grumbled. "I'm worthless. I'm finished."

"Hank Winston," I said, holding out a hand that was suddenly trembling.

He took the hand, squeezed once in a kind way, and said, grumpily, "God."

"I . . . I . . . I . . ."

He watched me for a moment and a tiny smile burned the edges of His mouth.

"My friends call me Hank," I managed, at last, dumbly repeating myself.

"Nonsense," He said, in that same grumpy tone. "You were given a fine name at your last birth; you shouldn't be ashamed of it. Look at me, look at all the ridiculous things I've been called over the centuries. You don't see me shying away from any of them. Be proud of your name, Fins-Winston." He brushed back his wild white hair with one hand. "Now, listen, we have work. The tee's open. Grab a set of clubs and let's go. I'm in a slump like nothing anyone has seen in a million years and you're going to make my game right again, or I'm going to quit the damn sport forever and take up needlepoint."

THREE

God stepped out on the tee (even now, even after all the time I spent in the Holy Presence, it still seems strange to write those words) and without the smallest hesitation, without even a single waggle, He drew His driver back and hit a shot that my former contemporary the great Ben Hogan would have given anything in the world to have been able to hit, just once in his career. The sound of the club striking the ball—I can tell you that God uses the old-fashioned persimmon woods—was like an artillery round hitting the trunk of a tree two feet from your ear. *Crr-ACK!* The ball rocketed away from the tee about a foot inside the treeline at the fairway's right edge. For a moment I thought it would brush the limbs there, that God's problem was that He was blocking everything to the right. But He'd put what we call "drawspin" on it, which means it began to turn gently leftward, toward the middle. It rose and rose, curling slightly, seemed to hang at its apex for several seconds, then dropped neatly onto the perfect carpet of green fairway, dead center, 390 yards out.

"You, now," He said gruffly, brushing back His hair. "Hit."

"I thought I was just here to give a lesson."

"I want a playing partner, not just a teacher. Hit, I tell you."

One does not disobey a direct command from the Lord—not in heaven, at least. Why this is so, I'm not exactly sure. I mean, I and most of my circle of friends had broken moral laws on earth, flagrantly in fact, but it was just something we didn't consider doing in heaven. I suppose it was because all doubt had been removed from the equation: There's no chance of not believing in an afterlife when you are, in fact, part of it.

Certainly there was no chance of me not believing in God—not after a 390-yard tee shot with a persimmon driver. But He was rougher than I'd expected, more ragged around the edges, a sort of stevedore with flashing eyes.

I can tell you this, too: After what I'd just witnessed, it wasn't easy to stand up on that tee, knowing I was there to help Him. Still, I'd had some practice dealing with nervousness on earth. I'd talked to my best pupils about it hundreds of times, and so I simply followed my own advice. The tendency is to shorten the swing, to worry about making an error, to keep your body from doing what it naturally wants to do. You can't stand over the ball too long; you can't try to steer it. You just have to get up there, settle yourself for a second or two, stare at the ball as if it might jump up and bite you at any second, trust your body, and make a nice, big, easy swing.

I did that. My ball flight actually took the same route as God's, a little right-to-lefter. But, compared to His shot, mine looked like something a teenager might be proud of, 255–60 yards at best.

"Decent ball," God said. "No carts at Eden Hills. The game was invented to be walked. Any objection?"

"No." And then, after a moment, I added, "Your majesty."

God looked at me and smirked. "Oh, come on," He said.

"But, the second commandment?"

"Thou shalt not take the name of the Lord thy God in vain, I remember it," He said, with just the smallest glint of good humor in His voice now. "A good friend of mine wrote that one up for me. It doesn't apply here. There's no such thing as 'in vain' here, you see. And I have no name in any case. Just God will be fine. The only rule around me is No fuss."

"No fuss?"

"That's the only real commandment . . . after you learn

to stop hurting people, which I assume you've done or you wouldn't be up here in the first place."

Assume, I thought. Assume? Don't You know? Haven't You been keeping track of me all these years?

I said nothing, haunted, for the thousandth time, by the notion that I didn't really belong in heaven, that my ascension had been a clerical error, that one day soon I'd be found out and sent packing.

I picked up my bag. God hoisted His onto one shoulder. As we strode up the beautiful fairway I saw that although He had taken on the face and hair color of an older man, there were tremendous muscles in His shoulders and forearms, and He walked with the springy step worthy of a twenty-year-old Olympic gymnast. We went along for two hundred yards in silence.

"Judging from that tee shot, and the putts I saw You hitting on the green, I'd say Your game doesn't need much help. Is this some kind of a trick? A test?"

Again, He shot me a nasty look with the hint of a grin beneath it. "I don't test," He said. "And I don't play tricks."

Well, You could have fooled me and a few billion other people, I thought, but I did not say that either. Strange as this may sound, I could tell that God had something on His mind, that He was legitimately troubled. As a pro, on earth, I'd always had an especially good intuition about my clients' state of mind. And I had always taken my responsibilities extremely seriously, sometimes worrying over a particular twelve- or twenty-eight-handicapper so much that, in the middle of supper, I'd go to the phone, make a call, and offer a suggestion I hadn't thought of on the practice range. This inability to leave my work on the course was part of the reason why my one attempt at marriage had ended in failure. There were other reasons; I don't really want to get into them now. The fact was that I'd been asked to help God Himself—the reality of it was still sinking in—and I wasn't about to fail to pay attention.

That first hole at Eden Hills, it turned out, was a 666-yard par four named Serpent's Advance. My "decent" tee shot had left me 400 yards out. There was nothing to do but take out a three metal and blast away. My shot went straight, at least, 225 yards, so that I was, after two hits, just a little ways farther up the fairway than God's ball after one. We walked silently up to it. I stood back and watched. He took out His eight iron and, again, without any hesitation, blasted the ball into orbit. A huge divot followed after it, flying probably thirty yards. The ball seemed to go twenty stories into the air, hover there as if eyeballing the pin, then it dropped down between the tops of the birch trees less than a club length from the hole. An eight iron, I thought, from 270 yards! My God!

"Nice," I said.

God replaces his divots.

I made it to the green with two more shots and two-putted from thirty feet for a double bogey. God's second shot, it turned out, had stopped three feet from the pin. He took out His putter and stood over the ball . . . and stood over it . . . and stood over it. I saw that His powerful hands were shaking. He calmed them at last, took aim, and yanked His birdie putt two inches off line to the left. More muttering. He walked up and tapped in for His par and we moved toward the second tee in a terrible silence. Just before I got there I summoned the courage to say, "You have the yips then, that's the problem?" but my voice turned up and cracked on the last syllable as if I were fourteen. God teed up on the second hole without saying a word.

FOUR

After an affliction called "the shanks," the yips are golf's most dreaded disease. It almost always attacks the better players and it consists of not being able to make short putts. This may not sound like much to the nongolfer, or even to the high handicapper. After all, it's hard to feel much pity for people who are on the green in regulation and putting for birdie or par. But the yips are maddening. I know this from my teaching career, from watching pro tournaments up close, and I know it from my own experience. In my second year on the tour, when it looked like I had found my stride and would finally fulfill the promise of my college career (I'd been twice voted to first team

All-America, only the third British citizen to achieve that honor), just then I came down with a horrible case of the yips.

It began, I'll never forget it, at something called the Western Pennsylvania Open, a fairly big tournament in those years. I was eleventh coming into the fourth and final day, hitting the ball beautifully. My friends—including my wife-to-be, Anna Lisa—had come out in force to support me. As the day wore on, I made my way slowly up the leader list. I was eighth after eight holes. In third place with four to play, two shots behind the leader. And then, suddenly, my hands became the property of some demon spirit. My mind turned into a circus. As I stood over a four-foot birdie putt on the fifteenth hole, I started thinking all kinds of crazy things. What I was going to have for breakfast the next morning. What kind of bird that was, chirping away in the distance. Exactly what Anna Lisa's kisses tasted like, what single adjective could best be used to describe them (*tobaccoish* was the word I was looking for). With Anna Lisa and my friends watching from just off the fringe, I jerked the putt left, two and a half feet past the hole. Incredible! Then missed the two-and-a-half-footer coming back, turning an almost certain birdie into a bogey, dropping myself to ninth place again, and detonating a hydrogen bomb a few feet from my confidence.

I dreamed about that putt for decades. Literally, decades. I heard imaginary taunting voices (sometimes not so imaginary: In subsequent years, during our worst fights, Anna

Lisa would sometimes say, "Herman at the Western Pennsylvania Open," in a certain voice, always a knockout punch). I was never the same after that round of golf. I had a few decent showings—twenty-fifth once, at the Phoenix Open. But I was never the same golfer, or the same man.

God's problem, it turned out, was a bit more complicated. He had the yips, yes, but not on every hole. And to compound that problem, He also would occasionally take out His sand wedge—a club designed for hitting the ball high up in the air and stopping it quickly—lift up His head at the last minute, and drill a low liner that shot over the green and into the rough beyond.

Neither of these problems was impossible to fix. I had, in fact, fixed them for hundreds of people on earth. But, at their essence, they are psychological problems, not technical, not physical ones. I watched God play the par-three, 355-yard second hole, a long downhill teaser over a huge pond. He drove the green with a four iron, ran up a nice lag putt to two feet, and, hands trembling again, left the two-footer four inches short. I thought I heard Him curse.

Before we were halfway to the third tee, I found myself saying, "I had the yips once myself, you must know that. It's nothing to be ashamed of."

But, to my complete astonishment, God *was* ashamed. So ashamed that He refused to speak to me for the rest of the front nine. Even with the yips, and even on a front side that measured 4,900 yards (3,500 or 3,600 is a typical PGA tour length now), He was one under par at the turn. And furious at Himself.

FIVE

It has always been my style of teaching to spend a long time observing the student before making any suggestions, to say very little while he or she is actually hitting balls on the practice tee or on the course. I did not deviate from that style with God. We walked the eighteen holes of Eden Hills without indulging in much conversation. I was happy to finish twenty-three over. God, at three under, seemed miserable. For the most part, His game followed the pattern I'd seen on the first hole: tremendous booming drives, beautiful iron shots, then . . . the occasional misplayed wedge followed by a stretch of the yips. The only variations were those times when He sank a long putt, or, once, chipped in from off the green—that is, those times when He wasn't faced with a three- or four-footer, the kind of putt you are supposed to make, the kind that any half-decent player is ashamed not to make. But on the eighteenth hole, a wicked 598-yard dogleg par four, something rather peculiar happened. After the usual amazing approach shot to two feet, God walked up and calmly knocked the ball in the hole without so much as a quiver. He's cured, I thought, though I knew a single putt didn't mean the yips had been conquered. I even let myself imagine, briefly, that He'd think I'd somehow helped Him. Just my presence had been curative.

When the round was completed and I'd put my clubs back where they'd come from, God and I walked into the clubhouse restaurant for what He called "a little nip." He seemed completely unembarrassed by His ragged clothes and shaggy hair.

Now, I should tell you that it is not necessary to eat in heaven. Eating is an option, something one does for pleasure, but the body can be sustained in perfect health without any nutrition other than light, which is plentiful. Still, for those of us who visited there from earth, eating had become a habit, and it was still practiced in social situations quite often.

We sat at a corner table in the empty café, two glasses of Guinness stout (there are several thousand Guinness breweries in heaven) and a large plate of onion rings in front of us. "So," I said, hoping to calm Him down with some small talk. "Is Eden Hills a private club?"

He looked at me again in a way that made me feel utterly stupid, as if, by now, I should have had a better grasp on the laws of paradise. The waitress stopped by to flirt with Him briefly—she said she liked His eyes, and it shocked me that she obviously could not see who He was. When she left, God picked up an onion ring and slowly chewed it. He seemed to be wondering if He'd made a foolish choice after all, asking me to assist Him, when there were thousands of smarter golf professionals in heaven. But when He spoke it was with the kind of loving patience you'd expect from God. "Not at all, Fins-Winston. Nothing is private in heaven, except a few isolated communities for people who were madly jealous of the rich when they were on earth. They live behind their tall hedges for a while, get it out of their system, and then move out here with the rest of us."

"But, excuse me, I've been here only a relatively short while, how could those people get to heaven in the first place if they were madly jealous?"

"You're not perfect, are you, Fins-Winston?"

"Far from it, Lord—"

"Neither are they. You don't have to be perfect to get here. You only have to try, to want it, to be sincere about wanting it. You have to not have hurt anyone too badly in your most recent previous life. Rapists and murderers and con artists don't make it up here. Kidnappers, wife or husband or child beaters. That's why this is heaven—we keep those bastards out."

It was all fascinating, of course, but the words "You only have to want it" had shaken me to the core. I took refuge behind my dew-coated glass. That was precisely the thing I used to say to my golfing students. You don't have to be perfect, you only have to want—really, sincerely want—to play better. I must have used that phrase ten thousand times. When God sipped from His glass I checked to see if there was a sparkle in His eye or a smile playing on His cheeks. But no, He seemed serious.

"You'll see Buddha here at Eden Hills—likes the layout."

"Buddha golfs?"

"Of course he golfs. Very intense about it, too. I saw him throw a club here once, on the sixteenth."

"Buddha threw a club?"

"Well, you saw the sixteenth, didn't you? That wicked two-tiered green. Who wouldn't get upset? He threw his putter into the damn lake."

"But Buddha is renowned for his—"

"He's calmed down now, again. I'm thinking of sending him to earth on another mission. But he has a regular weekly foursome with Krishna, Christ, and Moses—Muhammad sometimes joins them as a fifth—and I want to let him enjoy their company for another century or two. You'll see them around, I'm sure. I'll point them out to you if they happen to be playing in some kind of disguise."

"I'll be back then? That is, there'll be other lessons?"

"Other lessons? Well, this didn't count as much of a lesson, did it now? I haven't heard a single word of advice from you, not a single word."

"That's my style," I said. "Especially with problems that aren't, well . . . that aren't technical. This is a mental issue, if You'll forgive me. I need to go home and sleep on it, give it some thought . . . if that's all right with You."

God smirked and sipped His Guinness, and I could sense that He had the game in perspective again. There was a certain strange aura of humor surrounding Him. Everything had a slightly comic edge to it. Everything, that is, but His game when He was on the course.

"Well, Fins-Winston," He said at last. "This is your shot. This is the big leagues. Don't blow it."

And, having said that, He simply disappeared. The glass remained, half empty; the onion rings, half eaten. A certain sense-memory of Him persisted in the room. But God himself was elsewhere. The waitress came by to tell me the tab had been taken care of, then, somewhat shyly, she asked: "Who was your cute friend with the wild hair?"

I told her His name was Albert.

Julian Ever did not reappear, but he'd arranged for the beautiful helicoptress to ferry me home again. Back in the condominium, lying in my perfectly comfortable bed, preparing to slip into another in an endless succession of delicious nights of sleep, I tried to imagine what could have given God the yips, what could have messed up His short game so, when His swing was absolutely divine. I tried to do this, but, in fact, I was struggling with the echoes of His last words, so un-Godlike: "Don't blow it. This is the big leagues." Weren't those the very things I had said to myself on the morning of the last round of the Western Pennsylvania Open? My big chance. I tossed and turned that night as if I were still in the cauldron of earthly life, as if I weren't in heaven at all, but only some staging area, a base camp, the minors, the mini-tours.

SIX

God didn't call for me the next day, as I expected, nor the day after that. I thought about Him—that's what I'd been asked to do. I had some ideas about what He might work on, a couple of drills, some positive imaging. But I felt I was nowhere near getting at what might be bothering Him, that I needed to watch Him play another few times, watch Him miss a few dozen more putts, before I could unlock the mystery. But when a week passed and no one came for me, I was certain I'd been replaced by a better coach, or that God had solved His problems on His own.

By the way, I've been saying things like "a short while" and "a week," but these are just concepts I'm using to communicate with you, not precise measurements of heavenly time. It is true that there is night and day. And that some people have chosen to reside in parts of heaven where there are identifiable seasons—the autumn leaves turning, the first snow, the monsoons. Veterans of earth are attached to such things. In fact, though, the idea of time, so much a part of life here on the blue planet, is lacking there, or, if not lacking, extremely muted. You sense movement; certainly there is change and growth. But without death as an ending point, or some sort of irreversible old age as a marker, that movement loses most of its power.

It's complicated. Some people there actually choose to age, knowing they can reverse the process at will—believe it or not, it does get tiring to be mired in one's twenties or thirties. Many souls enjoy the feeling of early childhood and wish to go back to that from time to time, or they like the idea of being seen as a wise elder. And, in some cases I've heard of—mine, obviously—one is called upon to return to earth (where time, despite human assumption to the contrary, actually moves backwards and forwards and in historical circles, not in a straight line, so we are sometimes allowed to project our spirits into different eras) for the span of sixty or seventy or a hundred years, to help a loved one from a previous incarnation, to perform a certain mission, or to learn a certain lesson.

It's clear to me now that, when I am on earth, I know who these people are—the ones who've spent a lot of time in heaven, I mean. There is a persistent happiness shining through them, no matter what their mood or circumstance. An indifference . . . no, that isn't quite right. Perhaps a detachment. As if they are playing a role and, on some level, know it. In my previous earthly life, I had a grandmother like that; she died when I was fourteen. And, before I met Anna Lisa, I'd had a college girlfriend named Zoe who'd been that way. It was the great regret of that life—greater even than my failure on the PGA tour— that things hadn't worked out between Zoe and me. She was such a kind and giving soul. I've always thought it was she who arranged for me to rise up to heaven after that life was finished. Surely nothing else explained my visit there, brief as it was. But I am drifting.

A certain amount of what you would call "time" passed, let's put it that way. Roughly ten days. During that period I was sure I'd failed in my assignment to help God, and there was a flickering shadow of regret about that, something that would have been painful on earth but up there was just background music. The present is so powerful there—that is perhaps the single greatest difference between heavenly and earthly life—that it is almost impossible to be haunted by past failures and obsessed with as yet unrealized dreams. Almost.

In any case, after ten days of my usual social schedule—golf, time with friends, swimming, dancing, and more golf—I was again sitting out on my patio on a fine summerlike morning when a stranger came hurrying across the condominium's small and always perfectly mowed lawn. This stranger had skin the color of a coconut husk, but somehow when he got closer I realized it was Julian Ever, come to pay another visit.

"Where have you been?" he demanded without even so much as a "good day." "Almost two weeks have gone by. God's beside Herself."

"I thought God would contact *me*."

Julian was clenching his fists. He looked over at the fairway in exasperation, then turned back to me. "People are always doing that. It drives me crazy!"

"Doing what? Rolling the ball over?" I thought I'd seen someone on the fairway adjusting his lie with the club head. This is one of the parts of golf that people don't talk about very much because it's a form of cheating. Advised by well-meaning coaches and friends, beginners get into the habit of giving themselves "improved lies" in the fairway. This makes it easier to hit the ball cleanly, and it is also against the rules. The problem is that, if people learn to do this when they first start playing, they often continue doing it when they've become better players. On earth, I saw fights break out over this issue. I heard of friendships that were ruined because someone insisted on reserving the right to "roll the ball" or "play the ball up" or "improve" his lie, long after he should have been playing from the lie God had given him.

"I don't like it either," I said to Julian.

"Then why do you do it?" he said.

"Do it? I've never done it! Even when I was a beginner I didn't do it. My father was Scottish, he would have had my head if he'd caught me rolling the ball over!"

Julian was staring at me now, boring his eyes into me. But, God's lieutenant or no, this was a point on which I was going to insist. The record was clear: I had never rolled the ball.

"What in the kingdom of kingdoms are you talking about?"

"Rolling the ball."

"Who's talking about rolling the ball?"

"I thought you were. You looked out at the fairway at that older gentleman there, you said it made you crazy."

Julian looked out at the fairway again, then back. "I looked away because *you* were making me crazy. This attitude makes me crazy."

"What attitude?"

"That God will come to you, that you don't have to make any effort whatsoever, that you can't be bothered to pick up the phone, say Her name aloud, whisper it to yourself. You have no idea how many billions of people just sit back and wait for God to show. The Second Coming, the Third Coming. On some planets, in some universes, it's the Ninetieth Goddamned Coming and they still don't get it."

"*I* should have called *Him?*"

"He is a She today, and yes, you should have made some gesture of reaching out. Do you think I have nothing better to do than chaperone you into and out of God's presence?"

"What's Her area code?" I asked, but Julian didn't smile. In another minute we were in the gold-trimmed cart, racing west on another cart track I'd never seen. Another landing area, another helicopter with its blades already turning. Another beautiful pilot—that, at least, didn't seem to change.

At the door, over the sound of the motor, Julian shouted: "From now on, you're on your own with God. Call Her when you have something to say."

"Call Her how?"

"You already know how. Just do it!"

"This is a regular thing, then? The lessons, I mean?"

Julian gave me the stare again. I looked for the glint of humor—it was strange to see a resident of heaven who seemed to be actually angry—and thought I detected it. "Why in God's name wouldn't it be?" he said.

And, with that, he was off in his cart, and so were we, in our copter.

The pilot, whose name turned out to be Livinia, was not as sedate as the previous flier. She took her copter out in a left-leaning swoop (something like God's tee shot, I mused) and swung it back and forth as we went along a few feet above the treetops.

"Were you afraid of flying in your last lifetime?" I shouted over the sound of the blades.

Livinia nodded happily and grazed the top of a fir tree with the helicopter's landing gear. "Were you . . . did something happen with golf?" she yelled back.

"No, no, I love golf!" I told her, but as soon as the words were out of my mouth I sensed a sort of false tone in the air. I did love golf, of course, but it wasn't exactly true that nothing had happened. Golf had broken me, though I had never admitted that to anyone. I'd always told family and friends, and told myself, that I was perfectly content to leave the PGA tour and live the quiet, settled life of a country club pro. But there, flying over a last ridge and across an enormous desert, I saw, finally, that I had been cleverly lying to myself all those years. Anna Lisa had said as much in one of our last arguments, before we stopped talking to each other altogether except through our lawyers.

But I had resisted that theory to the end. (Isn't it often the case, on earth, that we bury the most difficult truths beneath all kinds of rationalizations?) I earned a decent salary as a club pro, made a lot of friends, had a fair amount of respect. Sure, I was obliged to deal with some of the more annoying members. Sure, I felt a twinge sometimes when I watched a match on TV, or when I heard stories of touring pros who'd overcome humiliation and failure and come back to win a tournament or two. I hadn't wanted to fight that hard. I'd told myself I hadn't wanted to. There, in the helicopter, I saw what an enormous mistake that had been.

Livinia, in some strange fashion, seemed to see it, too. She went silent on me, as if the lie had been aimed at her, as if she were offended. We passed over an oasis—I could see green golf links laid out there—and she set me down rather roughly in another landing area just off the practice range. I stumbled out, and she swooped away like a maddened falcon, dipping behind a row of palm trees, a long plume of dust rising up behind her.

When the dust settled, I found myself caught in some interior windstorm, my emotions swinging this way and that—shame, embarrassment, anger, self-justification—in a fashion that was utterly unfamiliar to me since I'd risen up. For a little while all I could do was stand there and stare dumbly at people hitting balls on the practice range. I felt somehow unprepared to look God in the face that day. Unworthy. Later, I would learn something about that kind of shame: It is exactly that feeling, exactly that sense of unworthiness that forms the fertile ground from which most spiritual troubles sprout. Trite as it may sound, the fact is that the Being that created us loves us, approves of us, expects the best from us—to steal a phrase from a fellow named Walt Whitman. So often, in the whirl of earth, amidst the complexities of family life and our professional ambitions, we lose sight of that existential approval. We turn away from that love. And after that, well . . . no place to go but down.

SEVEN

After a short time, some of that negative emotion subsided and I was able to get my bearings. The usual magnificent clubhouse, the usual fairways floating off into the shimmering distance. Gray mountains there at the edge of the sands. It was a desert course, this one, strips of emerald green laid out over a wasteland of cactus and silvery stone. In my time on the tour I had never been partial to desert courses—there are no deserts in England, after all, and none in Pennsylvania.

But it was another gorgeous layout, I could see that much at a glance. While I was waiting for God to manifest Himself, I wandered over to the practice range and picked up a new driver and a bucket of balls. I should probably mention here something that may already have become obvious: Even though heaven is heaven, one's golf game is not perfect. It could be, I suppose. I imagine there is some mechanism by which citizens of heaven can apply for the perfect swing, the perfect score every time, an eternity of chip ins and one-putted greens. But no one seems to want that. Heaven's residents understand that the imperfections are, in fact, what makes the game as thrilling as it is. People improve, gradually, with occasional lapses. But there is always something new to learn, some bad habit to conquer, some better player or more difficult course against which to match themselves. What fun would it be otherwise?

On the range that day, I worked on my middle irons for a while, adjusting my swing so I could move the trajectory of the ball right or left depending on the configuration of an imaginary hole. *Drawing the ball* is what we call making it curl gently to the left (for a right-handed player) and *fading the ball* means a move to the right. A *hook* is too much of a draw, and a *slice* is too much of a fade.

So I worked on my drawing and fading, bringing it right up to the edge of hooking and slicing, then straightening things out again. It's a matter of physics, really. A change in swing path, a change in grip or stance or movement through the ball, and voilà, the fade draws.

When I rested from this labor, I noticed that there was a very attractive Asian woman working on her fairway metals a few stalls down from me. One tries not to ogle in heaven. In one way this is easier—beauty is more widely defined there. But in another, since there is no such thing as adultery or sexual misconduct, it's more difficult. Anything can happen at any moment; you can find yourself in bed with the woman of your dreams, both of you ecstatic. Sounds wonderful, doesn't it? And that kind of ecstasy *is* nice enough, very nice indeed, but once you've tasted the deeper spiritual ecstasy of heaven it's like, well, it might be compared to eating a handful of good fresh grapes after you've been exposed to the complex sensations of a bottle of Chateauneuf du Pape, 1938. I believe you catch my drift.

But, for me, on that day, there was a further complication. Zoe, the college sweetheart I believe I've already mentioned, Zoe my soul mate, had been an Asian American girl. Even in heaven I could not quite get her out of my thoughts. I kept hoping I'd run into her there, that we could fix what had gone wrong, spend a couple of millennia together. For years and years I had been clinging to that hope. Dozens of relationships, a hundred ecstatic couplings, she still haunted me.

And, very strangely, the woman practicing on the driving range with me that day in the desert bore a striking resemblance to my Zoe. I made myself turn away, made myself hit fifty middle irons. But I could not keep from looking again, and when I did, closely, I saw the overpowering gleam in her eyes that could mean only one thing.

Before I had a chance to speak, She said: "Fins-Winston. Some fine-looking five irons you're hitting today."

"Thank You, Lord."

She walked over to me. At closer range I could see that She did not look exactly like Zoe, but could easily have passed for her sister. I swallowed, composed myself. "Good morning, God."

"Goddess," She corrected me.

"Yes, Lord, of course. I—"

She laughed, and it was almost Zoe's laugh. "I'm joking, Fins-Winston. Lighten up, would you? Let's go."

Another amazing course it was, but this one much easier than Eden Hills. Normal length par fours, a few water hazards, flat greens where you could find yourself with a hundred-foot putt. For the most part, the fairways were lined with expensive single-family homes set among date palms, with swimming pools behind, and gleaming, air-propelled autos in the drive. But on the third and fourth holes we passed a series of caves with a few emaciated-looking men sitting around out front in the hot sun. "The Desert Fathers," God said quietly. "Wonderful group of guys. Very funny once you get to know them."

"Do they golf?"

She shook Her head so that Her shining black hair swung this way and that. "Given it up for a while."

One of the Desert Fathers waved to me as we passed. I waved back, feeling as though I had just been granted a blessing.

Goddess had a different swing on that day. Her tempo was better suited to the musculature of a woman, a bit slower and looping, but She hit the ball just as solidly, if not nearly as far.

"So," She asked, when we'd played the front nine, each of us two under par, "what's your advice?"

"You don't seem to need any today. You're putting like Bobby Jones."

"It's the driving that needs work, though, don't you think?"

She had, in fact, pulled two of Her tee shots left almost into the front yards of the spectacular homes and taken bogey on both occasions. So focused had I been on the putting, that I hadn't really given it much thought. "I guess I'm confused," I admitted. "The other day it was putting troubles, with the occasional bladed sand wedge. Today it's driving. Someone of your caliber ought to have consistent and very small flaws in her—"

"Someone of my caliber." She laughed at me, openly but in an affectionate way, another bruise to the heart.

"You remind me of someone," I said, because this time the laugh had been Zoe's laugh, exactly.

"Really?" She took out a four iron and drilled a shot onto the 178-yard tenth. Eight feet from the pin.

"And You hit your four iron about three times that far the other day. I'm confused. I feel like I'm being toyed with."

"Want to resign your commission, Fins-Winston? Want to forego designing that links course on the new lands and just go back to your buddies at Rancho Obispo?"

In answer, I hit a four iron myself, a pace or two closer to the hole than God's ball. "No," I said. "I just want to be clear about my assignment, that's all."

"*That's* the way to assert yourself, Fins-Winston," She

said, walking off. "Way to take up the challenge. I've never liked people who don't want to move forward. Goes against the whole system of soul evolution I set up a while back."

On the green She yanked the putt left, I sank mine. On the eleventh She drove into the cactus, left side again. I made another birdie. On the twelfth, a long par five over water, She hit a ground ball tee shot, then just barely reached the green with Her second, and three putted. I felt like She was acting a role. I missed an eagle chip by a fraction of a centimeter.

By the time we stood on the thirteenth tee, I'd had enough. "Yes," I said, "I want to resign my commission. I'd like to go back to my nice comfortable condo and my regular foursome of Brits at Rancho Obispo."

"Really? You're sure?"

She was staring at me now, the beacon of Her eyes going full tilt, a sort of hard-handed love emanating from Her entire body. I felt—this will seem strange to you perhaps—a twinge of what might be described as lust. Though I'd never been particularly religious, I'd done a bit of religious reading in my spare time on earth—the pain of my divorce turned me in that direction for a while. And I remembered that some of the Christian saints and many Hindu mystics liked to describe their relationship to God in terms of a spousal love. I felt, at that moment, that I finally understood them, though it was, of course, somewhat disconcerting to feel the twinges of lust in God's presence.

"No," I said. "But . . . what do You want from me? How can I help You?"

"You said one wise thing the other afternoon, Fins-Winston. You said you believed my problems were 'mental.' I assume you meant 'psychological' and I agree with that. A brilliant observation. Exactly why I chose you for this lesson."

"All right," I said. I've never been impervious to flattery, not least coming from a beautiful young woman, not least from God Herself.

"My problem *is* psychological," God went on, flipping a strand of hair out of Her eyes. "A few years ago I felt I was in danger of becoming bored with the game of golf. That frightened me, I'll be candid with you. It frightened me, because, you see, golf is my one place of rest. I have great responsibilities, Fins-Winston, responsibilities you cannot even begin to imagine. It's like having a hundred billion young children and being required to look after them twenty-four hours a day, seven days a week, for eternity. Think about that. . . . And on the other side of the ledger I have golf. . . . So what I did to keep from becoming bored was this: I imbued myself with a human mind—on the golf course only. The body is still God's, male or female; the spirit, the intellect, the compassion—all supernatural. But the mind-body connection on the golf course isn't. Some days I can't putt to save my life. Some days I can't drive. Some days I hit my long irons fat. Sound familiar?"

"Of course. Everybody's like that. That's golf."

"Now you're getting it, Fins-Winston. And you're a golf teacher. So teach."

"We'll have to go to earth," I blurted out.

"What's that?"

"We'll have to go to earth."

You must believe me, I had not the smallest, not the slightest intention of saying those words. They seemed to have been drawn from me by some sort of divine—or devilish—magic.

"Ah," Goddess said, grinning. "Earth. I believe I've heard of the place."

I felt then, somehow, that I couldn't backpedal. I felt that God was on the verge of exiling me from Her presence, recognizing Her mistake and casting me out of heaven, and I simply could not have borne the pain of that. Not to mention the loss of my designing job. "It doesn't do any good for You to have a human mind in heaven," I went on, as if I knew something about the subject. "It just doesn't work. The courses are too perfect, for one thing. And there's no real pressure, no bad weather, no aches in the joints or money worries or family worries. If You really want to fix this You're going to have to go to earth."

"Permanently?"

"Of course not."

"Perhaps you would like to go back permanently, Fins-Winston."

"Absolutely not," I said.

"Perhaps you'd like to go back for a while, then. You

feel you missed out on something there, played things wrong. And you're saying this to me just to get, as it were, a free trip back into that messy karmic situation you call 'earth'?"

She was taunting me now with Her perfect understanding of how I thought. It was so much like Zoe that I felt completely bewitched. "Not really, no," I said. "That is, I don't think so."

"Perhaps you feel it would be good for you."

"I've had that thought, but I don't want to leave here. It's so restful."

She put Her club back in Her bag. "Ah, restful. Now we're getting to the truth, at last," She said. "Restful, though, is not a good motivation. Be completely honest with me, Fins-Winston."

"All right. . . . At this moment I feel like I want to ask You about how things are set up, how they're really set up, I mean."

"The Big Picture," She said. We were standing alone on the tee, not another golfer in sight. I had the sensation of being observed. I looked away for a moment and thought I saw one of the Desert Fathers holding a telescope up in my direction. The front lens of the scope blinked in the bright sun.

"Yes, the Big Picture."

"You want to know how the universes work."

"Yes, I confess that I do."

"Well, I'm not supposed to, but I'll tell you. They work exactly the way golf works."

"Meaning what, Lord?"

"Meaning: Golf is a metaphor for creation, for the spiritual path, the secret structure of the universes, whatever words you want to use. The Big Picture." She swept one thin, muscled arm around Her at the course—its hazards and inviting greens, its temptations and humiliations, so much joy and so much frustration, all in the shape of a game. "It's all here, Fins-Winston, but I believe you already knew that."

"I suspected it," I said. And then: "That's all? That's the whole secret of Your creation? That it's like golf?"

She raised an eyebrow at me. I thought She might wink. "All? You say that as if you believe you have mastered the game, as if it's a simple challenge."

"I haven't mastered it. I never will. Never. That will never happen."

"But you want to master it?"

"Of course I want to."

She lifted Her bag onto one shoulder and started to walk off the course. I had no option but to follow. A few minutes of silent walking and we found ourselves beside the clubhouse. "A little nip," Goddess suggested, and I could tell that no more Big Picture information would be forthcoming on that day.

Inside, we found a window table looking out on the pool—kids splashing about, mothers and fathers watching them. It might have been a millionaires' golf resort on Florida's Atlantic coast, I thought. But it wasn't. It was heaven. God ordered two Guinnesses and a plate of onion rings. Her tastes in snack food, at least, were consistent—and, I must say, identical to my own.

I was hoping She might have forgotten about the earth junket.

But after we'd sat there a while, She said, "So. Do you have a favorite place down there where we might go? It's early spring right now in the northern hemisphere, remember. I don't want to be playing in Pennsylvania—or Scotland for that matter—with long underwear on. It's going to be enough of a shock for me, going back to that planet. And, besides, in all of human recorded history God has never made an appearance where it's cold. Think about it."

"You're serious about the earth trip?"

"Deadly serious."

"Well, I did have some places I used to go—we used to go. Down south. The American South, I mean."

"You don't say," God said, but She was practically bursting out of Her skin with subdued laughter.

"When it got cold, once I closed up the clubhouse for the season, Anna Lisa and I used to like to pack up the Buick and head to Miami. We had these, well, I had favorite courses, I had friends there—"

"Ah," She said. And then: "Let's do it this way: Since it was your suggestion that we go to earth, why don't you allow me to make up the itinerary? I have some friends there myself, people I'd like you to meet. You be the teacher and I'll be the travel agent. Sound good?"

"Yes, of course, Lord. Whatever You wish."

She looked at me, that same enticing love in Her eyes, that frankness. She pursed Her lips, studying me now, starting a wee fire of fear in my innards. I wondered if there might be some way for me to take back my remark about going to earth.

"So you truly want to help me, Herman?"

"Yes, of course, Lord. I'll do whatever I can."

"You're not afraid? Not spiritually timid?"

"No, Lord."

She nodded, smiled at me. Zoe's smile. A last sip from Her glass of Guinness, an onion ring for the road, and, once again, my black-haired Goddess vanished into the bright, heavenly afternoon.

EIGHT

For the next four days I tried calling on God, as Julian had advised me to do. I prayed in all the traditional ways—standing, sitting, on my knees. There are no chapels or churches, no temples or mosques in heaven, the idea being that everything there is already holy and so it doesn't make sense to single out one place or another for worship. All this praying was done in my condominium, or while I was out for a walk, or between golf shots. "God," I said, "I'm ready to go back to the blue planet. The truth is, I wish I'd never mentioned it in the first place. I'm afraid You won't let me back up here. I've always worried that I somehow arrived here by mistake. But if You want me to go, I'll go. I've thought about Your troubles and I have a few exercises You can try, a few ideas for different mental approaches. So please get in touch with me when You can. Amen."

Nothing happened. I sent up this prayer, or some version of it, for four days, ten or twelve times a day. Nothing, no answer. No visions in Einstein disguise, no forceful taps on the shoulder by beautiful Asian women, no blazing eyes looking back at me with a packed suitcase nearby. Nothing.

Again, the usual doubts poured in: God had abandoned me; I wasn't the teacher He thought I was; the whole thing had been some kind of a lesson, or joke, from the start. Who was I to think I could actually be assigned to teach God something about a game He'd invented? I wrestled with this nonsense for four days and nights and then just decided on a kind of surrender. I did what I'd always done on earth when things felt beyond my control: I went out and played a round of golf.

I think one of the reasons golf is such an addictive pastime is that, after you've achieved a basic level of proficiency—somewhere around the fifteen handicap zone—you can, to a certain degree, control what happens on the course. Not every shot, no one controls every shot, but you can control a high enough percentage of your shots that you have at least the illusion that you're in charge. It's a small amount of authority, but on certain days that's about a million times more than you have in your married life, or in your work life, or in world politics, is it not?

You hit a nine iron stiff from 135 yards and you think: All right, I did that. I made that explosive white ball fly 405 feet through the air and stop an arm's length from where I aimed it.

It's rather a special feeling.

So I went out to play a round and get my mind off God and His or Her troubles. But, for some reason, I didn't go to El Rancho Obispo. It was right out my back door, literally, and challenge enough. And I had friends there. But I guess I wanted a little bit of anonymity, some thinking time, because I took a shuttle over to a tight nine-hole gem called Nirvana Meadows, where I'd played once, in a member-guest, with a woman I was seeing for a short while.

Nirvana Meadows has a tropical feel to it. The air is humid and hot, the fairways dotted with palm and breadfruit trees, the clubhouse done up in bright colors as if it's sitting on the shore at Cozumel, or not far from Bombay or Kinshasa. It starts off with a tricky dogleg right that has a large tree blocking part of the fairway just at the turn. Sometimes you'll see a spectator or two sitting beneath that tree, picnicking in harm's way, calmly watching the golfing goings-on.

On that day I took out a three wood and hit a nice little draw down the right side, about 240 yards. The ball bounced just perfectly, squeezing past the tree and into the open area beyond, leaving me only a pitching wedge to the green.

"Nice swing," someone behind me said as I was about to leave the tee.

"Thanks, want to join me?"

He nodded and I saw then, too late, that he was carrying one of those tiny golf bags that hold only about three or four clubs. This can be the sign of either a very good or a very poor golfer—the former just out for practice with a few sticks, and the latter so bad that he can't yet really tell the difference between hitting a nine iron and hitting an eight.

This fellow was on the plump side, of indeterminate age. He might have been thirty and he might have been a well-preserved sixty. Receding hairline, some type of Middle Eastern or South Asian blood. In a very relaxed way he set his little bag down, drew out his driver, dropped a ball on the ground without even using a tee, and hit an amazing power fade—probably 380 yards—that curled around the tree on the fly and bounced and rolled to within ten paces or so of the tiny first green.

"Beautiful," I said. He didn't seem to hear me. We started off down the fairway with the sun beating down on us and the smell of bougainvillea in the air, and I held out my hand and said, "Hank."

"Buddha," he said.

I looked away. If it hadn't been for the tee shot, and my recent experiences with another impossibly good player, I would have taken it as some sort of weird practical joke. But, in the first place, practical jokers don't make it into heaven—God harbors a particular dislike for practical jokers and punsters, though He loves a good comedian—and, in the second place, Old Tom Morris couldn't have hit that tee shot, with a driver off the turf no less, on his best day. I suppose that, after having played with God, my mind had been opened to a certain degree. I saw that there were no limits to how well a golf ball could be struck, or how far it could go. Well, perhaps it is incorrect to say *no* limits, but the limits were different than I had always assumed. Besides, there was an air of calm about this fellow, a way he had of smiling, of seeming to be still while he was in fact moving, that was extraordinary.

I hit my wedge to ten feet and just missed the birdie putt. Buddha took out his driver again and bumped one along the tight fairway and right into the hole. No exclamation of joy accompanied this remarkable shot. Calm as could be, he walked up and plucked his ball out from between the pin and the edge of the cup with two fingers, made the little smile for which he is famous, and walked toward the second tee.

He made eagle on the second hole, again. I made par. And as we walked toward the third tee he felt obliged to say, "My home course," hoping, I suppose, that I would feel less inept in comparison.

What a fine golfing companion he turned out to be. It was a bit intimidating at first, just as it had been, playing with God. Buddha never used a tee, never took a practice swing, seemed not even to have to line up his putts. And he started off eagle, eagle, birdie, par, birdie!

But there was something so . . . egoless about him. Not the smallest hint of a swagger. Not the smallest sign of aggravation when he finally missed a putt, on number six, and made bogey. In a strange way it was like playing with a reflection of your best self and, in fact, as if he'd infected me, I did start to play with a calm precision I hadn't known since my prime.

We stopped after our first time around the nine holes for a quick glass of coconut milk, and then, as we worked our way into the second nine, I decided to take advantage of the situation. Rather than mincing along bashfully, I reminded myself that I might never play with Buddha again (there were, after all, several billion of his followers in heaven and I assumed he'd prefer their company to mine) and I ought to make the most of it.

So, after working up my courage for several holes, on the downhill, par-three seventeenth, I said, after we'd both reached the green with our tee shots: "I've always had a question about Buddhism. Would you mind?"

"Not at all."

"When I was on earth it always seemed strange to me that the other religions all sooner or later ended up with a war of some kind. The Catholics were fighting the Protestants. The Sikhs and Muslims were fighting the Hindus. The Jews and Muslims."

"The Crusades," he put in, helpfully.

"The Crusades. But I don't remember ever hearing of a Buddhist war—one faction fighting another, or Buddhists fighting Christians over some piece of territory. Did I miss something?"

"You didn't miss anything," he said.

"Then there's a secret involved."

"You used the word, not me," he said.

We both sank our birdie putts and walked on through a grove of breadfruit trees to the last tee.

"Could you share it with me?"

"Share what?"

"The secret. The answer to my question."

He shrugged. "The nonviolence thing," he said, as if the subject bored him.

"But a lot of religions have the nonviolence thing, and they still get involved in wars."

He shrugged again and looked at me full in the face. Whereas God's eyes had seemed to be blazing with light, Buddha's had a sense of emptiness to them, as if you were looking into a bottomless valley. Kind enough, but large and echoing. "Be careful, Fins-Winston," he said. "You know what they say: that if you have too much curiosity about earth you'll end up back down there again."

"I am going down there again," I blurted out before I could stop myself. "I'm going down there with God."

"God?"

"Sure, God. He wants help with His golf game. It's not a secret. You must know."

"I do know," he admitted. "God and I are quite close, actually. He's been talking to me about you. He says if I ever need help with my game you're the go-to guy."

"Sure," I said. "Anytime. I—"

"He was fibbing about me throwing clubs, you know. I've never thrown a club. Not even on earth."

"But, what about the nonviolence question? I mean—"

"I'll give you a question in return. Answer it and . . . we'll see."

"A koan?" I said. "One of those Zen things. The sound of one hand clapping and all that?"

Buddha smiled and hit another 350-yard drive. Then he turned to me and said: "What do you call someone who just barely made it to heaven in the first place, and only because of the enthusiastic recommendations of a few of his old friends, and then risks his place here by going back to earth again on a crazy errand?"

He was staring at me now. It felt as though he were peering deep into my past, seeing every life I'd lived, all my errors and thrills, seeing the little hungers and prideful places I'd carried with me to paradise. I stumbled and stuttered for a while beneath the force of that gaze, then managed: "A faithful servant?" with my voice creaking and squeaking like boiled cabbage.

"Ah," he said, the little smile breaking into a full grin, then a drawn-out laugh that echoed through a banana plantation to our right.

"Not the right answer?"

He let the light from his laughter bathe me for a little while, until I squirmed uncomfortably, and then he said, "No," and we walked up the last fairway shoulder to shoulder.

Unlike God, Buddha didn't seem to feel the need to eat and drink once the round was over, and didn't just disappear. We shook hands on the last green, then he bowed to me in a formal way and shifted his little bag to the other shoulder. "I'll walk with you a while," he said, and we carried our clubs off the property and out along an abandoned country road.

I have always had a special affection for country roads. Once in my previous incarnation, traveling in southern France on some kind of golfing junket, I lost my way and accidentally ended up in a small town not far from Montpellier. There was a road there—I'll remember it forever—with graceful poplars to either side and ancient, dusty stone walls behind them. It turned out that the Tour de France was passing through town that day, so I pulled over and watched. I remember leg muscles pumping, team cars following, the cloud of dust; and I remember that the moment had a kind of magic in it for me. Not long afterward—about six weeks—I died. And just as I was dying a vision of that road came back to me, and brought with it a sense of profound calm. Next thing I knew I was in heaven.

So Buddha and I walked out on this road. It was the tropics, as I've mentioned, and we both sweated as we went along. As had been the case when I'd been with God, some of the time at least, being with Buddha gave me a warm feeling, the certainty that I was lovable, and loved. How exactly they conveyed this I don't know, but, in earthly terms, it might be compared to taking a walk with a new lover. You've just broken down the walls that keep you in your individuality, your loneliness. You want to be with this person so badly, and you are sure they want to be with you. There is a kind of dense sweetness to the air, and you breathe it in.

There was no particular rush. We weren't walking anywhere, just walking. After a time Buddha said: "Have you played Bo Tree Village?"

"Never," I said.

"Fantastic layout, lots of water, you hit over rice paddies, the whole thing. We'll play it together sometime. I'll have you as my guest."

"Thank you," I said. "I'd like that." And then, after another few paces, I could no longer maintain my facade of nonchalance. "Tell me something, would you?"

"Anything."

"What did I do to deserve this? I mean, God wanting to take lessons from me. Buddha inviting me out for a round of golf. I was perfectly happy in heaven, and all this seems like an extra bonus on the one hand, and . . ."

"And a pain in the rear on the other."

"Right."

"You almost want to be left alone, correct?"

"Sure. Almost, I mean—"

"Well, since you have such a great curiosity about the nature of things, I'll tell you this, Hank: You'll never be left alone."

"But it's supposed to be paradise."

"It is. But, believe me, if we left you alone you'd get really tired of it after a few years. You'd switch from male to female, African to European, old to young, golfer to bowler to cricket player to scholar to stamp collector, and you'd eventually get so bored you'd go out of your mind. That's one of the secrets: Things grow, the universes expand."

"Einstein said so."

"He was right. Things expand, which means you expand. No stopping it."

"But it hurts a little, or, not hurts exactly, but it's difficult."

"That's called 'work.' We're programmed to work."

"Even you?" I said.

He nodded.

"Even God?"

"Especially God, since God does the programming. As a soul evolves it begins to enjoy work more and to fight it less. That's one of the reasons you made it up here, Fins-Winston." As he said that name he actually clapped me on the back, an American-style congratulations. "You loved your work. You devoted yourself to it. God doesn't forget a thing like that."

"So you make it up here, rest a while, then you're given another assignment?"

"Bingo!" Buddha said.

"And you have no choice?"

"Of course. You always have a choice. Always. You can say no and wallow in the pleasures of being here, though I wouldn't recommend doing that for more than a few hundred years. What 'no' does is just put off the work. You come to it eventually, but the attitude is bad and it's more of a struggle. Just say 'yes,' push yourself out of that armchair, run through the flames, the heat of re-entry, and things will always turn out for the better. You'll have to trust me on that."

"I do," I said.

"Good. Travel well, then. Give God my regards and tell Him I'm still, you know, ticked off about the club-throwing remark."

"I will. And, thanks, by the way."

Buddha waved off my gratitude, smiled with one corner of his mouth, and drifted away toward a large tree at a crossroads. I glanced back once, before turning toward home, and saw him sitting there with his legs crossed and his small bag of clubs at his side.

NINE

Buddha's helpful comments made me certain of what I had suspected all along: God was not learning from me; He was teaching me. What, exactly, was the nature of this instruction I did not yet know, but the wonderful aspect of having been a teacher for so long is that I've become acutely aware of what it takes to be a good student. Some of the clients I'd worked with never really listened to what I was telling them on the practice tee or the putting green, did not have the ability to open themselves to the experience, weren't humble enough to really change. But others, the better students, came to our appointments with a sort of basic trust. They knew they had something to learn, and they believed I could teach it to them. Most important, they knew they would have to change something about their swing and that there would be a degree of discomfort involved in that process.

So I tried to put myself in their shoes. Buddha had shown me that even though I was in heaven, my happiness wasn't a static thing. I was supposed to grow. I could accept that and work through the difficulties of it, or I could resist. I vowed to accept it.

The problem is that, in golf as in life, difficulties don't usually take the shape we want them to. We see our troubles through the filter of our own imperfection, which makes solving them much harder. Even good golfers, even those who understood they had a problem, often would come to me with an inaccurate assessment of their flaws, some idea of what the cure should be, and that would get in the way of the learning process. For example, if they were hitting slices, they'd think they had to come at the ball more "from the inside" as we say, when, in fact, all they had to do was relax at the top of the downswing and that inside move would happen naturally. But try getting them to see that! Try getting them to stop thinking about coming at the ball from the inside and working their upper body into a sort of small panic.

And the same was true with me, I see that now, in retrospect. After my encounter with Goddess, and my talk with Buddha, it was starting to become apparent to me that I was going back to earth to help God with His game, but also, more important, to help myself. And once I saw that, of course, I started to lie awake at night wondering what I needed to change. I went through my habits and failures on earth, wracking my brain to find the trouble, the offensive aspects of me, the things God wouldn't like. Later I would be shown that this was an absolutely idiotic approach.

But that would be a long while in the future. For the moment, I was concerned about preparing to go back to earth, a re-entry I can't say I was looking forward to. Again, God made me wait. A day went by after my round with Buddha. Another day. What was I supposed to do? Pack? Shave extra close? Eat? Refrain from eating? Keep a journal? Change my underwear twice every day? What did God want from me? In my impatience to find an answer to that question, I stopped working on the single problem God had actually assigned me: I stopped trying to figure out what was wrong with His game. And that's the typical pattern, as I've discovered. You have one simple thing to accomplish in order to fulfill God's wishes, and you mess it up with a thousand unnecessary concerns. It was exactly, precisely, astonishingly like what happened on the golf course when one was playing poorly.

I waited. Two more days went by, three days, four. I got tired of playing at Rancho Obispo, tired of getting down on my knees and asking God what I should do, tired of watching out my back door for Buddha to arrive and take me to the Bo Tree Resort, as he had promised. I went back to Nirvana twice, hoping to bump into him and perhaps be granted another measure of wisdom, but the place was crowded with older, slower golfers, and I didn't even bother teeing off.

Finally, in exasperation, I ventured off to try a different course, one I'd heard about from some of my friends. Scarlet Sands it was called. Because of the name, I suppose, it was said to be popular with people who'd been communists during their last lifetime on earth—even in heaven people are allowed their quirks and inside jokes, their clubbishness and clannishness. And that rumor was precisely what had always kept me from trying the place, because I'm put off by communists, I tell you that frankly. I'm a compassionate and open-minded soul, but I'm also a free market type of fellow, as are most of my golfing pals.

But here I am, drifting again. My apologies. In any case, I was tired of my home course and the conversation of my friends there, impatient to be off on my new assignment, to see God again. But, since there was no way for me to rush the process, I called up and made a tee time at Scarlet Sands.

The club turned out to be nothing like I'd expected. No leftist intellectuals hanging around a shabby clubhouse reading each other passages from *Das Kapital* and poems about The Struggle. No signs at the door requiring that everyone dress alike. No portraits of Lenin or Ho Chi Minh on the walls. It was a modest place, I'll say that. Though by the standards of Eden Hills everything now looked rather modest to my eye. A wood-sided clubhouse, unpainted and already scarred by the sirocco that blew from time to time in those parts. (Isn't it amazing:

Some of heaven's residents actually missed the siroccos of their youth, just as others missed hurricanes and heavy snowstorms, monsoons and tornadoes. So, to accommodate them, heaven offers every imaginable climate zone within a few minutes' travel.) Lots of bunkers, naturally, but nice-looking green fairways, too. The pro at the desk, John something-or-other, a sort of hippie in sandals and beard, told me the holes were straight, narrow, cluttered with obstacles, but eminently fair, and advised me not to try to overpower the course. "Scarlet Sands kind of humbles you," he said.

Too bad, I thought, I'm not in the mood to be humbled.

The first hole was a tight 430-yard par four with an enormous waste bunker running the length of the left side, and a canal to the right. The canal is out-of-bounds, which encourages you to play it safe and aim too far to the left, which brings the waste bunker into play. I knew this was just one of the little tricks good course architects play on a golfer, and so I spent a moment visualizing a perfect drive boring straight up the middle of the greensward. When I stood up to swing, though, my mind was suddenly filled with worries, and I pulled my tee shot a tad left, got an ugly bounce, and ended up playing my second from a patch of hard-packed sand behind a mesquite bush. The bush caught my club on the downswing and the ball skittered forward, still in the sand. I tried a risky shot—hitting a runner onto the green with a five iron—but played it too low, caught the lip of the bunker, ended up lying three at the edge of the rough, still 167 yards from the tiny green. I could feel a particular kind of anxiety coming over me then, that tightness you experience when you're playing badly, thinking badly, and it's still only the first hole. It was not a feeling I'd had since coming up to heaven, so I worried that my mind, or my soul, already was slipping back into its earthly posture. I even thought I felt an old ache in my formerly arthritic left shoulder—the kind of thing that is completely absent in heaven. (People might miss the sirocco, but never their arthritis pain.) All of which put me in an ugly, festering state of mind.

Trying to make a heroic shot, I took dead aim at the sucker pin—which was tucked in the left corner of the green, between deep, wicked bunkers in front and the winding canal behind. The ball came out of the rough quite hot, flew all the way to the back edge of the green, bounced hard, and plopped into the canal. I took my drop, chipped, two-putted from six feet, and walked over to the second tee. *Snowman* is the American slang for a score of eight. I could not remember ever having made a snowman in heaven. I could not remember ever being so upset at myself.

To make matters worse, just at that moment, I saw a threesome standing on the second tee, looking as though they were waiting for me. They must have played incredibly slowly because, when I'd teed off, they'd been putting out on the first green. Given my own slow pace of play on the first hole, they should have been at least on the second green by then, but there they were, lounging about, watching me carefully as I walked up. Two men and a pretty young woman. The men had beards, flaming eyes. This time, I knew almost from the first moment that they weren't your ordinary heavenly occupants. I had learned that much, at least, in the bizarre past couple of weeks.

"Why, you must be Christ," I said to the younger of the two fellows.

He smiled at me very kindly. "Yes," he said, shaking my hand. "And this is Mary, my mother. And Moses, a very old friend."

"Of course," I said, perhaps with a bit of sarcasm. "Call me Hank."

"Oh," Christ said, as if he were disappointed. "We were told to expect someone called Herman."

"Herman Fins-Winston," Mary put in gently.

But there was nothing gentle about the third member of the trio. Moses was staring at me with an intensity that could have severed the columns that support the sun. He was a fearsome-looking fellow, enormous muscular forearms and a tremendous beard flowing out beneath piercing eyes and a broad forehead.

"That's me," I squeaked. "But I like to be called Hank."

They did not seem to hear very well. "Well, we want to join up with you, Herman," Moses rumbled. "That is, if you don't object to playing with people of color."

They were, in fact, of a shade something between that of a resident of Stockholm and one of Ouagadougou. Cinnamon brown, a beautiful tone. But what was this refrain of hints about my being racist? I am not racist, I want to say that very clearly. Never was. Naturally, it was true that I'd played my golf almost exclusively with white people, but that had been the nature of golf in those years, and no fault of mine.

But I wasn't sure I wanted to join up with them, for reasons that had nothing to do with skin color. I mean, judging by the first hole, I was playing embarrassingly badly that day, and in a foul mood besides. Others may approach it differently, but on earth, when I am in a foul mood, I prefer to work things out in solitude rather than salve my raw spirits with companionship. Anna Lisa had always been annoyed by that aspect of me—the occasional sour moods, the penchant for solitude. Just as I was about to ask the holy trio, in a respectful way, of course, if I could play through and be left alone, I remembered my ex-wife's annoyance and bitterness. I might even say I had a feeling for what it must have been like for her, how she must have felt excluded and frustrated by the way I'd behaved. So I stifled my words, made a stiff nod, and stood to one side to watch them tee off.

Jesus's swing was long and smooth, as effortless as God's. His ball had a low trajectory, with a slight fade at the last. Three-hundred and thirty or forty yards, dead center. Moses was a different type of player, a power swinger, someone who used the large muscles. He ripped at the ball and pulled it well out over the palm trees before fading it back to the middle, close to Jesus's ball. I hit a modest drive and then we walked up a few paces and stood quietly while Mary hit from the women's tee. She had a wonderful grace to her—her walk, her voice—but seemed a beginner at the game. Her drive bounced and rolled down the middle, but only about a hundred yards, and she let out a charming laugh at herself. We plodded off down the fairway.

Except for yours truly, it was a happy foursome. They knew I had been a teacher, of course, and so they asked if I wouldn't mind helping Mary learn to play. It was, as things turned out, her first time on the golf course— amazing to me, given the number of years she'd been living there, in such close proximity to such great golf. (It was explained to me, much later, that, after what she'd been through on her last earthly visit, God had arranged for her to have a special place in heaven, to be waited on hand and foot, to spend her days soaking in mineral baths, listening to fine music. Bach is in paradise, as you would expect. Chopin, Beethoven, Billie Holiday. Elvis, of course.) Amazing, too, that she could play as well as she did for a first timer. I gave her some basic tips—changed her grip, showed her how to shift her weight down and into the ball rather than trying to gain the extra distance by swinging mightily with her arms (Moses was a bad influence in this respect). She would spend the day playing double- and triple-bogey golf, but it didn't seem to bother her in the slightest, nor should it have.

But how I struggled with my own emotions on that sunny morning! Bad decisions, hideous tee shots, faltering putts. Jesus played steadily, perfectly. Moses bombed tremendous drives and fairway woods but had an abundance of trouble with his short game. Mary laughed a great deal and slowly improved. And I positively stank up the course. On the ninth hole, a long par three over a huge lake, I hit three balls into the water before finally putting one on the green. Three water balls, three wet ones, three dunks! This from a former tour player, in heaven no less!

As we approached the green, Moses walked ahead of us and parted the waters—it seemed to be some kind of a running joke among them. Mary walked through, hitting her ball along the bottom of the lake with an eight iron as she went. But Jesus took a side route, stepping across the surface of the water as calmly as you please. I was afraid part of the joke would be to have the waters close over me if I tried to follow Mary and Moses, or swallow me up if I went the way Jesus had gone, so, as inconspicuously as possible, I skirted the edge of the hazard on dry land and tried to control my urge to scream at the fact that my heavenly golf game had gone to hell. But I did manage to sink a long putt on that hole, which made me feel a bit better, and there was a food stand at the turn so we stopped for some refreshment. By the time we teed off on the tenth I was a notch or two calmer.

"You're really a pretty good sport, you know, Fins-Winston," Moses said bluntly, "considering the awful state of your game."

"I usually play better," I mumbled.

"We know that," Mary said generously.

"No wonder God has taken a liking to you," Jesus

added. "You bear your difficulties with a certain amount of, well, grace."

I looked at him again. What a kind fellow he was, trim, lithe, his face lit by an expression of such joy and goodwill that you wanted to stay close to him, touch his golf jersey, carry his bag. "Where I come from," I said, "most people usually say *you* are God."

"He isn't," Moses put in, rather quickly. Jesus looked at him, smiled, and then, as if to prove something, he hit the single most amazing shot I'd seen in the remarkable past few weeks. His drive simply rocketed off the tee, there is no other word for it. I don't believe it reached a height of more than twenty feet, but it just kept going and going, so fast we could barely track it. Naturally, once it touched down—a good three hundred yards out—it ran like the wind. In all, he must have hit that ball over 420 yards, and with what looked like a three-quarter swing, besides. Mary beamed; Moses harrumphed and hammered his own impressive drive. I more or less followed suit. We started off down the fairway in the perfect sunlight, a fresh breeze in our faces, stopping only to watch Mary hit.

After another hundred yards or so, Jesus dropped back even with me and let the other two walk on ahead. "Don't mind Moses," he said. "He's just a little bitter some days, feels he never quite received the kind of widespread recognition he deserved on earth. Tough childhood, too, you know."

"He needs work on his short game," I said.

"Little bit. But a good old fellow just the same. Did great things when he was down there, you know. A true leader, whereas I was more of the political radical type. A troublemaker, some would say."

We walked on a few paces, stopped to let Mary hit. "Beauty, Mom," Jesus said. And then, in a quieter voice, "This might be difficult for you to understand, but, in fact, to answer your question about the difference between God and me: There is no difference; we're all part of God. Chips of the Divine, is the way we sometimes put it. You've only really known the laws of biology and physics from a human standpoint, you're still probably caught up in the idea of separating bodies one from another. It takes most human beings thousands of years to get over that."

I did not really like or approve of this notion. I wanted my separateness, my blessed individuality. But, rather than admit that to Jesus, I changed the subject slightly: "I used to think, when I first got here," I said, "that I was at the end of something. I used to think I'd arrived, as they say."

"And now?"

"And now, every day it seems like there's farther and farther to go."

"Yes," Jesus said happily. "Isn't it wonderful?"

By that time I'd reached my ball. I stepped off the distance to the nearest yardage marker and discovered that I was still 327 yards out. By that point I had no confidence in my swing whatsoever, my mind was spinning down into an old depression, something straight out of the

Western Pennsylvania Open. Having been in heaven for seven good years, having been so far from such feelings, I can tell you that I almost wanted to throw down my clubs and walk away weeping. Imagine your worst, your very worst moment on a golf course. . . . My feelings were that times a hundred. I was in the process of thoroughly humiliating myself . . . and in front of a trio of some of the great sacred souls of all time.

But just as I was setting up over the ball, Jesus came up to me and said, "Can I show you one thing?"

"Of course."

"You're dipping your left shoulder a tad." With that, he touched me there, on the shoulder, just a light touch with two fingers, and I felt something go through me, a current of some kind. I looked up at him. He was smiling as if I were the finest specimen of man he'd ever met. "Just swing away now."

I had a three wood in my hands. I swung away. The ball flew 310 yards, bounced once on the green, and rolled to within ten feet of the flagstick. And I hadn't even swung hard. I hadn't swung hard at all, in fact, and had hit a three wood close to a hundred yards longer than I had in my best days on tour. "What did you do, Lord?" I said, looking at him. I felt, at that moment, an almost overwhelming urge to kneel before him.

"You had a tightness in your left shoulder from an old injury, three lifetimes ago. I loosened you up. You were just paying for old sins there on the first few holes, some kind of old egotism. You should be fine now."

And I was. For the rest of the game I regained my balance, with a little something extra added in. There were no more three-hundred-yard three woods, but I swung easily and naturally, hit the ball 20 percent farther than I usually did, and played the back in two under. Moses was seven under, Mary somewhere twenty or thirty over; Jesus didn't keep score.

On the dogleg, par-four twelfth we came upon two men having an argument in the shrubbery about halfway down the fairway. "Followers of Muhammad and Krishna," Moses whispered to me when we were safely past them.

"Fighting?"

He nodded. "They're arguing about which one of their teachers is going to have more influence in the coming centuries on earth. You know, the Jews were on top for a while. Then it was the Christians' turn, in certain parts of the world, at least, Catholics here, Protestants there. Now, naturally enough, the Hindus and the Muslims are hoping to be number one—not in numbers so much as in political power, military might, those ridiculous things. Jesus has been trying to talk with them but they won't listen. The teachers themselves, of course, are outraged."

"What about the Buddhists?"

"They don't seem to care."

On the long par-five fifteenth, Jesus dropped back with me again while Moses and Mary were off in the left woods looking for her ball, and I decided, as I had with Buddha, not to waste the opportunity.

"Would you answer one question for me?" I said.

"Anything, Fins-Winston."

I winced at the name. "I'm going back to earth for a while, as you know, and you left heaven to go back there, and I've always wondered, you know . . . why things are designed the way they are?"

"I'm not sure I follow you."

"I mean, look what they did to you on earth. Why are we, why are they always killing each other and hurting each other down there: rape, molestation, war, and so forth?"

"They're afraid," he said, as if it were the most obvious thing in the world.

"Of what? Dying? Illness?"

"Oh, just generally afraid. On that level, poor people, most of them at least, are living in a sort of constant, low-grade terror. Any little thing can spark it: Someone who doesn't look like them, or talk like them, or think like they do. Someone who wants to unify rather than divide. They insist on their individuality, their separateness, as if they have no connection at all to every other living thing. Your earth is just one planet in one of the millions of universes, you know, just a stopping place on the road. A stopping place for fearful types, a place of pain for many people, I'm sorry to say. No offense intended, but earth is not exactly my favorite of the so-called heavenly bodies."

"Stopping place on the way to what?"

He only smiled and motioned for me to be silent while Mary hit. "Another beauty, Mom!" he called over to her.

Moses gave him the thumbs-up sign without turning around.

"Wasn't it awful for you, though? Being tortured like that. Surely you didn't deserve it."

"Sure, sure," he said. "Pretty bad there. Worse, having my beloved mother witnessing the whole thing. Worse still that people ended up using me, us, to sow dissension, to hate. The Protestants and Catholics, the Christians and Jews. Some of my best friends are Jews, you know. My parents, for instance. And the Protestants and Catholics, well, I mean, they're much more alike than different. It hurt, no question."

"But why? I mean, why does God allow it?"

"It's like golf, my friend, that's the sum total of it. If life were too easy, most souls would flounder, sorry to say. Humans complain, but it's really their troubles that move them toward grace. The pain is very real—sometimes it even cripples a soul for a life or two, the way one traumatic hole can seem to destroy a golfer's composure forever. It's not forever, that's all, in golf or in living. Down the road you might want to ponder all the parallels. But for right now you shouldn't really think about it too much. Just do your best. Go forward with courage and goodwill. You're a little bit afraid of your upcoming trip, it seems to me. Afraid of disappointing God—-He really does need help with that short game of His, you know."

"I am afraid, I admit it. Of going back. Of failing."

"But you can't play golf that way, Fins-Winston, and you can't live that way either, on earth or up here. Any tightness, any fear, the fear of failure especially, is going to limit you. Remember that. Just go forward, don't think too much, trust in the process, and you'll be fine. I can't go into details, but God has something pretty special set up for you a little ways down the road."

"The designing job, you mean?"

"Oh no, that's just a tiny dessert. Your true reward will be something considerably grander than that. You'll hear about it before too much more time goes by. Let's just finish up the round now, okay my friend? I have a little business to attend to after this."

What business? I wanted to say. What do you do up here now? How did you get chosen in the first place? If we're all part of God, then why do some of us seem to understand it so much more powerfully and fully and so much earlier than others? But I'd had my ration of wisdom for the day. I knew that, and was thankful for it. I ought to mention here, in passing, that one of the prominent emotions in heaven is gratitude. Wonderful as things are there, people don't take them for granted the way we do on earth. I felt so lucky to have had the conversation, to have been in his presence. I mean, Jesus, Mary, Moses, Buddha, a blessing from the Desert Fathers, Guinness and onion rings with God Himself—what, I wondered, had I ever done to deserve this?

The round ended as strangely as it had begun. We shook hands on the eighteenth, as was the custom. (In heaven and on earth this graciousness is one of the beautiful aspects of the game of golf. I mean, one doesn't usually see hockey players taking off their helmets and shaking hands with one another after the match.) And then, as we were walking off the course, the three of them . . . the three of them turned into, well . . . into trees.

I know I know, all my credibility is going to be washed away in that one sentence. But they turned into trees, I tell you, trees that hadn't been there. I went up and touched them, tried to talk to them, but they were three palm trees just off the eighteenth hole of Scarlet Sands, no sign of their clubs or clothing. But let me add this: Since that moment, in heaven and on earth, I have never looked at a tree in quite the same way, never again had quite such a firm belief in the separateness, the individuality, of things.

TEN

Reading back over what I have written here so far, I see I've given the impression that heaven is composed of little else besides golf. That is not the case. Golf is available, of course, abundant in fact, but if you loved gardening on earth there are hundreds of thousands of fertile plots where you can exercise your green thumb. If you loved fishing there are streams packed with trout, oceans full of marlin, and so on. It would almost be true to say that we engineer our own life in heaven—age, friends, activities. But, in fact, there is always a component over which we have no control. The situation on earth is similar, I suppose—some things within our control, some things not—though in a harsher and rougher way, and, for most of us, without the soothing balm of God's presence.

During the period when all this golf drama was occurring, I had a special friend. Her name was Juanita and she had chosen a body that was quite a bit older than mine—the equivalent of her early sixties, in earthly measurement.

Juanita had chosen a Hispanic identity for this stage of her heavenly life, partly because she had a passion for the tango, and partly because some of her soul mate children were living in Argentina for that stage of their evolution, and she felt it was important to maintain a linguistic and cultural connection with them. (Those who dread the apparent finality of death might be comforted by the actual chemistry of the universe, a system of attraction and spiritual linkage that binds certain souls to each other for many centuries at a time. Juanita enjoyed this kind of bond with the souls who had been her children in her most recent life. Their connection had persisted through many deaths, and it meant a great deal to her, and, good mother that she was, she worked hard at nurturing it.)

In any case, twice a week, Juanita and I would go to one of the tango clubs. Imagine the thrill of that: being in your early sixties and tangoing the warm nights away with a man half your age. I think it was partly that thrill that made Juanita choose to be in her sixties, when she could have been almost anything: sweet sixteen with a boyfriend her own age, a thirty-year-old happily married wife, a vastly wealthy middle-aged man with a very young woman at his side. Love takes as many forms in heaven as it does on earth.

For me, there was a different attraction to our friendship. Juanita and I never actually made love, but we did share a deep intimate connection that I never remembered feeling with anyone else. Succinctly put, talking with her, spending time with her, felt to me the way making love with a beautiful woman had felt on earth, only there was no orgasmic end to the experience; it just bloomed and bloomed. We would meet two or three times a week for breakfast or lunch, then get together again and tango on Wednesday nights. Sometimes we'd even spend the night together at her place or mine, sleeping in the same bed. No sex, as I've said, but this delicious sense of closeness, of unity, as if we were two halves of the same person. That day on the golf course, when Jesus had talked to me about the illusion of separateness, I'd thought immediately of Juanita. If it were true that we were all actually one spirit in billions of manifestations, then Juanita was the only other soul I had ever met with whom I could actually feel that.

She did not enjoy golf, however.

On what would turn out to be our last night together before my trip back here to earth, we went out to a tango club called Old Rio and danced for hours with our usual assortment of friends. Juanita knew all about my encounters with the Holy Ones, about my upcoming but as yet unscheduled trip, about God's putting problems. Perhaps she sensed that we wouldn't be seeing each other for a long while because she asked to leave the club early—unusual for her.

We found a promenade along a tropical shoreline that reminded me of a beach I'd once visited on the west coast of Mexico. There, arm in arm, we strolled along under a display of northern lights, past other happy couples, young and old. In the background was the steady pulse of a heavy surf. The air was sweet with tropical flowers, a touch of sea salt. For a long while we simply rested in this beautiful intimacy we shared, in our comfortable silence.

"A drink?" Juanita suggested, nodding toward an all-night café that was perched on a small bluff overlooking the water.

We found a table, ordered some fancy fruit-and-liquor concoctions, and sat there sipping and staring out at the pounding surf.

Juanita spoke, after a time: "Your ex-wife, Anna Lisa, came to see me the other day."

I gagged on my pineapple-banana-mint julep, coughed and coughed, and had to discreetly spit out a mouthful into my napkin. Juanita was smiling at me.

"Sure, smile," I said, "I nearly choked to death." She kept smiling. When I recovered, I said, "I didn't know she was up here. In fact, I was pretty sure she was someplace else."

"She's here. A recent arrival."

"What did she want?"

"She talked obsessively about a certain Herman Fins-Winston."

This was different. Juanita knew how much I hated the name, and had never allowed it to cross her lips. I looked at her, perplexed, even slightly stung.

"Sorry, Hank, I was just quoting her. She loves you, you know that, of course."

"I most certainly do not know that."

"She does, though. She was a sort of teacher for you, as it turns out."

"Well, then I hope I thoroughly learned the lesson and never have to repeat it."

There was a smile, followed by an uncomfortable pause, another rarity where Juanita and I were concerned. I mentioned earlier that painful emotions like jealousy and regret are drastically muted in heaven. You barely feel them. But over the preceding few days, along with the temporary slippage in my golf game, and a new achiness in my joints, I'd noticed that the volume seemed to have been turned up in my emotional life. I was sensitive to things that had stopped troubling me years before. I was being reminded of what it felt like to be worried, fearful, ill at ease.

"She feels badly about the way she acted toward you. She feels a great deal of regret. The problem is that she had been sent to help you with a particular assignment, but something went wrong. She became frustrated, turned against you when in fact she was simply ashamed of her own failure. Does that make any sense, feeling-wise?"

"What was the assignment?"

"You know, don't you?"

I shook my head.

"Well, you were designed to be not just a good golfer but a great one, perhaps the greatest who ever played, and she was designed to support you in that."

Feeling-wise. Feeling-wise it made about as much sense as taking a more lofted club into a thirty-mile-an-hour headwind. The only nugget of truth was this greatest golfer idea. Not that I had ever come close to that, but I'd felt, in my college days, especially after my second selection to the All-America squad, that I was . . . well, *destined* might be too strong a word . . . but I felt that I was meant to play very well, to have great success on tour, perhaps even to inspire some numbers of people. I suppose a lot of very good young golfers feel that. But in my case it was less conceit or confidence and more something that might be called mystical, a voice whispering close against the skin of my soul.

Somehow, shortly after I actually arrived on tour, that voice had gone silent and that feeling, that sense of destiny, evaporated. Sitting there with the surf pounding and the other cafégoers sipping their drinks and laughing in the sweet tropical air, I believed, for a few seconds, that I could almost touch my finger to the moment when that voice had been drowned out. It was a week or two before the Western Pennsylvania Open. I had been playing down south—South Carolina or Georgia—and something had happened, something, something. . . . Some premonition of an encounter with an evil, soul-destroying force. It hid in a cleft of memory and would not show its face.

The only residue of that special feeling was what I experienced in my teaching life. There, I had moved people, inspired people. I had full confidence in myself. But the rest of it had been lost.

Juanita moved the swizzle stick around lazily in her drink. "Anna Lisa apologized, through me. She said she'd even gone to God, or one of His lieutenants, and asked for another chance with you. The offer was refused."

"Praise be to God," I said.

"But she wanted me to tell you that this trip might have some connection to all that."

"She's not going with me, is she? Juanita? Say she's not going with me."

Again the smile. I was, in fact, overdoing it a bit for comic effect.

Juanita was shaking her head happily. "I told her you wanted to make the trip alone. That is, just you and God this time, no intermediaries. I told her you had been chosen to cure God's golf troubles, the yipes, or whatever—"

"Yips."

"She plays now, apparently, and understands what He's going through. She wishes you luck. She says she'd like to play a round or two with you at some point in the future, here or on earth."

"Tell her I'm booked with my regular foursome for the next few eternities."

Juanita laughed then, her wonderful free laugh, lifting her head slightly and throwing the sound out into the night. Such a carefree soul she was, so open and warm. I hated to leave her, even temporarily.

We walked back toward Rancho Obispo arm in arm. I invited her to spend the night with me, but she just shook her head, kissed me on the mouth, and went off into the heavenly night humming a tango tune.

PART TWO

ELEVEN

On the morning after my night out with Juanita, I woke up old. I felt it as soon as I tried to get out of bed. My joints were stiff, my eyes slow to focus, my bladder summoning me urgently to the bathroom. When I'd first arrived in heaven and been asked how I wanted to live, I'd decided I would be a thirty-two-year-old man because, on earth, thirty-two had felt like the prime of life to me. At that age, I had been in my first year on the tour, playing better each month. Things with Anna Lisa had been going fairly well. I felt strong, virile, capable, content. So, naturally, my first heavenly request was to inhabit the body of a thirty-two-year-old man. Seven years later, I was still thirty-two, and had come to the conclusion that I would happily remain at that age for a long while.

Imagine my shock, then, when I looked in the mirror that morning and saw the face of what appeared to be a fellow in his midseventies. It was my own face, no escaping that, and a nice enough face it was. Wrinkled, though. White-haired. Some sagging of the skin around the eyes and mouth and below the chin. A sudden burst of hair from my ears and nostrils. And this from the God who said He did not believe in tricks!

As I was thinking that, somewhat bitterly I'm afraid, there came a knock at the door. I looked out the window before answering and saw a side view of a trim blond woman who was loaded down—ears, fingers, wrists—with expensive jewelry. People are, as I've mentioned, quite used to making new friends in heaven. It wasn't especially unusual to have someone walk up to the door of your cabin, condominium, or seaside mansion and say she wanted to get to know you, that you'd had some connection on earth a dozen lifetimes before, that she'd heard about you from a friend, so on and so on. It had happened to me a number of times. And yet, I had the sense that there was something different about this visit, although I don't know exactly why. For a moment I hesitated, peering through the blinds. I could not quite see the woman's full face, but, from my angle at least, she had a beautiful physique and profile; I watched her with a surprising echo of old lust—something else one rarely feels in heaven, as I would like to mention here again. She was studying the fairway much as Julian Ever liked to do, and for a few seconds I thought that's who she was: God's lieutenant in another of his disguises, come to fetch me at last. My old heart beat faster.

But then the woman turned and knocked again, and I caught a glimpse of her eyes.

"Lord," I said, when I opened the door.

She looked me up and down and said, in a flirtatious voice, "Herman! Do you always greet visitors in your boxer shorts?"

Oh, the embarrassment! On earth I had always worn briefs. Now, here I was, half naked. Seventy-five years old. At the front door. Facing a beautiful young woman I knew to be my creator. And, during the night, someone had fitted me out with boxer shorts festooned with small animals. Leopards, they seemed to be, or perhaps tigers. I could not bear to look very closely.

"I've come to take you to earth," She said.

"You've made me old, Lord."

"Exactly."

"But, I died when I was fifty-eight. I'm not used to this. Would it be possible to—"

"No. Get dressed, honey. Grab your clubs, let's go."

Honey?

"We're married, by the way. You are Herman Fins-Winston, not Hank Winston. And I'm Alicia Fins-Winston."

Honey?

Without even thinking to invite Her inside, I hurried to the bedroom and put on my best golf pants (at least my waist size hadn't changed, though the cuffs dragged a bit), a jersey, grabbed a sweater. I heard Her step into the kitchen. "Should I pack anything special?" I called out.

"It's all taken care of," She called back. I could hear Her helping Herself to something in the refrigerator. "You might want to take your clubs, though, hon. No fun playing with a rental set."

"We're going then?" I said, when I walked into the kitchen. "Today?" She was an incredibly beautiful woman, the kind of woman who seems to grow more attractive as she ages, prettier at twenty-five than she was at eighteen; prettier at thirty than she was at twenty-five. No doubt she would grow more attractive still as she moved into her forties. She was sipping from a glass of grapefruit juice.

"Today's the day?"

She nodded, looked me up and down the way a wife or lover might, then set Her glass on the counter. "Ready, honey?"

"Yes. No. How do we get there? A shuttle? A ferry? A subway train with EARTH on a placard in its window?"

"We take a breath," She said.

"Take a breath?"

And that was it. At the start of the inhalation I was standing in the tidy kitchen of my cozy condominium on the thirteenth fairway of El Rancho Obispo Golf and Country Club, talking with a gorgeous woman half my age, bag of clubs beside me. And by the time my lungs were filled, She and I were in the garishly decorated plasticized office of a car rental company just outside Washington, D.C. United States of America. Earth. The Universe of Pain.

There were these hideous posters on the walls, and strange music playing in the background. A young man stood behind the counter, bobbing his head to the rhythm. He looked at me, then at God . . . that is, Alicia, and barely suppressed a mocking smile.

"Mr. and Mrs. Fins-Winston," I said firmly. "We reserved a . . ." I turned to God. "What was it we reserved this time, hon?"

"A Cadillac."

"That's right." I turned back to the smug young fellow. "A Caddy. Pastel color if you have one. Largest model."

More smirking. He was flipping through a file of orders. The strange music was being piped from speakers near the ceiling. The clothing was bizarre, the hairstyles unappealing. I looked down at the piece of paper in his hands and saw the year printed there. Seven years had passed since my death. Alicia put Her hand over mine on the countertop, Her enormous diamond sparkling.

"Cash or credit card?" the young wise guy asked me, and in such a tone that I wanted to answer: Listen, I've just come from heaven, okay? And this beautiful woman with me is God, understand? So let's leave out the sarcasm and smirking, shall we? You'll be old one day yourself, believe it or not. You may even be lucky enough to have a beautiful younger woman by your side, though looking at you, I doubt it. So let's show a little humility, shall we, and just do what our customers ask.

But all I said was: "Credit card."

I had no idea where the words were coming from. The young man was looking at me expectantly. Alicia took my hand and moved it gently off the counter and, as if it had a will of its own, it found its way into my back pocket. There I discovered a wallet, alligator hide, the type of thing I never would have owned. Inside the wallet was some cash and credit cards. I chose one of them at random and handed it over. The youngster ran it through a machine, gave me a receipt to sign, and in three minutes' time Alicia and I were driving away in a pale pink Caddy, two sets of expensive golf clubs in the trunk, three pieces of luggage. In all my years on earth I had never sat behind the wheel of a Cadillac, never mind a pastel model. I must say I liked the feeling quite well.

Still, I felt like I was moving through swirls of confusion. "What on earth is going on here?" I said.

"Meaning what, honey?" She was looking out the passenger window, admiring the scenery.

"How has all this been arranged? How do I know what to say to these people? How did I have all that in my wallet?"

She shrugged. She fiddled with the radio until it spat forth a thunderous voice saying something about eternal damnation.

"Almost amusing, aren't they."

"Who?"

She snapped the radio off angrily.

"God?"

"You must call me Alicia, honey. People will wonder."

"People will wonder? I'm wondering! What is happening here? Who are You? Why—"

She sighed impatiently. "All right. I'll say this once and only once. I'm God. You're Herman Fins-Winston, just as you were in your most recent life, just as you would have been had you let yourself live beyond age fifty-eight. Though, as you know by now, heavenly time moves at a different pace."

"Let myself—"

"Please don't interrupt. We are here to work on my golf game and to enjoy some southern hospitality. The rest is on a need-to-know basis."

"But I need to know now."

"You don't, believe me. Just simply relax."

"I cannot function without knowing. I demand to know."

"You demand?" She said, toying with the enormous diamond.

"All right, I ask. I ask You to tell me. I implore You. It's difficult enough as it is, You know, leaving heaven and landing in the office of a rental car company, in an old man's body, with some young punk smirking because—"

"Here's our story," God said impatiently. "Your first wife died six years ago. You married me for my looks. I married you for your money. I'm a little bit on the, well, on the moody side, and you can be an absolute crank. But we get along, we both love golf, travel, and fine dining. And if you call me 'God' in front of other people, once, one time, then the deal is off and I'll go back up to heaven without you. I'll find someone else to cure me of the yips and you'll have to figure out how to get back there on your own. Clear enough?"

"Yes. All right."

"Now, can we enjoy our little vacation, or can't we?"

"We can."

"Good. I may have a slightly different body while we're here, but my golf troubles are no less aggravating. This is your element, after all. And this trip, in case you've forgotten, was your idea. Your job here is to worry about curing me. I'll take care of the rest. Just go with, as they say, the flow."

"Fine."

Her voice, which had gone harsh and almost manly, abruptly changed back to the voice I'd heard in my kitchen that morning. She said: "Sorry, Honey. I'm just a little anxious about these roads." She put Her hand on my thigh and I nearly drove into a bridge abutment. "You're such a wonderfully confident driver, though. I'm sure it will all be fine."

"Where are we heading? Can I ask that—I mean, just so I know which road to take."

"Colonial Williamsburg," She said, and She turned the radio on again and found a kind of bouncy, annoying music I would later learn the name for. Disco.

TWELVE

I have to admit, reluctantly, that there was a good deal of pleasure associated with being back here on earth. The aches of an old body weren't pleasant, of course, nor were the heightened emotions of the human realm—worry, anger, pride, embarrassment. But, in a strange way, those difficulties gave a fresh quality to the feeling of being part of creation, a hard-edged clarity to the air and light. Probably I hadn't been in heaven long enough to lose the sense-pleasure and emotional orientation all humans have, because driving south along the highway into Virginia was like revisiting one's childhood home: the same mix of nostalgia and pride, the same acute sense of feeling one's way backward along a thread that wound into the center of one's identity. An aching knee, a neck that wouldn't turn very far, my eyes drinking in the green rolling hills and bare trees. I reveled in it.

Williamsburg is a quaint village of restored old homes and a battlefield/museum from America's Revolutionary War. I'd been there once, with Anna Lisa, for a charity tournament. By the time God and I pulled into the town proper I'd gotten to the point where I was more or less taking Her advice and trusting in the moment, and I was speaking and acting—and driving—comfortably enough.

Following the last of Alicia's directions, I pulled up to the front of a fine old hotel. We got out of our coral pink Cadillac and strolled past the doorman and through the carpeted lobby. They were expecting us, of course. I don't know why I should have been surprised. When I gave my name at the desk the young woman there did not even need to look us up in her records. She smiled, handed across a large envelope and a set of keys, and said there would be no charge. The keys were to a suite of rooms on the second floor, and, once we were ensconced there with our luggage, I opened the envelope and found a warm welcoming letter from a man I had never heard of.

"Does the name Charles Pysher mean anything to you?" I asked.

Alicia had stretched out on the bed with Her high heels still on and Her gold bracelets resting on Her wrists. She was wearing a fairly short skirt, and I admit with some embarrassment that I could not keep myself from noticing what beautiful legs She had. She said: "Charlie is a dear old friend."

"Well, your dear old friend has included here a letter that entitles us to a complimentary dinner at the Dining Room restaurant at a place called Ford's Colony. Plus two complimentary greens fees for tomorrow morning on one of their four courses. Do you know this place?"

"Of course I know it," She said. "How could I not know it? Some of my angels play here."

"Are You all right, honey?" I heard myself say, because there had been irritability in Her voice, a note of pain. "Do You want to rest a while before going out to dinner?"

"It's always a strain for me, coming to this place."

"Williamsburg?"

"Earth. People don't understand how hard it is."

"Why don't you rest then? Take a soak in the tub."

She nodded in what seemed a grateful way, and sat up. In another minute She was in the bathroom with the door closed and the water running. I suppose this was some kind of terrible sin, but I couldn't help myself: I imagined Her in there, taking Her clothes off, slipping naked into the tub, the water rising up around Her beautiful legs and breasts—I was human again, after all, if somewhat past my sexual prime.

At that point in history at least, Ford's Colony was one of the only golf resorts in the world with a five-star AAA-rated restaurant. I don't know why that should have surprised me, either. But it turned out that, among Her other quirks, when She returns to earth, God likes to eat well.

More than that, He, or She in this case, is a connoisseur of the planet's fine wines.

After Her bath we drove out of town a few miles, up a long access road, past large brick homes, and to the door of the clubhouse restaurant. It was a chilly night—mid-April—and in the dusk I could see fairways, greens, and bunkers in the near distance. The sight made my old heart swell with joy. This was my element. This was golf, real golf, not golf in heaven but earthly golf where there is something really at stake—money, a career, your pride. I'd missed it more than I ever would have thought.

Inside, we enjoyed a sumptuous meal: a nice fillet of beef, garlic mashed potatoes, carrots and squash in a sugary glaze, a nice fresh salad. Alicia suggested I order a certain bottle of sixteen-year-old Bordeaux—I'm forbidden from writing the name here—and I did so, and it was like drinking the nectar of life itself.

"Are we going to play tomorrow?" I asked Her, when we were dipping silver spoons into our crème brûlée, trying to stretch out the meal as long as possible.

She nodded.

"Something's bothering you," I said. I had, it seemed, turned into a sensitive husband, a role I'd never quite mastered on earth. I must say I liked it quite well.

"Just a tinge of bad memories." She spoke quietly so the people at the next table could not hear. "Earth, as I may have mentioned, is not my favorite place in the universes. They've never treated me particularly well here, during my various manifestations. I hope I don't offend you by saying this, honey, but there's something perverse about human beings. They seem to have this urge to kill and torment the very best souls among them."

"You're safe though, now, aren't you? I mean—"

"Of course I'm safe, Hank honey. I'm always safe. What can they really ever do to me, after all? . . . Doesn't mean I like it."

"Well, we'll have a nice relaxing round of golf tomorrow. We'll get your game straightened out, and we'll head back up to—"

She stopped me with a frown. The waiter came by to inquire after our comfort, to refill our cups with coffee and our glasses with water. When he departed, I thought Alicia was going to lecture me about thinking in the future, but She said: "Do you really think I'm curable? I mean, the yips are so much trouble to so many fine golfers. And there are the occasional other problems, as well."

"Absolutely curable," I said. Slightly drunk from the wine—I'd grown completely unused to alcohol in that kind of barometric pressure—I reached across and rested my hand on top of Hers. She gave me a warning look. I took my hand away and said, in a professional tone: "No problem in golf is incurable. . . . Listen, I made a lot of mistakes when I was here, as you well know. And there was a long list of things I wasn't good at—swimming, courtship, spelling, playing under pressure. But no one ever accused me of failing as a teacher of golf. There was almost never a student who came to me for lessons and went away dissatisfied. I say this in all modesty: I am going to cure You."

Alicia gave me a small, sweet smile. I paid the bill with one of the plastic cards in my wallet and we went back to the hotel and spent the night in separate beds.

THIRTEEN

The next morning, God and I enjoyed a pancake breakfast (my, God likes Her coffee!) at a little roadside place
on the way to Ford's Colony, and arrived at the clubhouse
just after eight. It was, the pro told us, an unusually cold
morning for that time of year, temperatures only in the
high forties, but the forecast promised a sunny, clear day
with just a bit of wind coming up late.

Alicia and I were given two buckets of balls and offered a complimentary electric cart, which, despite my
age, we refused. We strolled over to the driving range. It
was set up on a rise to give poorer golfers the illusion that
they had suddenly improved, and older golfers the illusion

that they could hit the ball as far as they'd been able to hit it in their youth. It turned out, though, that, in my case at least, it wasn't an illusion. Thanks to all the golf I'd been playing in heaven, I hadn't lost my swing. And the balls were more "advanced" than what I'd been used to playing with on earth, so advanced in fact that I was getting almost the kind of distance I got in heaven, and much more than in my PGA days. There were a couple of men on the practice range—one middle-aged, the other in his twenties—and as I stooped to tee up another ball I noticed them looking in our direction. Admiring an attractive woman, I thought, at first. But these were golfers and had their priorities arranged differently: They were admiring my swing.

So I began to show off a bit, drawing and fading my tee balls from one side of the range to the other, hitting knock-down shots with a two iron, dropping a dozen wedges into a circle not more than five yards across, booming long drives that would have made any retiree's day.

Alicia was struggling, though. I couldn't be sure how much of it was an act, and how much just the difficulty She was having adjusting to the atmosphere of earth. Somehow, between heaven and Williamsburg, She'd shortened Her backswing drastically. Now She had a choppy, quick stroke that was as likely to send the ball drizzling along the turf as popping up into the cold morning. I stopped and gave Her a couple of pointers. I encouraged Her to twist Her hips more without going loose in the lower body, and to start the downward move with a shift of the weight rather than a jerking of wrists and arms. I suggested She remove some of the jewelry and store it in Her bag. Strangely, however, except for taking off Her sapphire and diamond bracelets, She didn't respond to these tips; or, that is, Her golf swing didn't respond. She was trying, I could feel Her trying. And the advice I was giving Her was sound advice. But, for some odd reason, Her body did not get the message: The balls kept dribbling along the ground or flying off wildly to the right, with the occasional straight pop up. It almost seemed as though She was putting on a performance for the benefit of the two strangers on the driving range. But what a peculiar performance!

At one point I said, quietly, "What's going on, Lord?"

This well-meaning inquiry was met with a glare that could have knocked a fellow sideways. Her eyes, even on earth, were striking. The irises were a dark blue, almost purplish, with a silvery circle at the outer edges, and the overall impression was sort of an echo of the glare and glow I'd seen there in heaven. There were sparkles, too, chips of silver that flashed and twinkled. "It's all gone to hell," She snarled. Her voice was a woman's voice, of course, and in kinder moments it had what I'd always thought of on earth as the lilt of money in it, of wealth and comfort and a sleek, shimmering power. But I noticed that when She was angry or impatient it took on the timbre of the booming voice of the masculine God I'd first encountered in the disguise of Einstein. Pure authority.

Pure power. So, intimidated, put off a bit, I let Her hack Her way deeper and deeper into frustration.

At last, it was close to our tee time. By then the air had warmed a few degrees. We pulled our bags around to the first tee of the Blue Heron course (I had always liked to carry my own bag—except when a caddie was available—but I wasn't strong enough to do that now, at this age, so I was using a pull cart). As we did some final stretching there I noticed that only the fairways were green: At that time of year the unwatered rough was hay-colored dormant grass. It didn't matter to me. It wouldn't have mattered if we'd been playing on gravel. I was about to golf again, on earth.

The starter asked if we were ready. "I've been ready for an eternity," I said in a cheerful voice. Alicia, still fuming from Her warm-up debacle, shot me another vicious look.

"Northerners, are you?" he went on.

"Way up north," I said.

"Well, you'll enjoy it here then. I've paired you up with a father and son from upstate New York, couple of real players, from the looks of things. They came down here to escape the snow, too." He put a hand on my old shoulder and said, "You two take it easy on them, now."

"Oh, we will," Alicia piped up. All of a sudden Her fury had dissolved and She was chirping out words in the voice of a not particularly bright rich woman. I'd seen—and heard—so many of them in my days around the country club that I recognized it immediately. That voice is a peculiar combination of stupidity and superiority, a false camaraderie, as if they are trying to pretend they are also human, but know they're really something finer. Even the expression on Her face had changed. She'd made Her beautiful eyes dull. She smiled at the starter in a dumb, flirtatious way. "We'll let them go on ahead after a few holes if they're too fast for us."

"That's what we like to hear," the starter said, as if he were talking to a cute eleven-year-old.

The father and son were standing not far away, listening in on this conversation. It turned out that they were the same fellows we'd seen, and who'd been watching us, on the practice range. Brian and Charlie, from somewhere outside of Syracuse, dressed in the very finest golf attire, carrying the most expensive clubs, and exhibiting the same strongly clefted chin and rather large ears that had, I imagined, been passed down through their family's genetic code for centuries. I must interrupt here just for a moment to tell you how odd this was. Odd, you see, because my father and I—both of us golfers—carried similar genetic identifiers. You can, in fact, look back through several generations of the portraits of Fins-Winston men and see that tiny pot bunker, midchin, that makes shaving such a challenge. And you can say the Lord cursed us by giving us auditory receptors capable of picking up every cawing crow and coughing spectator in the middle of our backswing.

Obviously, during my brief golfing forays with the Divine, I had been made sensitive to the possibility of supernatural occurrences. Oversensitive, perhaps. Because when I saw the cleft chins on these two good fellows I immediately suspected a trick. I was hurled back into a thousand memories of my father, the man who had taught me to golf. A flood of feelings washed over me, and those feelings run as deep as anything on heaven or earth. I felt as if I was being made to revisit that relationship in its entirety, and I suspected that God was up to one of Her strange lessons when, in fact, it all might have been just some meaningless coincidence.

In any event, I introduced us as Hank and Alicia and we shook hands and exchanged greetings all around. And then I heard myself saying this: "Would you boys like to make the round more interesting? Put a little money on the outcome? Total score, stroke play, no handicap?"

Please trust me, I had not had the slightest intention of speaking those words. The second they were out of my mouth I was tossed back hard against more memories of old Pop, a man who'd place a bet on whether or not the sun would rise the following morning, if there were any takers to be had. This quality had always amused me, his only child, and infuriated my mother, his only wife. But there it was, leaping out of my genetic history like some ancient, unresolved karma. There it was.

"Total score?" Brian said, and I could see that I had him. He was the twenty-something son, bit of a rogue if my instincts were correct. His father, a patient, forgiving sort, stood quietly by, but seemed willing to indulge the boy's impetuousness.

I nodded. He and his father exchanged one glance

and then Brian said, "What kind of money were you thinking of?"

"Two thousand dollars a stroke," Alicia said, dumbly.

Two thousand dollars a stroke! This would have been an absurd sum in my past lifetime; even my Pop wouldn't have made such a wager on his wildest day, against the club's worst player. In these modern times, I couldn't be sure how outrageous it was. I watched Brian's face to see what kind of an impression it would make. He was studying us in return, glancing at our clubs, and what he no doubt saw was a foolish and very wealthy couple that had nothing better to do with their money than give it away to young upstate New Yorkers and their dads. I had been hitting well on the range, as mentioned. But I was twenty-five and fifty years their senior, respectively, and Alicia was, well, Alicia had not been at Her best.

The figure seemed worrisome to the father, but Brian was not fazed in the slightest. He plowed right ahead. I could see, as soon as the young fellow accepted the wager, that there was a kind of hubris at work within him. You could read it in his eyes and arms, even the way his brown hair hung jauntily over the grand ears. God, it turns out, despises hubris. It turns out that pride is the one human failing that He or She simply cannot tolerate. Alicia must have sensed something in Brian at first glance, some attitude having to do with the fact that She was a woman, perhaps, or beautiful, or that I was an old man, or that I was an old man with a young, beautiful woman, or that I had managed to preserve a fairly decent swing into my seventies, or that their bags were festooned with tags from the most exclusive golf resorts on two continents. Perhaps they'd seen me drive up in the Cadillac and had some prejudice against Cadillacs. I don't know. But She sensed something off-tone in them, a dearth of humility, and She put this idea of gambling into my head and then onto my tongue. And Brian and Charlie went for it. Hook, line, and sinker.

The first hole was a sharp dogleg right, slightly downhill off the tee and then gently up again as it approached the green. Brian stood on the first tee and, trying to show off for his dad and us and boom his drive across the corner of the dog's knee, he got it caught up in the rather gnarly brown rough. His father tried the same trick with the same result.

To my surprise, I was a bit shaky-legged on the tee—there's nothing like a long layoff to make one nervous. But I played conservatively, as had been my style, and hit a three iron with a slight fade on it. The ball reached the corner easily, rolled just right, and ended up in good position, midfairway, 160 yards or so from the flag. Alicia walked up to the women's tee and, after spending a lot of time setting and resetting Her feet, whiffed on the ball. A complete miss. She'd swung so hard that, for a moment, I thought She'd slipped a disk. I could see the anger building up in Her again, but it might have looked like embarrassment to Brian and Charlie because the older of them called out cheerily: "Don't worry about that one! We won't count it. Everybody needs a practice swing."

On Her second attempt, the Lord and Creator of everything we were looking at hit a ground ball forty yards down the left edge of the fairway. It trickled into the rough there. The four of us walked after it without saying a word—the "Savage Silence" Pop and I used to call that when we played. "Ah, Hermie and I had a bit of the Savage Silence going there, Mum, off the first tee," he'd tell my mother when we got home. "Ba' then we come around, we did. Stroked some fine ones."

Once She reached Her ball, Alicia took Her position, waggled a few too many times, and hacked at the miserable little object like a blond bejeweled Russian peasant woman scything hay on the steppe. The ball moved all of two feet. She hacked at it a second time and managed to nudge it out onto the short grass. From there, She hit a fair fourth shot, not too far from my ball. While She was replacing Her divot, I went up to our opponents and said, quietly and apologetically: "She's usually much better. A bit of the first-hole jitters I suspect, playing in front of men she doesn't know, and so on."

They did not seem in any way upset.

Charlie took a wedge and popped out of the rough— had a nice rhythm, Dad did. Brian tried more heroics and flew one over the green. I hit a modest seven iron, pin high, thirty feet right. The senior member of the group, at least, was on in regulation.

I ended up with a par. Brian and Charlie each bogeyed. Alicia made an eleven. So we were five strokes and ten thousand dollars down. After one hole.

On the second hole God made nine. On the third, a fairly short par three, She took a seven. I went along playing my calm, easy game, getting into a nice mental groove while Charlie and Brian kept trying to outdo each other, and impress my beautiful young wife. At the turn, I stood at thirty-six, Brian and Charlie forty-three and forty-five, respectively, and Alicia at sixty-seven. One hundred three to eighty-eight, we were fifteen strokes and thirty thousand dollars down, a sum that, in my playing days, represented three times the yearly winnings of some very accomplished professionals. I was tempted to look in my wallet and see if She had magically put some large bills in there next to the credit cards, but I did not do that.

We were in deep trouble, it seemed. All through the front nine we fell deeper and deeper into debt. I'm convinced now that the only thing that saved us from a year of indentured servitude was this: As we were putting out on the ninth, young Brian made a terrible error. Not in his game, but in what might be called his spiritual life. All through that first nine he'd been condescending to Alicia—and even to me, really, though I was giving him a thorough thrashing. He was one of these young men who is bursting with health, a thick neck and shoulders, powerful forearms like his father, a wide, coarse, not unattractive face anchored by the cleft chin. He looked to be the type who would cut you off in traffic without a glance. Even Charlie, his own father, seemed a bit dismayed by him now and again: Across his face you'd see a fleeting wash of disappointment.

In any case, on the ninth, Alicia had an eight-foot putt for what would have been Her first bogey of the day, and She stood over it too long, then made Her stroke and left it a good four feet short. Brian was unable to disguise his joy at this misfortune. "Still some meat on that bone," he said, gleefully. Alicia stood over the second putt and I could see Her hands shaking. She waited and waited, finally pulled the trigger, and pushed the ball an inch right of the hole. The yips, and then some. We had fallen seventeen strokes behind.

Now Brian smelled blood. He knew he could throw Alicia off balance with a remark, knew they were so far ahead that almost nothing short of a miracle could save us, knew he stood to make a very fancy piece of change for a few hours' play, but he could not resist putting the needle in and wiggling it around a bit. The refreshment cart came by as we approached the tenth tee, and as we were munching on our hot dogs, he started to flirt with Alicia, shamelessly. No doubt he was thinking: I've thrown her off her game, now I'm going to throw him off his. "Let me show you one thing," he said, deviously. Standing behind Her, he took hold of Her arms and helped Her bring the club back, then demonstrated the weight shift by moving his hips sharply forward, pressing himself against Her in the process. He was a master at it, really. He made it look almost innocent, but it wasn't innocent, and the rest of us understood that perfectly well.

This kind of thing had happened to me a few dozen times on earth. Anna Lisa had been quite an attractive woman, and since, in the golf world, we were so often surrounded by men, there had inevitably been some flirtation— of both the harmless variety and Brian's variety. Brian's variety, I understand now, has something to do with a desperate inferiority complex you find in a small percentage of men. In spite of his impressive physical presence, there was an immense lack in him, an insecurity I could sense but not pinpoint. Perhaps it had something to do with his father, who seemed such a calm and pleasant sort that Brian, with his surges of pride, might have felt perpetually immature and unwise in comparison. I suppose that, at moments, we all behave this way to a greater or lesser degree. Faced with the calm majesty of the world, we're sometimes frustrated by our own incapacity for perfection and compensate for those feelings by bravado, petulance, anger, and ungratefulness.

Perhaps not; I have strange theories about things, I admit. In any case, it was clear enough that, rather than face his feelings honestly, Brian attempted to soothe himself by controlling the behavior and feelings of those around him, as if to prove to some panicked interior judge that he was no worse than his dad, no less fine and strong than the rest of creation. Ah, what a pathetic mess underlies the flirtatious impulse in such men! More often than not, sad to say, my Anna Lisa had gone along with such games, touching these men on the shoulder or knee, dancing close with them at weddings. Of course, all that had stimulated my own insecurities, knocked against my own soft spots. We'd had some terrible fights over it, though I was never sure whether she'd been actively trying to hurt me, or just carried away by her own subtle troubles.

Now though, truly, I could not have cared less, perhaps because I was playing so well, or perhaps because there was no romantic connection between Alicia and me, or perhaps because a bit of the carefree ease of heaven had stayed with me as I'd made the transition to earth. Whatever the reason, I was not upset by Brian's antics, and I felt a great power and freedom because of that.

In any case, even Charlie seemed uncomfortable with his son's behavior. And, though Alicia smiled and played along, I knew Her well enough by then to see that She was positively livid. As we were tossing our paper napkins in a trash container and getting ready to begin the second nine, She whispered: "Well, that's it for him, then." And I hoped the poor lad hadn't condemned himself to some awful semieternal punishment.

As if to spite him, She hit a marvelous drive on the tenth hole, die straight and almost two hundred yards.

"Maybe you shouldn't have given her that little lesson, son," I heard Charlie say, but Brian just laughed, oblivious.

For Her second shot, Alicia pulled out a three iron and laced it to the apron of the green. Though She'd been having trouble putting all morning, She sank the eighteen-footer. I birdied the hole, too. The magnitude of his transgression hadn't yet been made plain to Brian; he knocked in a carefree bogey. They were still fourteen strokes ahead with eight holes to play; no doubt he was already thinking of ways to spend his winnings.

But on the next hole, Alicia did it again. "My goodness," She squealed in Brian's direction after Her second perfect drive, "I should take lessons from you more often." This was accompanied by a sweet smile. As we walked off the tee, She put Her hand briefly on Brian's shoulder and looked at him as if he were an angel. He still did not understand. Alicia stumbled over Her putting on that hole and made bogey. Charlie also made bogey. Brian made what would prove to be his final par of the day.

"Oh, honey," Alicia said to me when She missed the putt. "Darling, I'm costing you a small fortune here today, aren't I?"

I shrugged as if the money meant absolutely nothing to me, which, of course, was the actual fact of the matter.

"You're paired up with the wrong guy, that's all," Brian said, winking.

"Oh, I hate men who wink," Alicia replied.

The blunt tone carried so much force in it that even Charlie, staring at Her in a new way now, understood that something had changed, that they might not be dealing with a dumb blond high-handicapper after all. Brian, alas, was slower on the uptake. On the twelfth, he pushed his drive to the right, far out-of-bounds, so far in fact that it bounced off one of the beautiful brick homes there and caromed into the shrubbery.

"Got my hands caught behind a little bit," he said. "Haven't done that in a hell of a long time."

Perhaps trying to compensate, he hooked his second drive deep into the left rough, lying there three. His father hit down the middle. Alicia and I also. It was a very short par five, dogleg left, 467 yards. When I went to my ball and paced it off I realized I was just over two hundred yards out.

"You can reach with an iron, hon," She said. "I have faith in you."

Out of the corner of my eye, I saw Brian grin. I took out my four iron, settled my mind, made a nice, smooth swing, and the ball flew down the fairway, bounced once, and rolled to the heart of the green.

"Beautiful, hon," She called out, and then, to the others: "He does that sometimes. He's very long, really."

Charlie flew his approach into the left bunker. Not surprisingly, Brian tried a spectacular escape from the rough. He met the ball solidly, too, but his club head must have gotten caught up a bit in the grass because the ball flew well off to the right, then bounced and bounced as if it had a little motor in it, and scurried a foot or so past the O.B. stakes. Four swipes later he was on the putting surface, lying nine. "What the Christ?" I heard him mutter.

Alicia heard it, too. "Now, now," She said. "Please don't use that name in vain in my presence."

Brian looked at Her, said "Huh?" and three-putted.

We were seven strokes behind with five holes to play.

It was truly enjoyable to play those final five. The Blue Heron course at Ford's Colony is a wonderful layout, nothing like the courses in heaven, naturally, but quite fine nevertheless: a series of pleasant, slightly undulating holes with water in evidence on all but the dogleg left eighteenth.

I probably don't need to tell you that Brian found the water on three of those final four holes. On the 174-yard fourteenth, he dubbed a middle iron off the tee and we watched the ball bounce crazily a few times then kick left into the drink. On the 350-yard fifteenth, he smacked his tee ball almost ninety degrees right, another splash. On the long, difficult sixteenth, second hardest hole on the course, he hit into the water again off the tee, and threw his driver in after the ball.

Alicia and I said nothing. His father looked rather sad, but remained quiet. By the time we stood on the tee of the par-three seventeenth, 173 yards, with a lake looming all down the left side of the fairway and Brian fuming and muttering to himself, the match stood all square.

I had the honors. On earth, my four iron had always been my 175-yard club, and I'd always felt confident and comfortable taking it out of the bag. But things had changed since then. I was a veteran of heavenly golf and the ball had been made livelier by advances in technology, so I pulled a six iron and stood up on the tee, surveying the shot. By then, the promised wind had sprung up, moderate, left to right, coming off the water. I strengthened my grip a bit, aimed at the flagstick, and played a draw. But, as I'd hoped, the ball could not draw into the wind. It flew straight, landed a yard or two in front of the hole, bounced up so that it struck the stick at waist height, then dropped down again and settled about four inches to the right of the cup. Alicia was squealing with joy, making little hops in Her expensive golf shoes. Charlie managed a "good shot there," but Brian was beside himself.

It is commonly stated that golf is the most frustrating physical activity ever invented, and I will not argue with that premise. What had just happened to Brian happens so often on the course: You're playing along well for a stretch of four or six or ten holes, and then, without explanation, the gift leaves you. Where you could do nothing wrong, you can now do nothing right. The ball has become an independent being, a petulant teenager of sorts, no longer willing to listen to logical suggestion. I'd seen it happen a thousand times — to myself and to others.

But, in Brian's case, I had the sneaking suspicion that some other force was at work. Maybe that's always true. Maybe God is behind all those triple and quadruple bogeys, those sudden disasters. Maybe it's all a kind of punishment for bad behavior, or a lesson in patience, or humility. I don't really know.

But I do know that Alicia did not like Brian. Charlie knew it, too. Even Brian himself might have understood it if he hadn't been surrounded by a fog of his own inflated self-approval. And when God takes a disliking to you, well, you can't expect good things to happen, can you.

So Brian stood up on the seventeenth tee at the beautiful Blue Heron course at the beautiful Ford's Colony

Country Club, and yanked his tee shot directly into the pond with what looked like a six iron. A moment later, the six iron itself followed the ball, making a somewhat larger splash. Perhaps he was thinking: I'm going to lose two or four or six thousand dollars or more, so what's a new set of clubs? But it was another childish display, and it made all of us uncomfortable. I thought, then, that Alicia might have some pity on him, but Brian took out a five iron and hit his second shot into the water, then his third. He found the front bunker with his fourth ball—so, with the penalty strokes, he was lying there seven—then stood off to the side with his back turned to us and actually started crying. Not the first time I had seen a grown man shed tears on the course.

It seemed a harsh punishment for one crude flirtation, but I said nothing. Charlie mumbled a word of encouragement in his son's direction, then made his swing and found the bunker, also. Alicia played the hole in much the same way as She'd begun the round—hitting little dribblers that went straight enough, eighty yards or so. She ended up with a seven. With my birdie, that made nine for our side. Charlie had trouble with the sand and recorded another bogey. And Brian hit a sand wedge—his eighth shot—right into the hole on the fly, which only added insult to injury. Nine shots against twelve. We were three strokes up going into the last.

The eighteenth is an easy par four, 352 yards. There is no water, good news for Brian. Lacking a driver and a six iron, he made five. His father made six. I managed another lucky par while Alicia played well and scored bogey. Nine to eleven. We finished the match five strokes, and ten thousand dollars, ahead.

As we shook hands on the last green there was a terrible awkwardness in the air. Brian was being talked to by his dad, and I wondered if he had been planning to accuse us of sandbagging and try to wriggle out of his obligation. But when we'd put our gloves, balls, and ball markers back in our bags I saw that Brian had taken out his checkbook and was walking over to me. There was such an awful expression on his face; the dimple in his chin wavered like a star on a windblown flag, a sorrowful dark flag tossing in the breeze. If it is true that pride goeth before a fall—and I see no evidence to indicate that it is not—then it is also the case that the fall is a terrible thing to witness. You can't help feeling just a bit sorry for the proud man fallen, even if he was an obnoxious boor only a few holes before. I felt this. I suppose Alicia felt it, too.

She came over, hooked Her arm in mine, and pressed against me affectionately. We stood facing Brian, with Charlie hovering in the background as if hoping his boy would show he'd learned something and behave with some dignity during this trial.

"Well, you hammered us," Brian managed, God bless him.

I could tell he was forcing the words out; it must have been difficult for him. Yet I gave him credit for at least pretending to be a good sport.

Alicia looked up at me and batted Her eyelashes, and I could see that Brian's attempt at humility had impressed Her, too. "Honey," She sang, "we don't really need the money, do you mind if I offer this young gentleman an arrangement?"

"Not at all, dear."

She looked straight at Brian and said: "Why don't we do this? Why don't you write that check out to your favorite charity and make it for, let's see. . . ." She turned to me, overdoing it a bit, I thought. "Honey, what's half of ten thousand?"

"Five," I said.

"Five thousand dollars. Why don't you make it out for five thousand and hand it over and we'll mail it in for you and ask that the receipt be sent to us when the check clears."

Brian was in equal measure offended and relieved. Offended because he wanted to be trusted to mail it in himself. But relieved, as anyone would have been, at having his and his father's substantial losses cut in half.

"You sure about this?" he asked, looking at me.

"Absolutely," I replied. "My wife is known for her soft heart."

He thought a moment, made the check out to a health charity, and handed it over. "I'll settle up with you later, son," his father said behind him.

We shook hands a second time, all around, thanked them for the enjoyable match, tipped very, very generously the young fellow who loaded our bags into the trunk of the Cadillac, and drove south out of Williamsburg in Virginia's tepid spring sun.

But I must add something here, before bringing this part of our earthly saga to a close. I have been devoting a good deal of attention to Brian and his follies, but in fact I should say that, during our delightful match, I was somewhat buried in myself. I have neglected to mention that, in the younger years of my previous earthly incarnation, in the days before I met and became seriously involved with Anna Lisa, I had been something of a, well, a hellion. Even as a boy I'd had so much natural golfing ability, you see. And that in a nation that elevates its golf champions almost to the status of gods. I'm afraid I must admit that this situation had gone to my head, especially in my teenage years. I'd strutted about the house, and school, like some sort of hero just home from the battlefield. Breaking hearts, drinking a bit, generally acting as if I knew everything and could conquer everything, and that my parents were kindly, if ignorant, old fuddies.

During the match at Ford's Colony, I'd remembered all that misplaced pride, in vivid hues, and seen much of my youthful arrogance reflected in Brian. I'd watched the suffering it caused his dad. I'd seen how badly he'd wanted to help his son, to save him, but how he seemed to know, as my own rather roguish father had known, as God the Father must surely know, that experience, not fatherly or motherly instruction, is what really teaches. Pain teaches. Life teaches.

After the money had been handed over I caught a

glimpse of Charlie wrapping one arm around his obnoxious boy and squeezing his shoulders as they walked toward their car. That gesture sounded such a sweet old chord in me that my eyes filled and I had to turn away from Alicia to keep Her from noticing. How many times had Mum and Pop made similar gestures in my direction—an embrace, a glance, a hand on the forearm, a word? And how many times, sailing along through my wild youth, had I completely failed to grasp their patience, humility, and love? God's love in miniature, of course.

gnarled hands, feeling again all the times Anna Lisa
d mocked the old-fashioned, more formal name.

She smiled another small, sad smile, so beautiful at that
moment that it was everything I could do to turn my attention back to the darkening ribbon of highway.

"It seems to me I could have done a better job."

"It seems that way to a lot of people," I ventured.

"From the human perspective, I suppose," She agreed.
"From the human perspective."

"The problem with the human perspective is that,
when you're human, it's the only perspective you have.
It's like being a child in that way. Children are just not
equipped to grasp the larger reality. They have no perspective on their pain."

"That's the smartest thing you've said since I met you."

"To a child," I went on, as if I, a childless man in my
previous incarnation, were an expert on the subject, "to
a child, the deprivations and troubles of childhood seem
eternal, tremendously unfair. If the parents play a role in
them, they can seem like demons."

In truth, I had never thought about these things and
had little idea I would say them. Alicia seemed impressed,
though—She mentioned that I'd been a loving father and
mother many times in various incarnations—so I stumbled on. "But I don't think You should feel bad about
Your creation. It's a marvelous creation, really. If people
only had the advantage of a little while in heaven, they'd
all realize—"

"What makes you think I feel bad about my creation?"

FOURTEEN

Being back on earth again, as I may have mentioned, was
a bit like revisiting the town you'd grown up in as a child.
I'd done that once, in fact. A year or so after Anna Lisa
and I were married, we took a sort of delayed honeymoon
to England, toured London and the Lakes District, and I
played some of the courses there. I brought her back to
the little hamlet where I'd been raised, a place called
Westbridge Ames, in the lower reaches of Nottingham-
shire. Partly due to Pop's gambling, and partly to Mum's
frustration with it, and partly due to the particular
makeup of my soul, the memories weren't all sweet. From
the age of six or seven, I'd known that I didn't quite be-
long in Westbridge Ames, but on that trip there was a

pleasant sense of connection. There is something so vivid and intense about childhood, the trials and terrors, but also the slow awakening of our senses, the majesty and enormity of the world, the relationships that mark us.

It felt something like that to be back on the blue planet again. There were the harsh memories—most of them having to do with my failed marriage and truncated career as a touring pro. But there was a kind of tastiness to everything, too, a way in which the smells, sounds, and sights brought back a hundred old friendships, a million happy hours. I do not in any way mean to imply that things are dull in heaven, that the happiness you feel there is somehow muted and false. I was happier in heaven, no question. But there is only one earth, just as there is only one Westbridge Ames, and returning to both places gave rise, in me at least, to a gritty, checkered joy.

That joy was still alive and new as Alicia and I rode south away from Williamsburg. It did not take me long to accustom myself to the ways of modern-day America, computers everywhere, hybrid golf clubs, and wonderfully light and impermeable rain gear. The country seemed blander than it had in my day, however. The food, especially, seemed to have become more artificial tasting, less real. And the things we heard on the radio shows were sometimes mean things, the mocking voice of intolerance. Perhaps I had grown spoiled in heaven.

There were moments when I almost felt as if we were a husband and wife team, traveling away our retirement, or my retirement, at least. Wherever we stopped—at traf-

fic lights on the side roads, for quick meal—people stared at headed man escorting a beautiful car, She was as distant as God, with the window in contemplation of the lan gers idly working the bejeweled bracelets, huge diamond ring. But in public, God made behaving like a dutiful, affectionate, if not very spouse. She'd take my arm at every opportunity, look ingly into my eyes when I spoke, occasionally plant a kiss on my cheek for the benefit of our audiences. Sometimes this behavior so captivated me that I lost sight of the fact that I was traveling with the divine Creator.

But when we were alone it was impossible to forget. I don't know if the people around us could feel it, but it was clear to me that She was emanating a magnificence, a power, that had little to do with the human realm. I never heard her sigh or complain. For long stretches of time it seemed to me that She wasn't even breathing, just staring at the world She had made, gazing out from a perfect interior stillness that nothing could trouble or harm.

Somewhere in southern North Carolina I screwed up my courage and said: "What has it been like for you so far, Lord?"

She turned to me calmly and smiled, as if She appreciated my asking. After a moment, She said, "Disturbing." And then: "Disappointing, if you really want to know, Fins-Winston."

"Call me Hank, please," I said, squeezing the wheel in

Alicia said sharply, as if, until that moment, She'd been only half listening.

"But You just said—"

"Said what?"

"That You were disappointed."

She laughed at me then. "Oh Herman," She said, "I didn't mean I was disappointed in my creation. I meant I was disappointed in my golf game. It's disturbing to play like I played with those men, to embarrass myself in front of people."

"But I thought that was all an act. I thought You were just setting them up . . . so we could win the money."

"Money is of no use to me whatsoever," She said.

"I know, but . . . what about Brian? Are You telling me You didn't work some kind of a spell on him?"

"I'm not a witch, Hank, I'm God."

"But—"

"Listen," She said, "people control their own fate."

"Control their own fate? That's absurd, it's irrational."

"No, it is not. I made this planet. I set the rules, so to speak, and since then I've stood back and more or less let things unfold on their own. Brian made the decision to bet with us, and then he made the decision to try and beat us, and then he made the decision to find devious ways of making us feel badly about ourselves, by flirting with me in such an ugly manner, for instance. He wanted to throw us off balance. Those were purely and simply his decisions. His behavior saddened me, of course, the way it saddened you. It even saddened his friend, what was his name?"

"Charlie. And that was his father, not a friend."

She was shaking her head. "Not really. There are some true father-son and father-daughter and mother-son and mother-daughter relationships. But most of the time people who appear to be parent and child are really only old enemies or old friends who happen to be thrown together for a single life in order to work out a debt or two. A true father-son relationship has a particular resonance to it, a power; you can sense it from the first word. And it goes on for many centuries."

"All right," I said. "His friend then."

"Yes, his friend Charlie. Deep in the recesses of Brian's psyche he knew that what he was doing was wrong, but he made a conscious choice to do it anyway. He disturbed the energy field of his own mind at a certain level when he did that, and that disturbance came back to haunt him a few holes later. His own ego was the source of his troubles, not me. It's always like that. It's a law of creation: Ultimately, you control your own fate."

"But if that were the case, then the best people, the best souls, would also be the most successful golfers. And I can tell you with absolute certainty that it doesn't always work out that way."

"Oh, but it does, it does," She insisted. "It's just that everything is set up on a time frame that is not the human time frame. To you, if someone acts badly this morning they should be punished this afternoon. Sometimes, in fact, that is the way it happens—look at Brian. But in other cases it takes weeks, years, or even a future lifetime for the consequence to be acted out. That's just the way this universe is structured. You can think of it as the architecture of heavenly time. Within that architecture, one's fate is determined by these millions of little invisible choices you all make, every second: how to think, what to think about, how selfish or selfless to be, how kind. And so on."

"It sounds very fair."

"Eminently fair," She said, with some pride. "It is nothing if not fair."

I let a bit of countryside roll past. We were in South Carolina by then. Darkness had fallen. The land was featureless and flat, with straight rows of pine trees guarding the sides of the road. "So are You saying then that everyone gets the punishment he deserves, the life he deserves?"

"He or she, yes."

"Then people who are tortured or maimed . . . are You saying they brought that on themselves?"

"Too simple," She said. "For one thing, sometimes certain especially generous or courageous souls choose to take the suffering of another soul upon themselves, just as one might pay a financial debt for a close friend or relative."

"But, in essence, if someone is treated very badly—"

"Too simple, that's as far as I'll go. I will say this, though: Things have happened over the course of human history that have been terribly, unbearably sad to me. Needless pain and death, horrible crimes—against the innocent, against children."

"Why did You let it happen then? Why didn't You step

in? I mean, people are praying to You all the time, beseeching You, asking for help."

"I always help them."

"But why do You let them suffer like that?"

"In the long run I always help them. Always. I pride myself on this: Not once has someone asked for help and not gotten it from me or one of my special assistants."

"But, I'm confused. I mean, why don't You stop wars, for instance?"

"I can't. Anymore than I can start playing golf well again."

"But you can't compare the pain of playing golf badly with the pain those people feel."

"I'm aware of that, Herman, thank you. The way things are set up, I feel, cumulatively, what each member of my creation is feeling at every given moment."

"It would be too much," I said.

She laughed. "For you, yes, of course. Just as the complexity of the universe is too much for a human mind. Look at Job; most people would say his suffering was too much for one soul to bear, yet he bore it fairly well. Did you have a chance to play with him while we were in heaven, by the way?"

"No."

"I'll set it up then, at some later date. Job is an excellent golf companion, patient in the extreme, if not especially lucky or talented. I once watched him hit eleven balls into the water at Eden Hills. Eleven balls in a row. And not so much as a 'damn it' came out of his mouth."

"Does that mean I'm going back to paradise? That I'll—"

She flashed Her eyes at me and I stopped. "I'll set you up for a game of golf with Job, is what I said. I didn't say when, or where. But yes, if you must know, you are going back to heaven."

"Thank God."

"Everyone goes back."

"But how could they?"

She let out an exasperated sigh. "That is simply the way it works. Everyone gets there, many times in fact. If you've done well on earth, you go there, get yourself rested up, rub shoulders with a few of the great teachers, enjoy the amenities for a time, then you return."

"To earth?"

"To earth in your case, at your level of development. At other evolutionary stages it may be to a different system with different challenges."

"And where does it all lead?"

She sighed. "Where does it all lead? Ugh. Oy. Your problem, Mr. Fins-Winston, is that you have some kind of pathological obsession with the future, with goals, with so-called 'end results.' Right now you are driving along a mysterious dark highway, with a beautiful younger woman, and you are curious to the point of obsession about where you will end up for eternity. It's incredibly stupid and wasteful of you. And ungrateful, too, I might add."

I knew it was. Somewhere inside me I knew. But I

simply could not resist the opportunity to ask God what I'd wanted to ask Him, Her, for every thoughtful adult minute of my earthly life.

"But where does it end?"

"It doesn't."

"The universe expands," I suddenly said, as if Einstein himself were whispering in my ear.

"Endlessly."

"We just go on and on, then."

"Exactly. On and on. Except that your idea of time is not accurate."

"There's no hell then?"

"You're looking at it," she said, gesturing at the dark view out the window.

"South Carolina?"

She smacked me lightly on the arm as a real wife might do to a husband who'd made a foolish joke.

"The idea of hell was developed by earthly minds because here, on earth, you can experience the rough equivalent, the feeling that you are being tormented forever—by illness, by a nasty spouse, by an evil, immature soul—with no hope of escape. The relationship between earthly reality and Absolute Reality is very similar to the relationship between a human being's dream and her waking consciousness. The difficulty or pain or fear in the dream seems utterly real, and then you wake up and realize it was an illusion. Just so with human misery— you should know this by now. It isn't really forever, of course, but that's what it feels like. You remember your pain from the years after your divorce, do you not? From the years of your apparent failure?"

"Apparent? It was a real failure."

"It felt real, of course. It felt eternal, too, if I am not mistaken."

"All right, yes. And people bring that on themselves?"

"I never said that."

"But you did, I just heard you."

"You misunderstood, Hank. You're making the immense subtlety of creation into a crude theory that fits the narrow abilities of your mind."

"Oh."

"Stick to golf—that's something you know."

"Okay," I said.

"No offense intended, honey."

"None taken."

My old eyes saw that we were approaching the turnoff for the highway to the coast. God pointed at the exit and told me to take it.

"Can I ask where we're going next?" I said, putting on the blinker and moving the Cadillac smoothly into the right lane. "In case You fall asleep or something?"

"You are hopeless," She said, and seemed to drift away from me again into Her own thoughts. It occurred to me that there were billions of other souls out there that She had to concern herself with, that I was being selfish, taking up Her time. And conceited, to think God would give me all Her attention. But another part of me just wanted to push and harangue and pester until I understood everything She did. I am, after all, a descendant of Adam and Eve—that foolish pair who refused to just do as God asked them, refused to let Him run the show. These kinds of things get passed down, you know.

A bit later, when we'd stopped for a light dinner of fried-to-death seafood, heavily sweetened iced tea, hush puppies, and a sumptuous piece of pecan pie, and were getting back into the car, Alicia said, "Follow the signs for Myrtle Beach and then keep going south. We're headed for a place called Pawleys Plantation, a golf resort. I have another old friend there. All you have to do is go into the welcome center and pick up the keys. And then, if it isn't too much trouble, when we wake up tomorrow morning, I would, in fact, like for you to do what I called on you to do. I would like you to fix my golf game."

"Yes," I said. "Of course."

And so, caught up in another real-seeming, earthly dream, I drove tiredly on.

FOURTEEN

Being back on earth again, as I may have mentioned, was a bit like revisiting the town you'd grown up in as a child. I'd done that once, in fact. A year or so after Anna Lisa and I were married, we took a sort of delayed honeymoon to England, toured London and the Lakes District, and I played some of the courses there. I brought her back to the little hamlet where I'd been raised, a place called Westbridge Ames, in the lower reaches of Nottingham-shire. Partly due to Pop's gambling, and partly to Mum's frustration with it, and partly due to the particular makeup of my soul, the memories weren't all sweet. From the age of six or seven, I'd known that I didn't quite be-long in Westbridge Ames, but on that trip there was a pleasant sense of connection. There is something so vivid and intense about childhood, the trials and terrors, but also the slow awakening of our senses, the majesty and enormity of the world, the relationships that mark us.

It felt something like that to be back on the blue planet again. There were the harsh memories—most of them having to do with my failed marriage and truncated career as a touring pro. But there was a kind of tastiness to everything, too, a way in which the smells, sounds, and sights brought back a hundred old friendships, a million happy hours. I do not in any way mean to imply that things are dull in heaven, that the happiness you feel there is somehow muted and false. I was happier in heaven, no question. But there is only one earth, just as there is only one Westbridge Ames, and returning to both places gave rise, in me at least, to a gritty, checkered joy.

That joy was still alive and new as Alicia and I rode south away from Williamsburg. It did not take me long to accustom myself to the ways of modern-day America, computers everywhere, hybrid golf clubs, and wonderfully light and impermeable rain gear. The country seemed blander than it had in my day, however. The food, especially, seemed to have become more artificial tasting, less real. And the things we heard on the radio shows were sometimes mean things, the mocking voice of intolerance. Perhaps I had grown spoiled in heaven.

There were moments when I almost felt as if we were a husband and wife team, traveling away our retirement, or my retirement, at least. Wherever we stopped—at traffic lights on the side roads, for coffee and doughnuts or a quick meal—people stared at the spectacle of a white-headed man escorting a beautiful younger woman. In the car, She was as distant as God, with Her head turned out the window in contemplation of the landscape, Her fingers idly working the bejeweled bracelets, earrings, and huge diamond ring. But in public, God made a point of behaving like a dutiful, affectionate, if not very bright spouse. She'd take my arm at every opportunity, look lovingly into my eyes when I spoke, occasionally plant a kiss on my cheek for the benefit of our audiences. Sometimes this behavior so captivated me that I lost sight of the fact that I was traveling with the divine Creator.

But when we were alone it was impossible to forget. I don't know if the people around us could feel it, but it was clear to me that She was emanating a magnificence, a power, that had little to do with the human realm. I never heard her sigh or complain. For long stretches of time it seemed to me that She wasn't even breathing, just staring at the world She had made, gazing out from a perfect interior stillness that nothing could trouble or harm.

Somewhere in southern North Carolina I screwed up my courage and said: "What has it been like for you so far, Lord?"

She turned to me calmly and smiled, as if She appreciated my asking. After a moment, She said, "Disturbing." And then: "Disappointing, if you really want to know, Fins-Winston."

"Call me Hank, please," I said, squeezing the wheel in

my gnarled hands, feeling again all the times Anna Lisa had mocked the old-fashioned, more formal name.

She smiled another small, sad smile, so beautiful at that moment that it was everything I could do to turn my attention back to the darkening ribbon of highway.

"It seems to me I could have done a better job."

"It seems that way to a lot of people," I ventured.

"From the human perspective, I suppose," She agreed. "From the human perspective."

"The problem with the human perspective is that, when you're human, it's the only perspective you have. It's like being a child in that way. Children are just not equipped to grasp the larger reality. They have no perspective on their pain."

"That's the smartest thing you've said since I met you."

"To a child," I went on, as if I, a childless man in my previous incarnation, were an expert on the subject, "to a child, the deprivations and troubles of childhood seem eternal, tremendously unfair. If the parents play a role in them, they can seem like demons."

In truth, I had never thought about these things and had little idea I would say them. Alicia seemed impressed, though—She mentioned that I'd been a loving father and mother many times in various incarnations—so I stumbled on. "But I don't think You should feel bad about Your creation. It's a marvelous creation, really. If people only had the advantage of a little while in heaven, they'd all realize—"

"What makes you think I feel bad about my creation?"

Alicia said sharply, as if, until that moment, She'd been only half listening.

"But You just said—"

"Said what?"

"That You were disappointed."

She laughed at me then. "Oh Herman," She said, "I didn't mean I was disappointed in my creation. I meant I was disappointed in my golf game. It's disturbing to play like I played with those men, to embarrass myself in front of people."

"But I thought that was all an act. I thought You were just setting them up . . . so we could win the money."

"Money is of no use to me whatsoever," She said.

"I know, but . . . what about Brian? Are You telling me You didn't work some kind of a spell on him?"

"I'm not a witch, Hank, I'm God."

"But—"

"Listen," She said, "people control their own fate."

"Control their own fate? That's absurd, it's irrational."

"No, it is not. I made this planet. I set the rules, so to speak, and since then I've stood back and more or less let things unfold on their own. Brian made the decision to bet with us, and then he made the decision to try and beat us, and then he made the decision to find devious ways of making us feel badly about ourselves, by flirting with me in such an ugly manner, for instance. He wanted to throw us off balance. Those were purely and simply his decisions. His behavior saddened me, of course, the way it saddened you. It even saddened his friend, what was his name?"

"Charlie. And that was his father, not a friend."

She was shaking her head. "Not really. There are some true father-son and father-daughter and mother-son and mother-daughter relationships. But most of the time people who appear to be parent and child are really only old enemies or old friends who happen to be thrown together for a single life in order to work out a debt or two. A true father-son relationship has a particular resonance to it, a power; you can sense it from the first word. And it goes on for many centuries."

"All right," I said. "His friend then."

"Yes, his friend Charlie. Deep in the recesses of Brian's psyche he knew that what he was doing was wrong, but he made a conscious choice to do it anyway. He disturbed the energy field of his own mind at a certain level when he did that, and that disturbance came back to haunt him a few holes later. His own ego was the source of his troubles, not me. It's always like that. It's a law of creation: Ultimately, you control your own fate."

"But if that were the case, then the best people, the best souls, would also be the most successful golfers. And I can tell you with absolute certainty that it doesn't always work out that way."

"Oh, but it does, it does," She insisted. "It's just that everything is set up on a time frame that is not the human time frame. To you, if someone acts badly this morning they should be punished this afternoon. Sometimes, in fact, that is the way it happens—look at Brian. But in other cases it takes weeks, years, or even a future lifetime for the consequence to be acted out. That's just the way this universe is structured. You can think of it as the architecture of heavenly time. Within that architecture, one's fate is determined by these millions of little invisible choices you all make, every second: how to think, what to think about, how selfish or selfless to be, how kind. And so on."

"It sounds very fair."

"Eminently fair," She said, with some pride. "It is nothing if not fair."

I let a bit of countryside roll past. We were in South Carolina by then. Darkness had fallen. The land was featureless and flat, with straight rows of pine trees guarding the sides of the road. "So are You saying then that everyone gets the punishment he deserves, the life he deserves?"

"He or she, yes."

"Then people who are tortured or maimed . . . are You saying they brought that on themselves?"

"Too simple," She said. "For one thing, sometimes certain especially generous or courageous souls choose to take the suffering of another soul upon themselves, just as one might pay a financial debt for a close friend or relative."

"But, in essence, if someone is treated very badly—"

"Too simple, that's as far as I'll go. I will say this, though: Things have happened over the course of human history that have been terribly, unbearably sad to me. Needless pain and death, horrible crimes—against the innocent, against children."

"Why did You let it happen then? Why didn't You step

in? I mean, people are praying to You all the time, beseeching You, asking for help."

"I always help them."

"But why do You let them suffer like that?"

"In the long run I always help them. Always. I pride myself on this: Not once has someone asked for help and not gotten it from me or one of my special assistants."

"But, I'm confused. I mean, why don't You stop wars, for instance?"

"I can't. Anymore than I can start playing golf well again."

"But you can't compare the pain of playing golf badly with the pain those people feel."

"I'm aware of that, Herman, thank you. The way things are set up, I feel, cumulatively, what each member of my creation is feeling at every given moment."

"It would be too much," I said.

She laughed. "For you, yes, of course. Just as the complexity of the universe is too much for a human mind. Look at Job; most people would say his suffering was too much for one soul to bear, yet he bore it fairly well. Did you have a chance to play with him while we were in heaven, by the way?"

"No."

"I'll set it up then, at some later date. Job is an excellent golf companion, patient in the extreme, if not especially lucky or talented. I once watched him hit eleven balls into the water at Eden Hills. Eleven balls in a row. And not so much as a 'damn it' came out of his mouth."

"Does that mean I'm going back to paradise? That I'll—"

She flashed Her eyes at me and I stopped. "I'll set you up for a game of golf with Job, is what I said. I didn't say when, or where. But yes, if you must know, you are going back to heaven."

"Thank God."

"Everyone goes back."

"But how could they?"

She let out an exasperated sigh. "That is simply the way it works. Everyone gets there, many times in fact. If you've done well on earth, you go there, get yourself rested up, rub shoulders with a few of the great teachers, enjoy the amenities for a time, then you return."

"To earth?"

"To earth in your case, at your level of development. At other evolutionary stages it may be to a different system with different challenges."

"And where does it all lead?"

She sighed. "Where does it all lead? Ugh. Oy. Your problem, Mr. Fins-Winston, is that you have some kind of pathological obsession with the future, with goals, with so-called 'end results.' Right now you are driving along a mysterious dark highway, with a beautiful younger woman, and you are curious to the point of obsession about where you will end up for eternity. It's incredibly stupid and wasteful of you. And ungrateful, too, I might add."

I knew it was. Somewhere inside me I knew. But I

simply could not resist the opportunity to ask God what I'd wanted to ask Him, Her, for every thoughtful adult minute of my earthly life.

"But where does it end?"

"It doesn't."

"The universe expands," I suddenly said, as if Einstein himself were whispering in my ear.

"Endlessly."

"We just go on and on, then."

"Exactly. On and on. Except that your idea of time is not accurate."

"There's no hell then?"

"You're looking at it," she said, gesturing at the dark view out the window.

"South Carolina?"

She smacked me lightly on the arm as a real wife might do to a husband who'd made a foolish joke.

"The idea of hell was developed by earthly minds because here, on earth, you can experience the rough equivalent, the feeling that you are being tormented for-ever — by illness, by a nasty spouse, by an evil, immature soul — with no hope of escape. The relationship between earthly reality and Absolute Reality is very similar to the relationship between a human being's dream and her waking consciousness. The difficulty or pain or fear in the dream seems utterly real, and then you wake up and realize it was an illusion. Just so with human misery — you should know this by now. It isn't really forever, of course, but that's what it feels like. You remember your pain from the years after your divorce, do you not? From the years of your apparent failure?"

"Apparent? It was a real failure."

"It felt real, of course. It felt eternal, too, if I am not mistaken."

"All right, yes. And people bring that on themselves?"

"I never said that."

"But you did, I just heard you."

"You misunderstood, Hank. You're making the immense subtlety of creation into a crude theory that fits the narrow abilities of your mind."

"Oh."

"Stick to golf—that's something you know."

"Okay," I said.

"No offense intended, honey."

"None taken."

My old eyes saw that we were approaching the turnoff for the highway to the coast. God pointed at the exit and told me to take it.

"Can I ask where we're going next?" I said, putting on the blinker and moving the Cadillac smoothly into the right lane. "In case You fall asleep or something?"

"You are hopeless," She said, and seemed to drift away from me again into Her own thoughts. It occurred to me that there were billions of other souls out there that She had to concern herself with, that I was being selfish, taking up Her time. And conceited, to think God would give me all Her attention. But another part of me just wanted to push and harangue and pester until I understood everything She did. I am, after all, a descendant of Adam and Eve—that foolish pair who refused to just do as God asked them, refused to let Him run the show. These kinds of things get passed down, you know.

A bit later, when we'd stopped for a light dinner of fried-to-death seafood, heavily sweetened iced tea, hush puppies, and a sumptuous piece of pecan pie, and were getting back into the car, Alicia said, "Follow the signs for Myrtle Beach and then keep going south. We're headed for a place called Pawleys Plantation, a golf resort. I have another old friend there. All you have to do is go into the welcome center and pick up the keys. And then, if it isn't too much trouble, when we wake up tomorrow morning, I would, in fact, like for you to do what I called on you to do. I would like you to fix my golf game."

"Yes," I said. "Of course."

And so, caught up in another real-seeming, earthly dream, I drove tiredly on.

FIFTEEN

Pawleys Plantation is a marvelous place. Though the resort fronts on a rather plain and unattractive highway, once you are past the gates and the security booth, you enter a peaceful world of southern homes—porches, mansard roofs—with a golf course winding through it. After a brief stop at the welcome center ("Yes, sir, Mr. Fins-Winston, everything is all set for you and your wife, sir") we checked into a charming two-bedroom condominium on the eleventh fairway, and I rolled our luggage in from the Cadillac.

Through the fragrant southern darkness, I strained to get a glimpse of the fairway and green that I knew lay just beyond our little screened back porch. Alicia enjoyed a glass of wine with me on that porch (She is partial to full-bodied reds), but was in a contemplative mood and did not say much. It was strange for me, seeing Her that way, distracted, working through some divine problem. I had the sense, I don't know why, that this particular problem had nothing to do with golf. But, after Her earlier reactions to my questioning, I was loathe to inquire. On that warm, Low-Country evening, God seemed far away.

When She went into Her bedroom without saying good night, and did not reemerge, I sat up long past what should have been my bedtime, listening to the symphony of crickets and the rustling of wind in the palm trees, then I stepped outside and took in the salt air mingled with that heavenly scent of a recently mowed fairway. Even in my achy old body, being on earth seemed such a wonderful thing at that moment that I had to struggle a bit to remember what it had felt like to live in heaven.

That night I had a strange, quick dream, and awoke holding to the pleasant memory of it. In the snippet of dream, I was striding confidently off the eighteenth tee of a magnificent golf course as if I were the great Ben Hogan, and there were fans six and eight deep along the ropes, cheering wildly. For me.

The next morning we took our breakfast in the plantation's café, the large, second-floor windows of which looked out on the eighteenth hole. We could have tossed the coffee from our cups down onto the sloping green, and, with a bit more effort, into a small pond protecting its left side. Beyond the water, an as yet empty fairway stretched toward the ocean. I was aching to play. The only trouble was that a storm had moved in during the early morning hours, and rain was streaming down the plate-glass windows and puddling in low spots on the green. It had been so long since I'd had a golf day ruined by the weather that I felt boiled in an irrational fury: How could God do this to me? Bring me to such an exquisite golfing venue, and then spoil all my plans with a storm? I thought of asking Her, but held my tongue again and just glared out at the drooping palms.

After we'd been sitting there a while, over our break-fast of waffles, fruit, and coffee, Alicia's "old friend," a woman named Jann Walker, came and joined us. From the first minute, she treated God as if She were just an-other visiting human. She was polite to me and welcom-ing, but there was an ease between the two of them that went beyond politeness, and I wondered if, at some recent point in her spiritual evolution, Jann had also spent some quality time with God. As they talked, I found myself wondering if God didn't spend this kind of time with everyone, if She or He was, in fact, capable of taking a va-cation with every single person who'd ever lived—play-ing golf with the golfers, talking vectors and momentum with the physicists, jumping rope with the children. It seemed a reasonable way for God to operate. But, some-where during that breakfast, sitting there sipping from a third cup of coffee and twisting in a wet, angry wind, while Jann and Alicia reminisced about mutual friends I did not know, I came to the conclusion that God was simply too large and complicated a subject for a brain like mine, for any human brain, to understand. I could catch little glimpses of Her true essence, I could speculate, I could decide what seemed fair and not fair according to my own sense of such things. But it was beginning to seem that, ultimately, God was simply God, and I was simply one tiny human, and so I tried to stop pretending to understand Her. I worked very hard at just living there, in that wet moment, with a lonely seagull swooping over the pristine fairway on the far side of the windows, and the strong coffee, and the green grass calling to me, whispering, beckoning like a lover.

During our breakfast with Jann, Alicia was vibrant and vivacious, but when we returned to the elegant condominium, She drifted away again, into Her pondering of the architecture of time, I suppose. I was frustrated at not being able to play. I was angry at Her—for Her distance, Her secrecy and games, for bringing me to earth in the first place when I could have been teeing it up happily with my usual foursome at Rancho Obispo. It was a foolish emotion, naturally. After all, what good can ever come from being angry at God? But that's what I felt. The God who had made me, the God who had disguised Herself as a pantsuit-and-jewelry-wearing, thirty-something blonde with old friends sprinkled across the American South like so many magnolia trees, the God who watched over innumerable universes and innumerable creatures in those universes, that God was perched on the comfortable salmon-colored couch at Pawleys Plantation with a remote control in Her hand, flipping through television channels while I waited to hear what we would do next, why we had come so far to play golf, why She'd arranged for weather that made playing golf impossible.

Finally, when I'd paced the rooms, poured myself two glasses of water, stood looking out at the drenched fairway for half an hour, glanced at the television for the twentieth time, I told Her I was going to put on my rain gear and go out for a walk.

"That's fine, honey," She said, immersed in some kind of foolish game show. "I'll see you around lunchtime."

I grunted, the reply of a grumpy husband, pulled on my rain pants and rain jacket, and, for the first time since our arrival on the watery planet, ventured out into the world without my God.

During my abbreviated time on the PGA tour, it had been a habit of mine to walk the golf course on the night before the first round. Like all the other golfers in a given tournament, of course, I would have arrived a few days early and spent some time playing the course: studying the roll of the greens, thinking about the placement of flagsticks and where best to position my tee shots. But on Wednesday nights, usually in the last hour or so of daylight, when the course would be empty except for the maintenance crews, I'd walk the course without my clubs or caddie.

Some of the finest and most peaceful hours of my life had come during those scouting walks. On those warm evenings, striding along the empty fairways and skirting the bunkers and greens, I was filled with a sense of some larger dimension I could not name. I do not mean to sound irreverent, but those beautiful golf links were like cathedrals for me on those evenings. I had a visceral sense of the closeness of God. Not the God of the gray, cold Protestant churches I'd attended as a boy. Not the God of rules and righteous anger, the God of punishment. But a nameless, faceless God, a spirit who emanated a feeling of acceptance.

So perhaps, when I went out in the wind and rain on that first morning at Pawleys, I was simply trying to retrieve those feelings.

I was also, I believe, hoping for some kind of help, some unseen celestial friend to tell me how to behave with God, which makes me realize that at this point, before I describe the rest of that day, I need to explain another one of the peculiarities of heavenly life: Those in paradise can keep up with events and people on earth to a degree commensurate with their interest in those events and people. So, like my friend Juanita, if you had a particularly close relationship with a son or daughter, say, and if you died while that child was still alive, it was really no problem to continue to observe, although from a great distance, what was happening to that person. A "deceased" father, mother, or friend can check in hourly with the situation on earth, watching over the progress of a loved one, sending a subtle code of communications that, unfortunately, most people on the blue planet do not know how to receive.

There is even a way in which they can be of assistance to important friends left behind. This is a fairly complicated procedure, and difficult to explain to someone who has not actually experienced it, but, basically, it involves making what might be thought of as a spirit-to-spirit phone call to one of the legion of saints and angels who take an interest in the fates of human souls, and who have the power to influence those fates. You can't overdo it and burden those spirits with one request after another. And, for a variety of reasons, your requests aren't always granted. For instance, I had lost contact with my old love, Zoe, and no amount of trying could get me back in touch with her.

But during my stay in heaven, if I knew an old friend on earth was having a rough go of it, I would make contact with one of the "helpers" and ask for a particular favor, just as one might intercede on earth for a friend in need. We are all involved in a web of helping and hurting one another — you don't have to spend time in heaven to understand that. It's just that, in heaven, it's entirely helping: The process of living through a single earthly life is incredibly arduous and difficult; it should come as no surprise then that there is assistance available, locally and elsewhere. So perhaps I expected a bit of assistance on that rainy walk. But there was no one on the course. The starter's shed was closed, the carts tucked safely away in a storage shed. After wandering for a while I decided to pretend I would be playing in the first round of a tournament the next day, and set off from the tee on the first hole, up the fairway, with the rain cascading down the arms of my jacket, and my shoes already starting to soak through.

The Pawleys course was an early Jack Nicklaus design (I'd passed away while he was still in the midst of his legendary career, and had watched him, with no small amount of envy, from heaven), and, as I'd expected, the master had made it a supreme challenge, from the back tees, at least. The first hole, a par five, was rather short—only 511 yards—but the fairway moved slightly to the right, and all along the inside of that slight curl lay a huge waste bunker. There were three small deep bunkers around the green as well, and the putting surface rolled and tilted like the North Atlantic in a hurricane.

The wind picked up as I turned onto the second hole, a monster 461-yard par four, and I felt as if I were in a hurricane myself. There was a pond on the third, a par three with a shallow green, another huge waste bunker on four, more water on five . . . and on six, and seven, and eight. On the ninth, the fairway was punctured by a huge, dripping live oak right in the center, right at the point where you'd want to be flying your tee shot; and there was a deep grassy gully between it and the elevated green.

By that point my socks were soaked, water dripping down the collar of my shirt. I had seen enough of the course to know what I would be up against—if the weather ever cleared—but I did not want to go back to the condominium and face God's distracted mood and the empty afternoon. Just as I passed the starter's shed for the second time that day, I noticed a few people coming out of the pro shop, in an adjacent building. It was still raining moderately hard, and the wind was strong, but the air was mild. Even squishing along in wet socks and shoes was not particularly unpleasant.

On a strange impulse, I stepped into the pro shop—just the kind of place where I'd spent my working life—and asked if I might hit a bag of balls. The pro's name was William Akers, a famous teacher in those parts, as I later learned. He raised his eyebrows at me, but did not otherwise object. It was only a short walk back to the condominium. Alicia wasn't there. I grabbed a few clubs—driver, three iron, pitching wedge—found a new glove in my bag, gathered up a half dozen tees, changed into dry socks and golf shoes, and went off to indulge my eternal passion.

Only the truest golf fanatics will understand this, but I loved standing out there in the South Carolina rain, hitting balls. The wind whipped at my back, the raindrops pricked my face, I loved it. Just the act of bending down to put the ball on the tee, then the address, the quieting of my mind, drawing the club back then moving my body fluidly down and forward so that all my weight was transferred to the clubface as it struck the ball—this was a kind of opium for me, it had always been that way. I did not understand at the time that golf was the secret language of my spiritual life, that in pursuing perfection on the course, I was in fact working on a different kind of perfection. I just loved the motion of the golf swing.

Ball after ball I sent flying out into the storm. My

rhythm had never felt so fine. At one point a raincoated maintenance worker came by in a covered cart and collected the little green mesh bags other golfers had left there the afternoon before. "Little wet for this, isn't it?" he said, in a tone that did not carry much admiration. I didn't answer him. I was engrossed, overjoyed. I thought: This kind of thing could never happen in heaven. And just then I saw Alicia standing there on the tee with a large beach umbrella over Her head. She was struggling with the umbrella, which was being tugged by the wind, and I could see that She had Her good shoes on. "Hi," I said happily, without thinking. For that instant it wasn't as if I was talking to God at all, but to a friend and fellow golf aficionado, someone who would understand my little crazy stunt. All the deference had been washed out of my voice. I was myself, and happy.

"You're practicing," She said.

I smiled and sailed a long straight drive off into the maelstrom.

"You're out here in a gale, practicing."

"If I hear thunder, I'll come in, honey. Don't worry."

"I'm not worried."

Something in Her tone caught my attention. I looked up again, expecting a lecture, but there was a look of what I can only call satisfaction on Her face. It was very strange. It was as if She'd somehow expected, or wanted, to see me doing this; as if my foolhardy urge had confirmed what She'd long suspected about me, and it pleased Her very deeply. "I walked the front nine," I said, setting another ball on the tee and sending it soaring. "Then I just had this urge."

She watched the trajectory of several more shots, stood there for another few minutes, then gave me the most beautiful, joyful smile you can imagine. She said, "I was right about you, after all," in a voice that sent a thrill from my navel to my throat. Then She turned and headed off to the café, and after switching to my pitching wedge and hitting a last dozen balls, I went off, sopping wet, old hands aching, to join Her.

SIXTEEN

The next morning I rose at first light. The storm had passed, leaving only a scattering of palm fronds strewn about the grounds, and small puddles in low spots on the tar parking lot. Before breakfast I stepped out onto the fairway behind our condominium and saw that the course had drained beautifully and was perfectly playable, if still a bit damp.

Alicia had gone out and bought some groceries the day before—I did not ask about money; it was simply there, in my pocket, in my wallet, in the folds of Her leather purse—and we had a light breakfast in the condo without saying much to each other.

In my excitement, my eagerness to play, I'd almost forgotten that I was supposed to be helping God with Her game. So I began working up a practice routine for Her—an hour on the putting green, a little time on the driving range, then a relaxed eighteen holes during which I'd try simply to build Her confidence. It was wonderful to be able to think like a teacher again, and wonderful to feel the anticipation of the golf round building in my old body.

But when we'd finished with our croissants, fruit, and coffee, God gave me the bad news that She wouldn't be accompanying me after all on that fine morning. "Jann and I are going on a little shopping trip, honey," She said, in her cute, not-so-smart voice. "You won't mind if I skip out our date just this once, will you?"

"But You said You wanted to work on Your game. I think I may have figured out what Your problem is and—"

She gave a casual wave of one braceleted arm. "Oh, Hank, honey. There will be plenty of time for golf. I haven't shopped in so long, and haven't seen Jann in eons. You understand, don't you?"

I mumbled something about understanding perfectly, gave Her a chaste kiss on the cheek in farewell, changed into my golfing attire, and strolled off in the direction of the starter's booth. Men were taking golf bags out of the trunks of cars; women were hitting wedges on the practice range; two young towheaded boys were horsing around with their father on the putting green. Near the starter's shed, carts were muttering, golfers slipping dollar bills out of their wallets—this was the busy little drama I had lived with for most of my adult life, and it sang a sweet chorus in my innermost ear.

In a moment I had made the acquaintance of the starter at Pawleys Plantation, a genial and hardworking fellow named Greg Stevens. Greg spoke with what I recognized from my Pennsylvania days as a West Virginia accent, and he had the natural hospitality of so many of the people I'd met from that state. In heaven, when I wasn't spending time with Juanita and my Brit golfing pals, I often sought out the company of former West Virginians. I couldn't remember ever having played golf there, but I had admired its most famous son, Sam Snead, and, perhaps because of that, I felt an instinctive link to the place. The real reason for that deep West Virginia link would not become clear to me until the very end of our trip, but I felt this connection with Mr. Stevens, and I believe he felt it with me.

I introduced myself as Herman Fins-Winston, and, when Greg heard the name, he said, "Long time ago used to be a golfer by the name of Winston, Hank Winston, I think it was, a tour player, I mean. Late forties, early fifties, I think it was, right around the time of Hogan and Demeret. My daddy used to talk about him having the sweetest swing he ever saw. You're no relation by any chance, are you, Mr. Fins-Winston?"

"That was a distant cousin," I lied. "When he came to America he dropped the 'Fins' and just called himself Winston."

"Well, I hope you have the gene for that swing of his,

then," he said, and setting my bag on a cart, he gave the irons a quick cleaning and sent me on my way with an "enjoy that round now, Mr. Fins-Winston" that sounded completely sincere.

Well, I was flattered, naturally. That someone had called my swing sweet, that someone remembered my name, my brief career, thirty years after its demise, that someone would even mention me in the same breath as my famous contemporaries. Looking back on that encounter now, it seems clear to me that the small exchange with Greg Stevens flipped a lever within me, began the change that God had intended all along. But, of course, I didn't know that then.

I liked playing alone, and have to admit that I was glad—God forgive me—for the chance to be on the course without Alicia for a while. If I was going to be an older man on earth, complete with arthritic knees, petulant bladder, and a full capacity for worry, then the least that was owed me was a little time to myself on a fine golf course. No teaching, no gambling, no worrying about what God was thinking. Just pure golfing pleasure.

There were a few other people on the course, but Greg said it would be no problem to play a solitary round and sent me off on the first hole, no one else within shouting distance.

So, I stepped up onto the tee, going back over my mental notes from the day before. I always play from the back tees, naturally, what we call "the tips." As a former tour player, even in heaven, I've always been too proud to do otherwise. And as I stood on the back tee of the first hole at Pawleys, even though I was swinging so well, I suspected I was in for some rough sledding on the Nicklaus course.

But something strange had been happening to me on that first day at Pawleys, even before I'd stepped onto the tee. From the moment Alicia said She was going off to the mall with Jann, I began to sense a small change in my muscles. At first, I thought it was only too much of the strong coffee.

But as I took a couple of practice swings on the first tee I felt it again. I hit a beautiful straight drive, and when I walked up to the ball I calculated that it had traveled almost 280 yards, or about 10 percent farther than I would normally hit a ball, even in my prime, even in heaven. Two hundred and eighty yards. Nearly the length of three soccer fields. And I was seventy-five years old.

I followed that small miracle with another: a high four iron that flew all the way down the length of the waste bunker and landed on the putting surface. I then sank a double-breaking, eighteen-foot putt for eagle.

Nothing so surprising there, you might say. After all, I'd played well at Ford's Colony, had raised an eyebrow or two on the practice tee. The new clubs and balls were giving everyone extra distance, and it was a rather short par five. But, I tell you honestly, my body felt different. I felt younger than my age, and had somehow just known I could reach the par five in three shots. More important, I felt that my swing had fallen into a groove I'd experienced only briefly during my years on earth, and had never actually rediscovered in heaven. More than once, Greg Stevens's kind words—"sweetest swing he ever saw"—echoed in my inner ear. I played the difficult front nine in even par.

But the real challenge came, and the real change in me occurred, on Nicklaus's wicked and gorgeous back nine. The thirteenth, fourteenth, sixteenth, and seventeenth holes play along an estuary, just a mile from the ocean itself, and so are subject, at that time of year, to blustery winds. The thirteenth tee sits on a sort of levee, and you hit across the estuary to a green surrounded by water on three sides. It is common, as I learned from playing there for several days, to see egrets and sandpipers, and, at low tide, hundreds of golf balls stranded in the muck like the hulls of unfortunate pleasure craft, victims of a devastating flood.

Standing on that levee, with at least a fifteen-mile-an-hour wind blowing in my face, and the green looking very tiny there, 145 yards in the distance, I thought I heard, or felt, an echo of my wonderful dream. I actually turned and looked over my shoulder, expecting perhaps to see a cheering crowd, but all I saw was a big-bellied middle-aged man slamming his club into the twelfth fairway as his ball wobbled sideways and skittered down into a deep trap. The memory of that echo of applause was very brief, but it seemed to trigger an electrical surge in the fibers of my old man's muscles. When it passed, I knew, I simply knew, that I was about to hit a marvelous shot.

And marvelous it was. I took a seven iron into that whipping wind and laced a shot that headed right for the flagstick from the moment the clubface made contact with the ball. It bounced once on the front part of the green, bounced a second time, and rolled into the hole as if guided by a divine hand. Immediately I turned to see if the fellow on the twelfth had borne witness. No, he was kicking sand and cursing. I searched the fourteenth tee and fairway, the sixteenth green—no one watching. Somehow, it did not matter. No witness, no official hole in one, but it did not matter. I had never made an ace in my previous life. Almost fifty years of playing, hundreds of close calls, but never an ace. I went and retrieved the ball from the cup, pushed it down into the rear left pocket of my trousers so I wouldn't lose it on one of the later holes, and walked to the next tee a very different man.

I'm almost embarrassed to boast like this, but over the next five difficult holes, I did not make anything less than a superb shot. Long straight drives, crisp approaches to the putting surface, putts that either fell right into the cup or stopped a millimeter to either side. When I pulled my bag back to the starter's shed, and Greg greeted me there with a "How did your round go?" it was all I could do not to tell him I'd played Nicklaus's masterpiece in three under. "Not bad," was all I said. I did not even mention the unwitnessed hole in one.

"The sun did some good things to your face, if you don't mind me saying," he said. "You're from up north?"

"Pennsylvania," I said. "I was a club professional for a while there."

"Maybe I can squeeze a lesson out of you late one afternoon then," he said, and for a moment I thought he meant it, and I was ready to oblige.

I walked back to the condominium—Alicia was still shopping—and took a long bath. As I was lying there I happened to look at my forearms. It seemed to me that the skin had tightened, that the muscle tone had improved since the night before. And I seemed to have gotten a slight tan here on earth. Nothing especially dramatic, but noticeable nonetheless, and a pleasant surprise for a pale-skinned Brit used to going beet red over the course of a single hour in the outdoors. After toweling off, I looked in the mirror and thought I saw a difference in my face, too. I looked, not exactly young, but younger. A fellow in his late sixties who'd kept in shape.

By the time Alicia returned, laden with fancy boxes from a variety of fancy stores and as happy as I'd ever seen Her, I'd done a complete examination of my body. When She walked through the door, I was sitting out on the screen porch with a gin and tonic, toying with my hole-in-one ball. She poured Herself a glass of wine and joined me. "It went well, honey?" She said, the way any loving wife might.

"You're making me younger."

There was a splash of surprise on Her face. She nodded at my glass. "How many of those have you had?"

"I can feel it. In my arms and legs. I could feel it in my swing. I hit a 280-yard drive on the first hole."

"Well, the prevailing wind is at your back on that hole, isn't it?"

"Look at my face. I'm younger."

"It's the Carolina sun," She said. "It changes the skin tone and at the same time affects the brain if you stand out in it too long."

I just stared at Her then, twirling the ball in my free hand. "You don't want to improve Your golf game, do You," I said. "It doesn't really need improvement. This whole thing is some kind of charade."

"I don't participate in charades."

I wasn't fooled. "Something is going on. You called on me to teach You, but you don't need teaching. Of course, You don't. How could You? You're God."

She looked at me for a long time without speaking, glanced away, looked back. "You're not a teacher," She said at last.

"No? Well, then I could have fooled several thousand happy clients a few years back."

"I mean, essentially, at the primal root of your soul. That is not your eternal identity."

"Oh, really," I said. "What then, may I ask You, might my eternal identity actually be?"

"You're a great champion."

"A great champion? A great champion? You've gone mad."

"Careful, Hank."

"Well, fine, all right. I'm upset. We had a deal and I thought—"

"The deal is off," She said.

"But—"

"I've changed my mind."

"But I . . . what did I do wrong?"

"Did it seem today, out on the course, that you were being punished for something?"

"No, just the opposite, in fact. I made my first ever—"

"Exactly, just the opposite. In fact, you've been remarkably patient, much more patient than I would have expected, given the behavior in your last several dozen lives. I turned you into an old man and you didn't object. I made myself into a beautiful younger woman traveling with you and, except for a brief lapse when I was taking a bath at the hotel in Williamsburg, you've kept your lustful instincts in check. I played so poorly on the front nine at Ford's Colony, yet you handled the situation with a gentlemanly good cheer that would have been beyond the capability of fully 99 percent of the male human beings in this universe."

"Fine, thank you. But—"

"Can you let go of being a teacher or can you not?"

"I can, I suppose."

"Can you be taught? Can you allow someone to lead you?"

I twirled the ball once and gave it a hard squeeze. I sipped my drink. "Absolutely."

"Now, I'll give you a bit more information, but only on the condition that you do not ask another question for the duration of our stay at Pawleys Plantation. Agreed?"

"Agreed."

"My friend Jann, like most of the people we'll be in

contact with on this tour, is actually a helper, an 'angel,' you would probably call her. Part of her duties on earth right now, a small part but an important one, is to effect a certain kind of change in you. The same was true for Charlie Pysher at Ford's Colony. Now, you met a man named Greg Stevens today, I believe. A West Virginian."

"The starter."

"Exactly. He has started you on something larger than a round of golf, a journey I've designed, naturally, but that you can either embrace or reject. Can you accept that without your curiosity and your infernal pride getting in the way?"

"My body feels different," I said, meaning it as a confirmation of all She had been telling me.

"Can you, Herman?"

"Of course, Lord."

She drew and released one long exasperated breath, then seemed to sink back again into a kinder Alicia. "Fine," She said, in a soft voice. "There's a little place called the Hanser House just up the road. I like the scallops there. Let's go have a nice quiet dinner and let things unfold as they will, shall we?"

I nodded. I squeezed the hole-in-one ball twice more, slipped it back into my pocket, and dressed for dinner.

SEVENTEEN

The next day, our third at Pawleys, Alicia and I had a light lunch and teed off at twelve-forty-five. The early birds had finished their morning eighteen by then, their daily prayer to the god of golf. Most of the rest of the resort guests were in one of the restaurants enjoying their fettuccine Alfredo or flounder sandwiches, so we had a couple of open holes ahead of and behind us. I had the smooth swing going for me again, and Alicia, well, Alicia played like God. Through seventeen holes She was four under par, and would have been several strokes better than that if She hadn't missed three putts inside three feet. The yips again. She would occasionally mutter to me, angrily, that I'd been assigned to cure Her and She had not been cured at all. I'd try to object, to remind Her of the previous evening's conversation, but She kept insisting I was not doing what I'd been asked to do.

On the eighteenth, a foursome of fellows came up behind us as She was teeing off, and I suppose She was uncomfortable playing like God in front of them. She dribbled one off the tee, smiled back at them and said, to their great relief, no doubt: "Honey, shouldn't we let these gentlemen play through?"

We stood to one side and watched the gentlemen tee off. The eighteenth is almost a mirror image of the first hole, except that it's a par four instead of a short par five. The fairway bends lazily left, with a long waste bunker there, and the green is tilted toward a small pond (where you might see a basking alligator), so that chip shots from the opposite side seem more difficult than they actually are. For a long hitter, the temptation is to try and cut the corner, fly a tee shot over the near end of the waste bunker and leave yourself only a 130- or 140-yard approach.

All four gentlemen tried to fly the bunker. Three of them ended up in the sand with what looked to be problematic second shots; the fourth went farther left and splashed his ball into the water.

"Why did You do that?" I asked God when they had thanked us and puttered away in the direction of their various disasters. "Why did You pretend You couldn't play as well as You've been playing?"

"I wanted you to see them," She said. "I wanted you to

have a lesson in course management, which is really only a lesson in humility. Which is actually the primary lesson of earthly life. I wanted you to remember this as things unfold—stay humble."

"Am I that arrogant?"

"Not at all, honey . . . by human standards."

"Are human standards that awful?"

She pretended to be watching the men hit their second shots, and for a moment I thought She was going to avoid answering altogether. But then she turned to me and I could see the fire in Her eyes, a kind of divine exasperation. "Let's put it this way: Everything is given to you. Everything. Everything is a gift—the sun, your breath, your food, your capacity for wonder, even the possibility of union with God. And well, let's just say I hear a lot more, 'Please, could you just do this one thing?' than I hear 'Thank you.'"

"All right," I said. "Guilty as charged. And, for the record: Thank You for all this."

She waved my gratitude away. "You can make it up to me by giving me a lesson on the putting green afterward. I know you have something in mind."

I did have something in mind. I'd been thinking about the yips as we played and had devised a little practice game that I thought might help Her. But as we strolled down the eighteenth in the late afternoon light—I had always enjoyed playing at that time of day more than any other—I was thinking about the peculiar kind of arrogance that afflicts some golfers. I was thinking, especially, about the arrogance of youth and strength, and how that might have been a factor in my failure on tour.

Part of why I was thinking along those lines had to do with the fact that I had grown younger that day, again. It was an incremental change—I'd gotten out of bed and discovered that I'd dropped perhaps another two years off my age and was now somewhere in my midsixties. Jann Walker, the angel with whom we'd breakfasted again, had either not noticed or decided not to comment. Greg Stevens had not seemed to notice. Alicia changed the subject anytime I brought it up, or categorically denied it if I confronted Her. But I knew my body. I could feel the change. And over the course of that walk down the final fairway I was wondering if being old had finally taught me what I should have understood when I was young: that a golf course has to be handled carefully, respectfully, just as life does. Life can seem benign, but, really, the price paid for a moment's bad judgment can be a terrible price. A single mistake on the highway, a single miscalculation in business, a single hour of carelessness in a romantic relationship—any of those can carry with them a punishment that seems to exceed the crime. In Bethlehem, for instance, I'd had a friend who'd made one careless step on an icy sidewalk when he was in his early thirties. One moment of inattention, and he'd fallen and cracked a vertebra and suffered decades of chronic back pain. Many, many times in tournaments I'd seen someone make one small mental error and lose a match.

On the putting green after our round, I had Alicia hit

one hundred three-foot putts, and I stood close to Her, always within Her range of vision. I moved from one side to the other. I stood directly behind the hole. I encouraged Her to imagine that there was a crowd of people watching, that the putt She faced meant the difference between winning the green jacket at Augusta and losing it by a stroke. I told Her to form a rock-solid preshot routine, and then to step up to the putt and stroke it without thinking, with a blank mind, with the certainty that it would go in.

This drill had just come to me; I'd never actually used it during my teaching days. But I liked it so much that, after Her hundredth putt (She sank eighty-nine of them), when Alicia pleaded exhaustion and went back to the condominium to shower and lie down, I gave the assignment to myself. One hundred three-footers, and before each one of the first fifty I imagined myself at the Western Pennsylvania Open, with Anna Lisa and my friends watching, with an opponent silently rooting for me to miss. Then, when I'd conquered that, I tried the second fifty on the last hole at Augusta.

I made them all.

EIGHTEEN

Over the next five days at Pawleys Plantation it seemed to me that I shed a year or a year and a half every twenty-four hours. It happened gradually enough that none of the people we dealt with—waitresses, starters' assistants, workers in the pro shop—made any but the most ordinary comments. Greg Stevens, who saw me several times a day, would occasionally say something about the seaside climate agreeing with me, or suggest I was looking happier so I must be playing well, something along those lines. But that was as far as it went. Every morning when I looked in the mirror I would see irrefutable evidence of this peculiar backward movement: a slight darkening and thickening of my hair; fewer lines around my eyes; some tightening of the muscles of my abdomen and upper arms.

I decided not to mention it to Alicia again. Perhaps I was learning to let the awesome magic of Her creation unfold, minute by minute. Or perhaps I was just afraid that, if I annoyed Her, She'd leave me stuck in my middle sixties and abandon me there in South Carolina, with no friends or family, no way of making a living, nothing but a collection of shiny plastic cards in my wallet and a set of golf clubs.

We played together every morning. As had been the case in heaven, She hit the ball beautifully tee to green, and then struggled with Her putting. Since She never again mentioned the fact that I was now supposed to abandon my teaching in favor of becoming "a great champion," as She put it, I went on with my original instructions, which were to help Her cure the yips. Day by day, I worked on Her. "Now," I would say, as She was taking Her putter out of the bag and walking up to a difficult, downhill twelve-footer, "You must believe, in Your heart of hearts, that this ball is going into the middle of the cup. You must make your stroke with pure confidence, absolute confidence, without hesitation or second thoughts. Get Your line, go through your preshot routine, and trust."

"Thanks, honey," She'd say, but half the time She'd stand over the putt too long, worrying about this and that, remembering all the bad putts of the past few weeks. And when that happened She'd inevitably make an uncertain stroke and leave it short a few inches, or pull it left of the hole. Still, I believed I could see some progress.

My own game was magnificent; I say that in all humility. I was consistently two and three under par from the
back tees. As it tends to do on a golf course, word of my
ability spread quickly, and in the bar in the late afternoons
some of the resort's better players would approach me
and suggest we play for money. On Alicia's advice, I refused them all. "We'll have time for that, hon," She said,
when we were walking along the cart path on a beautiful
spring evening. "Right now, all you need to think about
is etching that swing into the cells of your brain and spirit.
I want you to be so sure of it that, no matter what kind of
pressure you face, it won't break down on you."

"Your game is moving into a new dimension," I said in
return, and, to my surprise, She hooked her arm in mine
and we walked along like a real married couple. Previ-
ously these displays of affection had always occurred
when there were others watching, but we were alone on
that evening, a few seagulls coasting, a few seabirds calling out. I felt an impossible hope rise in me.

"Yes, you've helped me," She said, "though I'm still not
quite comfortable on the greens."

"Putting is the only part of the game that's almost totally mental."

"Everything is," She said.

"Well, there are physical mechanics to the full swing
that—"

"No, no." She patted my forearm. "Everything is mental, sweetheart. The entire spiritual path, as you like to
call it, takes place in the deepest inner workings of the

mind. Everything is formed there—your health, your swing, your fate. Even your death occurs there. You can't see that yet, can you, Hank?"

"No," I admitted.

"The mind is neglected on this planet," She went on. "Well, not neglected, actually, but understood in too crude a manner. It's more than mere intellect. There's something much larger and subtler that goes almost totally ignored. Human scientists know that only a small part of the brain's potential is actually used. Yet you humans spend so little time in mental cultivation—I don't mean learning, cramming your head with facts; I mean prayer, meditation, contemplation, even just the simple effort of changing a thought pattern in a positive direction."

My thought pattern at that moment brought me back to the palm readers and fortune-tellers of my earthly days, the frothy-headed ones who would say things like what Alicia had just said, who would deny the laws of the body, of physics, of reality, who'd try to claim that you could heal an illness simply by wishing it away. Or that you "created your own reality" by your habitual patterns of thought. So much airheaded nonsense, as far as I was concerned.

At that moment, we walked onto the long levee that ran between the thirteenth green and the fourteenth tee, and in front of us spread a magnificent vista of an estuary at full tide, marsh reeds stretching off toward a single row of houses on the horizon, right at the edge of the surf. The sun was just setting behind us, and the light on those reeds was a golden, salty light. We could hear the faint rumble of surf beyond the houses. As we paused to take in the scene, two magnificent birds rose up and made a graceful circular sweep not far above our heads. Graceful is not really the word for it: These were otherworldly creatures, and their flight was the kind of thing you wouldn't be surprised to see in heaven. There was a red patch on their heads, and black feathers—like mustaches—to the side of dark beaks. Their necks were long and outstretched, their wings pure white except for an ink-black fringe. But it was the way they moved that struck you, as if they were moving and not moving at the same time, as if their swooping flight required no effort at all but was simply part of the greater flow of energy that surrounded them.

"Whooping cranes," Alicia said softly, and with some pride. "There are only 183 of them left now."

I could not take my eyes from them, and suddenly, in the midst of watching them glide out over the marsh, I understood something. I cannot, however, properly cage this understanding within the metal bars of words. All I can say is that it felt as though the ordinary boundaries of my brain had dissolved, and I understood what Alicia had just been telling me, understood it in an utterly fresh way. I knew, I simply knew at that moment, that it was actually possible to transfer the perfect grace above me directly to my golf game, wordlessly, effortlessly, simply by placing my mind into this larger context.

I must sound like a palm reader to you. I must sound

like I'm being foolish and frothy headed. But knowing what I know now, I can't bring myself to apologize. It is true: Everything we experience in the external world, good fortune and bad, has its root in the subtle workings of the mind. And it turns out that those subtle workings, those patterns, can be changed. It's exactly like golf. The change occurs slowly, practice round by practice round, year by year, life by life. That's our real work, though. That's what Alicia was trying to show me.

NINETEEN

We left Pawley's Plantation without warning. After my exhilarating moment with the cranes, I should have realized that everything Alicia did with me was a type of lesson. I should at least have understood the link between expectations and disappointment. I should have seen that the human mind is all knotted up by a two-colored rope: hope and fear. You have a wonderful Hawaiian vacation scheduled for three weeks in the future, and the present gets diluted by that, dissolved in your visions of salty surf, tossing palm trees, and lush fairways. Or you have a root canal scheduled for three weeks in the future, and the thought of it keeps bumping the actual moment out of focus: You are talking with your wife or husband or child, you are playing golf, and yet you aren't fully there because part of your mind is taken up with the root canal, with Hawaii.

God doesn't feel bound by that rope, by human projections. When I heard Alicia say we'd be leaving Pawleys, I remembered a friend of mine at Rancho Obispo telling me that the most important thing he'd learned in heaven was "not to take the next breath for granted." "On earth, we were always making plans, weren't we Hank?" he said. "Well, here's what I've figured out: The motivation for that obsessive plan making came from fear. We couldn't control the future, and we knew it, and that made us afraid."

By refusing to give any kind of advance notice, Alicia was giving me this lesson: Don't take the next breath for granted. Live in the absolute Now, and you won't be afraid. Ah, how easy these things are to talk about.

She knew that I had started to imagine myself spending months at Pawleys Plantation, stringing together one beautiful round after the next, one great meal after the next, strolls along the beach, glasses of wine in our screened-in porch. She didn't want me to be wasting my time on earth that way, indulging in thoughts of some pleasurable future or worrying about getting back to heaven, my regular foursome, my nights out dancing with Juanita. There is a direct parallel to golf, naturally. I see it very clearly now. You cannot be a great champion without being able to shut out hope and fear, Hawaii and the root canal, eagles and double bogeys. You have to learn to take the very center of yourself, every ounce, every drop, every nerve and muscle, every cell, and concentrate it on the golf ball, on the shot you are playing and nothing else.

But obviously I had not learned that lesson yet, because I was upset to hear that we would be leaving Pawleys. That course, that setting, that screen porch on the eleventh fairway at twilight—it was a kind of paradise, and no one who has had even a small taste of paradise wants to give it up.

TWENTY

So there we were, going along on our pleasant routine—breakfast, a round of golf together, a bit of shopping for Alicia and a bit of putting-green time for me, another round for me in the afternoon, a few minutes in the Jacuzzi, a fine meal, a walk along the cart paths in the dying light. And then one evening—it was a Thursday—that sweet routine was broken. We returned from our quiet stroll and Alicia said, "Pack up, Hank honey, we have to be on our way."

"When?" I said, "Where? But—"

She turned those amazing eyes on me. I went off to pack my things.

In less than an hour I had stuffed the clubs and bags in the Cadillac's spacious trunk, and we were driving west, away from Pawleys, away from my happy projections.

God, naturally enough, refused to say where we were headed. When we came to a turn, She'd give me just barely enough notice: "Left here, Hank. North on this route. Up onto the interstate now, honey. Head west." If I said I needed to stop and use the facilities, or have a cup of coffee or something to eat, She was perfectly gracious and generous. There was no sense of impatience on Her part, only that same impenetrable calm I recognized from just about every minute of our time together on earth. God had something in mind. And when God has something in mind, well, try to resist it.

Late that night we finally stopped—in a not particularly nice hotel on the outskirts of Columbia, South Carolina. She asked for two rooms, for some reason, and I was left to lie tiredly in a sagging bed, surrounded by the stink of disinfectant and old tobacco smoke, feeling my body growing stronger and younger, and doing exactly what I should not have been doing: wondering where it would all lead.

Before dawn She was knocking on my door, dressed in a beautiful golf outfit—forest green slacks and a green-banded cream-colored jersey with a light jacket over it, earrings on, makeup on, Her eyes looking particularly bright and happy. It almost seemed to me that God, too, had grown younger during the brief night we'd spent in the chain motel. At least, She was more beautiful than ever, and I was more attracted to Her than I probably should have been.

She gave me fifteen minutes to shower and dress ("Your best golfing clothes, hon"). We stopped at someplace called the Waffle House for an inexpensive and quite satisfying breakfast, and then, with the sun rising like an even-edged ember over the Carolina landscape, we were once again on the road.

INTERSTATE 20 WEST, the signs said. Though I had played in the South numerous times in my professional career, I was unfamiliar with the particular stretch of countryside through which that highway sliced. To either side were rolling hills, just brightening; old southern farmhouses stood beyond the billboards, surrounded by fields that had been worked by humans for centuries—Native Americans, slaves, sharecroppers, hardworking southern farmers. I felt a strange nostalgia for that land.

In a short while we began to see signs for Augusta, Georgia. Just that word—*Augusta*—sent ripples of feeling along the skin of my arms and neck. Augusta. The Masters. Golf's hallowed ground. It was everything I could do to keep myself from asking Alicia if we might stop there, just for a quick look, on our way to wherever it was we were headed.

I didn't ask Her, though, which was a good thing.

"Now listen carefully, Hank honey," She said, when we'd passed the second Augusta sign. "We're going to play Augusta National, you and I and a very old friend of mine named Larry Five Iron, who is in charge of welcoming people to another resort not too far from here. Larry, I should warn you, is a man of humble birth, Brooklyn, I believe. As in Brooklyn, New York. Is that going to be a problem for you?"

"No, no, no, no!" I shouted in the Cadillac's posh front seat. "Why do You and Julian Ever keep asking me things like that that? No, the answer is no, it isn't a problem! I'm not racist, I'm not sexist, I have nothing against the working classes!"

"Calm down, honey. Just asking."

"But why do You even have to ask? Do I have some history of that kind of thing? Was I a bigot in a past life or something?"

I was answered with a grin worthy of the Buddha, and a truly awful, echoing silence. We rode along for a ways, God looking out the window into the vast terrain of human history, and me, Herman Fins-Winston, pushing my thoughts against the barrier of my humanity, the thin lining of guilt there, the borders of memory. On earth, I and everyone I knew assumed we had done nothing to deserve our pain and bad fortune. When things went badly we complained and wrung our hands. We felt mistreated by fate. How did we presume to be so sure?

In time, She told me to take the appropriate exit, and said, "The membership at Augusta National Golf Club is, as you know . . . well, how should we put it?"

"Selective," I said.

She laughed. "Yes, exactly. What a beautiful language English is. Perfect. Right, our friends there are selective.

Excessively careful about who gets into their little paradise. Imagine if I were like that."

"I'd never have gotten to heaven," I said. "I have a long history as a bigot, You practically said so yourself. I'd be burning away in the fires of Hades for all eternity."

"Now Hank, honey, don't be quite so hard on yourself."

"Well, it's a horrible feeling, knowing you were somebody you don't want to have been, and yet not really remembering it."

"You've been forgiven," she said.

"For what? When?"

"You are forgiven."

At the sound of those words—I had to hear them twice—it was as if a terrible weight slipped from the tops of my lungs. I felt an actual physical change in my body, a kind of internal release. I started to breathe differently. I lost four or five years in a phrase.

"Thank You," I said. "I'm sorry for whatever it was. I'm grateful You can forget it."

"Who said anything about forgetting? I never forget. In fact, there is still a tiny bit of work left for you to do in order to, well, *atone* is not exactly the right word. Let's say, there are still a few things you have to do to balance out your past."

"Another life?" I asked.

She frowned. "Always the future, always the future."

"All right, I'm forgiven. I feel forgiven. That's what matters. Thank You again, Lord."

She reached over and patted my thigh. "Just a simple 'Alicia' will be fine, honey."

"All right. Sure."

"Where were we?"

"Augusta. Selective. Bigotry in past lives."

"Yes. Well, it might upset our friends at Augusta National to have a person like Larry Five Iron playing on their beautiful course. He has traces of an old accent, you see, just a word now and again, you may not even notice. To his credit, he has never really shaken off some of the less-refined aspects of his background. Still, these people cling to their prejudices. . . . And it might upset them, too, if they saw me playing at my best."

"Women are allowed on Augusta National."

"Oh, how kind," said my ironic God.

"Some of the members must have been working class in their early days."

"Two of them," She said. "To be precise. And the first African American member won't be admitted for another decade. Wonderful that the powers-that-be are so open-minded."

I listened closely. God seemed, that day, slightly uncomfortable and out of character, almost nervous. "There's something You're not telling me, isn't there," I said. "Come right out and say it. Believe me, after what I've seen the last few weeks, I can handle whatever it is."

"This is your left, Hank."

"Hit me," I said, as I turned. "Give me the whole, unvarnished truth."

"Fine, I'll do that." She twirled her diamond ring and drew a breath.

"Do you remember the conversation we had on the porch one night at Pawleys?"

"Which conversation?" I asked, but I could feel a peculiar species of nervousness twisting my innards like a small eel.

"The conversation about your being, in the essence of your soul identity, a great golf champion?"

I swallowed. I said, "Yes." I felt a steady current of electricity start thrumming through my limbs, as if I'd been plugged into an outlet. It was not a particularly pleasant sensation. She directed me to turn into the parking lot reserved for members, and I did so, and to my astonishment the attendant there glanced at the license plate and simply waved us through.

"Park here," Alicia said.

I parked and turned off the engine. We sat looking at each other across the front seat.

She said, uneasily I thought: "Do you know what a scout is? A scout for professional sports?"

"Of course, someone who goes around to high school and college games looking for players who might make it to the big leagues someday."

"Exactly."

The electric current weakened and then ceased altogether. I wasn't worried any longer. "You're grooming me to be a scout, then, that's what this is all about. You want me to travel through the realms of heaven and earth, looking for great sports talent, or decent souls."

Alicia stared at me across the seat of the Cadillac. "Is that your idea of a joke, Herman?"

My arms started buzzing again, just my arms. "No, it isn't. I'm confused, if You really want to know. I mean, Augusta, some joker named Larry Five Iron, Your problems with putting, which, frankly, seem to bother You a lot more at certain moments than at others. And now something about baseball scouts? Who wouldn't be confused, I mean—"

"Hank, honey."

"What."

"Calm yourself."

"I'm calm, I'm perfectly calm, I'm just—"

"Hank, listen. Your fingers are trembling on the steering wheel. Just calm down for a moment and listen. Take a breath."

"I'm not nervous," I said.

"Yes you are. And with good reason. Take a breath now."

I took a long breath. *Good reason?*

"One more."

I breathed again.

"Now . . . up to this point I have been rather gentle with you. Don't interrupt, please. I like you, personally, that's not the problem. The problem is that you are not a particularly easy person to work with, and, believe me, I've worked with billions upon billions of souls, so I have some basis for comparison. In your most essential identity you are, as I've said more than once now, a great champion. A champion of historical proportions. But you simply don't seem to believe this. Like so many of your fellow humans, you are constantly limiting yourself, finding a thousand and one excuses not to live up to your full potential. Frankly, I've grown tired of that. As my good friend Juanita mentioned—"

"Juanita!"

"As my good friend Juanita mentioned," God went on more sternly, "during your previous life I sent down someone who was supposed to guide you—"

"Anna Lisa?"

"Yes. Your former wife, Anna Lisa. And you were so unwilling to take her guidance, so stubborn, so determined to avoid your champion's responsibilities—"

"But Anna Lisa made fun of me, she undermined my—"

"Hank. One more interruption and we're through. I mean it. We go back up to heaven. You hang out with your pals at Rancho Obispo and it will be five hundred years before we speak again. Clear?"

I nodded. The electricity had been turned up. My right leg was twitching. I tried not to let God see.

"Anna Lisa made her share of mistakes, but you made it unnecessarily difficult for her, just as you are doing for me. Now, my good friend and helpful associate Larry Five Iron is what you would call a scout. His job, not his earthly job but his secret spiritual job—you all have one—is to help me identify the essence of various types of souls. Sounds simple, but it isn't. According to the heavenly statisticians, 92 percent of the souls on earth have not yet discovered what it is they should be doing in order to fulfill their holy potential, and I don't have the time to enlighten them all single-handedly. So I have people like Larry who work with me. You following so far?"

I nodded.

"Larry has the ability to see beyond people's disguises and into the center of their sacred architecture. This would be the rough equivalent, in physical terms, of a person who could look at you and see your genetic code. Clear?"

I nodded.

"In your previous life, Larry saw the champion's architecture in you. He also saw the troubles you had trying to manifest it. He was, in fact, present at a particular moment a few weeks before the Western Pennsylvania Open, when you first really started to turn your back on your destiny. That moment occurred in the state of West Virginia."

"But I never played in West Virginia, I'm sure, I—"

"You blocked that memory from your consciousness. Believe me, you played there. It was there that you began to fail. Seeing that failure bothered my friend Larry, naturally. Bothered him so much, in fact, that he took to following you around from tournament to tournament, trying to pull you off the path you'd chosen, but to no avail.

"So," God continued, "in large measure it was Larry who arranged this entire trip. He helped you get up to heaven for a while, rest there a bit, and then he suggested to me, through Julian Ever, that I make contact with you and start this process. His work, as I mentioned, is to help you reach your true potential as a sacred creation. Now, this is the difficult part: In the coming week or so you will undergo a great test, a series of tests, actually, that will try your spiritual mettle in a variety of ways. I'm sorry to say there is not very much I can do to help you, other than giving you some warning, which is what I'm doing now. Even Larry can't really help you. Still with me?"

I was shaking so hard I could barely nod my head.

Alicia was not smiling. She said, "Now, here's the final and most important part. You can choose to accept all this and go forward, or you can turn away. If you turn away, there will be no punishment, but you will have to face these same tests at some much later date. The choice is yours and yours alone, but I recommend against procrastination here, Hank honey. The road to true salvation is narrow, the proverbial camel through the eye of the needle, you know. The proverbial razor's edge. Are you willing to try or not?"

I couldn't speak. I believe now that we all know—our spirits know, our subconsciouses, our bodies—when we come to certain crucial moments in our lives, key decisions on which our futures rest like huge oak logs balanced on an acorn. A tiny movement either way and the direction of our lives changes immensely.

"Hank?"

I hesitated, feeling myself teetering over some bottomless abyss I could not name. I stared into the silver-flecked eyes for a second, two seconds, and then I nodded. And when I nodded, God smiled.

After She smiled, She took a breath and said, "Oh, one more thing. Larry Five Iron is Anna Lisa's spiritual brother. He's hoping to engineer your reconciliation; I thought I should warn you of that."

TWENTY-ONE

And then! The columns of that fabled clubhouse, the boughs of the great live oak, the unbelievably perfect fairways, tee boxes, and sparkling bunkers! Augusta National. Every golfer's dream.

We did not venture into the clubhouse, but simply took our bags out of the trunk, borrowed two pull carts without asking, and strode onto the first tee. There, waiting for us, was a fellow with elaborately twirled mustaches, silver trousers with silver suspenders, white and blue golf shoes, a bright white collared jersey, and a cap that read: WORLD'S GREATEST DAD. He was smoking a thick cigar and twirling a pricey but well-scarred driver in one hand. He reminded me, instantly, of my father.

"Larry," Alicia said, when she'd accepted his kiss on both Her cheeks, "I'd like you to meet Herman Fins-Winston."

"Hank, baby," he said, crushing my hand in his, "I'm the famous Larry Five Iron." He was smiling an enormous, apparently genuine, incredibly warm smile at me from behind the twirled mustaches. "You, my friend, you are simply the cat's meow. I am familiar with your work, and your game, and I have to say it is truly an honor, an absolute honor, to make your acquaintance."

"Nice to meet you also," I said, but I was overwhelmed from the first minute.

"I've been waiting here all day, watching all these turkeys tee off, so me first." Larry stuck the cigar between his teeth, stepped up and hit a hard ground ball about ninety yards along the unblemished first fairway. He laughed loudly, looked up at the clubhouse, and made what might have been taken as an obscene gesture in that direction. I glanced at Alicia, who was watching him as one might watch a dear friend one had not seen in several years. It was clear to me then, if it had not been clear before, that angels come in many unusual disguises.

I hit my tee ball over the trap that guards the right side of the fairway, some 310 yards out.

"What was I saying," Larry said, very loudly. "He is the man! He is the cat's meow. He is the cat himself! He is just exactly everything we thought he was, Lishie, honey."

Lishie went to the front tees (there are no ladies' tees at Augusta) and hit what, by Her standards, was a modest drive down the left center. Larry hoisted his bag onto one shoulder, and with my two spirit guides, I walked off the tee box, marching straight toward the great battlefield at the outer edges of who I thought I was.

Augusta National, for those of you who have never had the privilege of seeing it in person, is everything you would imagine it to be. As fine as the perfected soul. The fairways and tee boxes are without blemish. The rough is cut more evenly than the neatly trimmed beards of some of the Scotsmen I played against in my youth. The course is hillier than it looks on television, and actually, surprisingly, appears rather easy until you get to the greens. The greens are monstrous, devilish, impossible, cut so tight you feel as if you are putting on green-painted asphalt, with bunkers placed in such a way that you step down into them praying for mercy. Not a difficult course to play, really: The members are not all known for their golfing prowess. But a difficult course to, well, master.

But made less difficult, on that cool April morning, by the unfettered exuberance of one Larry Five Iron. (So named because he used his five iron—and beautifully, I might add—for every shot from 170 yards in. When other people hit a wedge, Larry bumped and ran his five iron. From the fringe of the green, Larry popped a five iron. On tight driving holes, Larry teed off with his five iron. He was a genius with that club.) On the first hole, he hugged God three different times, he slapped me on the back twice, applauded when I stroked a nice nine iron onto the putting surface, laughed at his own mediocre opening shots, kept turning and making amusingly irreverent gestures in the direction of Magnolia Lane. "Trevino hated this place, you know," he said to me confidentially as we stood on the tee of the long par-five second. "Despised it. Took his freaking shoes off in the parking lot for God's sake—sorry, Lish, honey. I relate to Trevino, I don't mind saying. I want to see them humbled here. I want a poor or at least a middle-class kid to get the green jacket draped over his shoulders, a plumber's son, a bricklayer's kid. I want a nonwhite champion here. I want a woman."

"Larry, honey. Don't get carried away, dear."

"I want to carve some divots," he said, after he'd chunked a driver 150 yards dead center, cutting out a cutlet of perfect turf in the process.

After the opening four, and the long par five, you have a tricky short four and then a long par three. Lishie and I both played this stretch in one over par, although from different tees. She was swinging beautifully again, as She had in heaven, but looking a little shaky around the greens. With the sins of my past life forgiven, and my almost-youthful body (I felt in my late fifties by then, but believe me, once you've seen seventy-five, fifty-eight seems like adolescence), I was swinging the club as nicely as I'd ever swung it. Something about Larry's personality took the edge off the place, too, and at least some of the thrumming nervousness out of my arms and legs. I had approached Augusta in the same way I'd always approached the idea of God, with a kind of subservience. The place is magnificent, yes, but it is still and only a golf course, a former nursery, in fact, eighteen holes in the ground. Larry helped me remember that . . . and helped me forget, for moments at a time, about what Alicia had called my "great test."

In fact, not only was he irreverent in regard to the golf course, he was irreverent in the larger sense, toward God. Irreverent, and yet somehow properly respectful at the same time. He'd hug Her roughly, plant a wet kiss on Her cheek, kid Her mercilessly when She missed a short putt ("Lishie, baby, I could have knocked that one in with the end of my stogie"). But then he'd pick up a wedge She'd left at the edge of the green and hand it to Her in a gesture of perfect intimacy and respect. Or look at Her as if She were the woman of his dreams, a starlet, a goddess. They had, it seemed, gotten to the place some long-married couples get to: They no longer felt the need to be overly polite to one another.

As we went along the front nine, Larry would tell us the names of each hole—Flowering Crab Apple, Magnolia, Juniper, Pampas—pronouncing them, sometimes mispronouncing them ("Pamp-ass"), with a sort of bemusement. "Look at this, will ya Hank baby," he said, standing over his third shot, uphill, to a blind green at number eight. "What are ya supposed to make outa this? You can't even see what you're aimin' at. Yellow Jasmine, they call it. Yellow Jasmine, my butt."

And so on.

Still, after the first couple of holes, his game fell into a steadier rhythm, and he played, for the most part, a decent stretch of par and bogey golf.

It has to be said that every hole at Augusta National is a work of art, testimony to the vision and pure golf knowledge of the men who laid it out—Alister MacKenzie and the greatest of all amateurs, Bobby Jones. But the course's splendid character really becomes apparent at what is known as Amen Corner, that famous, devilish, two-and-a-half-hole stretch: the second half of eleven, plus all of twelve and thirteen.

By the time our peculiar threesome was making the turn and approaching Amen Corner, I was feeling like I'd known my playing partners for all eternity, that we'd been golfing pals since shortly after Adam and Eve had been tossed out of the garden. Larry was just a fine soul, I don't know how else to say it. He bounded around the course with a boy's enthusiasm—for the elegant fairways and greens, for my play, for the company of his "Lishie, honey," for the great gift of being out in the Georgia sunlight on such a day. Because of his duties at his own resort—I didn't catch the name the first time he mentioned it—he didn't get out to play as much as he would have liked, and his game reflected that: ground balls and fat shots mixed in with some pretty, left-to-right long irons and confident putts. His affection for me—obvious, unfeigned—was manifested in a steady stream of outrageous praise. When I hit a long, perfect, downhill draw off the tee on ten, he leaned his own driver against his belt buckle, clamped the cigar between his teeth, and gave me a big round of applause—as enthusiastic and sincere as anything ever offered a player on that tee. When I hit my second shot to two feet, he came all the way across the fairway to hug me, then called out to Alicia, to God, "I told You it was programmed into the genes. Can You see it? Can You see it now, Lishie, honey?"

On the eleventh tee, when I told him I was, after all, a man past my physical prime and in semidesperate need of a water closet, he said, "Listen, go water-closet the azaleas over there."

"But this is Augusta National," I said. "You don't just casually pee in the shrubs at Augusta National."

"No?" he said. And he proceeded to do just that. And I proceeded to follow his example . . . and felt much the better for it.

While Larry and I were thus engaged, and Lishie, discreetly averting Her divine gaze, was fiddling around in Her bag for a clean ball, three gentlemen came up the fairway of the previous hole, playing at a fast clip. We decided to let them play through. They barely nodded, then stepped onto the tee as if we were not there. Something about these men troubled me. I'm not sure what it was. They were dressed in expensive shirts and watches, and had caddies toting bags filled with the most expensive clubs. And they each in turn knocked a crooked drive down off the elevated tee. Nothing especially unusual in that; I'd seen it a million times at the club outside of Bethlehem, at charity tournaments, in pro-ams on the tour. You don't play well simply because you can afford the best irons, or a membership in the best clubs.

Of course, I never judge a man by how well or poorly

he plays golf. What bothered me about these fellows, was a certain air of presumed superiority, as if they were simply entitled to their great good fortune, and others simply were not. It was strange for me to see this attitude in the flesh again; I'd become unused to it in heaven.

"Captains of industry," Alicia said to me, when the men and their caddies were well down the fairway. "Did you notice anything about them besides the fact that they didn't say thank you when we let them through? A certain, well—"

"Sense of entitlement."

"Yes, good. Many of the members here aren't that way, really. I count some friends among them, in fact. But I wanted you to see this particular group."

"Why?"

"Because someday you're going to be in a position to be able to behave that way, and it would simply break my heart if you did so."

"Fine, okay," I said, putting my tee in the ground and setting my shining new ball on top of it. "So I'm destined to be a captain of industry, then, in a future lifetime. That's what this champion stuff is all about?"

At this remark, Larry burst out into such a roaring wave of laughter that I thought he was going to do himself harm. When he was finished, after a long stretch of coughing and gasping and spitting of cigar juice, he and God exchanged a happy, conspiratorial look, and I had to settle myself for a moment before blasting a tee shot well down the center of the fairway.

As I was retrieving my tee, Larry walked over and put an arm around my shoulder. "See that," he said. He pointed after my drive and squeezed my triceps—which seemed to be swelling by the hour. "See what you just did there, young fellow? Captains of industry don't do that, okay? Not when they're twenty-five, and not when they're sixty. All right?"

I nodded. "Young fellow" had been what Pop always called me. I could feel lines of energy running up the bones of my spine like mice along a rope.

"We're talking something bigger than a captain of industry here. We are talking—"

"Larry!" Alicia warned.

"Right, okay." He slapped me on the back, stood up, and laced a sweet drive of his own, and then all the way down the fairway he was beside me, filling my nostrils with the scent of cigar smoke (Juanita had given me a box of Havanas for my last birthday; how I missed her; how I wanted to ask her about her conversation with God). "Big," he was saying, "you are going to be big. You are going to be huge, my friend. Enormous."

"Gigantic," I said.

"Gigantic wouldn't be too strong a word. Gigantic."

The second shot on eleven is to a green as slick as the greasy countertop of an all-night diner . . . only with a small pond just to the left side of it. I hit the middle of the green and made par.

The twelfth, Golden Bell, is a short and impossibly difficult par three to a shallow green with water in front, sand in front and behind, and a margin of error of just about four feet either way. I made birdie.

The thirteenth is a relatively short, uphill, dogleg par five with Rae's Creek running in front of the green in case you're feeling powerful and try to reach the putting surface in two. I did reach the putting surface in two, then sank a snaking twenty-five-foot putt for eagle.

"That's it, then," Larry said, after he'd tapped in for his seven. He put the ball in his pocket and lit a fresh cigar. "That's it. From here on in I'm just a spectator, watching in awe."

"Me, too," Alicia said.

I thought they were joking. They weren't. On the next tee, though I implored them to change their minds, they refused to take their clubs out of the bag.

"We're watching you," God said, when I complained that I'd really rather play with them than be an object of observation. "It's something you must get used to, Hank."

"Listen, it's time for a little wager," Larry said, and I peered into him when he said those words, trying to see past the disguise of his face, because they were my father's words, my father's mantra. "Listen, young fellow, a little wager," Pop would say, as we were teeing it up at our home course, or setting off on a train to London, or bringing in some logs for the hearth on a damp Nottingham evening. Greens hit in regulation, exact time of arrival at Victoria Station, number of logs in the pile—he'd bet on anything. It was his odd way of saying: We're in this together, you know—you, your Mum, and I; let's make some fun out of it, shall we?

Larry's eyes were sparking. "A little wager," he repeated. "Just to get you used to performing, you know, under pressure. Play the next five holes in even par or better and I'll put you and Lishie up at my place just northwest of here. One week. Finest accommodations. Four golf courses and all meals and wine on the house."

"And if he's over par?" Alicia said.

"If he's over par . . ." Larry took a long drag on the cigar, studied me, looked off into the distance. For some strange reason, even before he spoke the next words, I felt my legs start to shake. "If he's over par, then in his next life he's born a captain of industry. He loves golf, adores it. Has all the money in the world, all the power, but no time. Has to sit in his corner office and look out at the scenery and think about night-shift nurses who get to play, and cabdrivers who get to play, and schoolkids who get to play. Give him a membership here, Lishie, for good measure, right? And maybe three, four rounds a year."

"Seems a bit harsh," I told him.

"Reincarnation is no picnic," he said. "Ask the Boss, here."

"So you know who She is?"

"Know?" Larry put his arm around God as if they

were brother and sister. "Sure I know. I'm sort of an un-paid advisor, aren't I, Lishie sweetheart."

"A scout," I said.

"Exactly."

She kissed him on the cheek.

"You're not serious about the bet," I said, when Alicia and I had a moment alone.

And, in a voice that had no mercy in it, She said: "I could not be more so."

"This is the test, then?"

"One small part of it," She said, and turned away.

So, for the last five holes at Augusta National they just walked around with me, watching me play. The enormity of the bet, the thought of living a whole life without time for golf, hung over me like the blade of a guillotine. The effect, of course, was similar to the effect of playing in front of a crowd on tour. A certain kind of self-consciousness rises up in you and does strange things to your muscles, to your mind. You place yourself inside the spectators' heads. You worry about failing, about look-ing bad. Only this time I was worried about something far worse. What rose up in me then—no surprise here—were visceral, horrible memories of the Western Pennsyl-vania Open. I could see those feelings spinning around me like the mocking faces of demons. We all have such demons, don't we? Some hideous regret, or series of re-grets. Some humiliating failure, or terrible, unforgettable pain. Some deep understanding that we should have been courageous when we were cowardly, or kind when we were petty; some sure sense that we could have become someone we did not become.

Perhaps the Christian purgatory is a metaphorical place, symbol of the opportunity to confront those leering, jeering memories anew. Conquer them, and you rise up to heaven. Fail to face them and you languish there, not quite in hell, but burning, writhing, desperate for a sense of God's love.

I played the last five holes of Augusta National with mocking voices in my ears and gruesome devil faces before my eyes. The deep shame of that missed putt at the Western Pennsylvania Open linked up with the shame of everything else I had ever failed at, and slithered around me like some hooded, hissing serpent.

But thanks to some newfound grace, I walked straight toward my former humiliations, straight into them. I saw the shame, I felt it, but I did not turn my back or cast my eyes down.

And I played the last five holes at Augusta National in one under par.

At the end of the round, standing near the huge oak in front of the clubhouse, Alicia hugged me tight, pressing Her body against mine, a tear or two dripping onto the skin of my neck. I felt as though I was about to rise up into the sky.

Larry was puffing away on his big cigar, beaming at me like, well, like a proud father. "I'd give him A-plus for the first round of things, wouldn't you, Lish?" he said. And then, as we were leaving the grounds, he added, "Hang on for just a second, would you, Lishie, sweetheart?" She nodded. He loosened his belt, dropped his trousers a little ways, and offered his bare behind to the clubhouse windows, and then we headed off, north, toward the resort God likes best in the world, in the company of the man who oversees it.

TWENTY-TWO

Larry's resort went by the rather unusual name of Château Élan, and was set on several hundred acres of pretty, rolling north Georgia land, just off one of the interstates there. Much as I'd come to like my new friend, the name of his resort put me off a bit, I have to say. Maybe it was just some old British prejudice: The French have never been our favorite neighbors, you know. Or maybe it was the way the place looked from the highway at night, as if it were an ancient estate spread around a candlelit castle set down there in the middle of nowhere.

Alicia and I were given our own "golf villa," and when I woke up and looked out, and then made an early morning walking tour, I began to appreciate the beauty of that

complicated knobby landscape, and of Château Élan itself. It was a kind of paradise in miniature. There were
three courses, plus a par-three layout, the castlelike main
hotel, one very fancy restaurant, some smaller pubs, a
wine museum, an indoor tennis center, an equestrian
show ring, even a race-car track off at the back edge of
the property, where you could train for the Grand Prix if
your heart so desired. As we settled in, I began to feel at
home there, just as I'd begun to feel at home in the other
places God had taken me. People who are obsessed with
golf like to be around other people who are obsessed with
golf. But there was more to it than that: On the round
stone we call "earth," as the Native Americans understood, certain places have a sort of sacred charge to them,
a sense of holiness. Château Élan was one of those places.

Larry arranged everything: the five-room villa with a
fairway view; succulent meals in the Versailles Room
where the offerings included things like roast lamb and
anadama panini, pumpkin risotto, and twin braised quail
Tagine, along with a selection of wines wide and deep
enough to satisfy God herself.

In all, we stayed at Château Élan ten nights, treating
ourselves to Jacuzzis and massages in the spa, to glasses
of Guinness and onion rings in the pub, to eighteen holes
of golf in the mornings and eighteen more after lunch, on
three different courses. Ford's Colony to Pawleys Plantation to Château Élan, I felt like we were working our way
through increasingly marvelous levels of heavenly life.

Perhaps some of this feeling had to do with the fact

that, with each passing day, there was less and less friction between God and me. If I had not yet passed the "great test," if I had not yet moved all the way out of purgatory, I felt as though I had at least climbed up a few rungs on the ladder. Thanks to Larry's lesson in fond irreverence, I was coming to understand that there was a way to be properly respectful without losing my dignity, a way to yield to the divine command without fighting and whining like a very young child, a way to sense the godliness in myself, if that doesn't sound improper.

On top of all this, I was continuing to grow younger. It was a gradual unaging, just a slight, steady change in the color and thickness of my hair, the loss of a little weight around the belly, a tightening and sun-darkening of the skin. I was more flexible in the joints. I no longer needed reading glasses. One day I noticed that my teeth looked stronger and whiter; another that my vision had improved; an increase in leg strength, arm strength, sharper hearing. None of the friendly staff of hostesses and waiters remarked on this metamorphosis, beyond the usual: "You're looking well this morning, Mr. Fins-Winston, sir." Alicia didn't seem to notice. We saw Larry for dinner every night in one of the seven restaurants, and for a total of two rounds of golf, and he didn't comment on the change in me either.

There was a downside to it, though I feel foolish complaining about such a thing. Going into detail about this downside is a bit embarrassing, to be honest. And more than a bit difficult for a well-bred Englishman like me.

But, well, you see, one of the side effects of my new youthfulness was a, well, an increase in what might delicately be termed "my interest in the opposite sex." As an ordinary golf professional in an ordinary body in good old ordinary Bethlehem, Pennsylvania, I had always had what I thought of as a normal, healthy appreciation for the beauty and grace of an attractive woman. I like to think, in fact, that I saw beauty and grace in places some of my coarser men friends didn't: in a gesture, a smile, warmth of heart, a certain confident posture or gait. During our years of courtship and marriage, I had been faithful to Anna Lisa, and had always made a point—unlike some of my fellow instructors—of respecting others' marriages, not flirting with my married clients, not flirting very much at all, in fact, though I had my share of lovers after the divorce was finalized.

But a detached appreciation is one thing. The vibrant demand of a young libido is quite something else. And as I moved backward through my fifties and into my forties, what happened was that my new blood chemistry started to affect my thought process. Let's put it that way. I won't, I suppose, be the first man to admit the affliction. I grew younger. I grew more virile, more interested. Which wouldn't have been a problem, I suppose, if I hadn't been living in close quarters with an especially attractive woman. Who happened to be God.

Alicia, for reasons known only to Herself, did not make this situation any easier on me. It did not occur to me at the time that this might be another aspect of my trial. She was tanned and fit, and, as the weather grew warmer, She took to strolling over to one of the swimming pools in the late afternoon and asking me to accompany Her. Never much of a swimmer myself, I would sit by the side of the pool and go over my golf game of that day, or page lazily through one of the magazines lying about, studying the advertisements and articles there, trying to make myself into a man of the modern era, when so much of me was still caught up in the past. In her tasteful, one-piece suit, Alicia would step to the edge of the pool, stand there with Her feet together, and reach up to the sky like some kind of yoga goddess. Then She'd knife into the water and swim a few laps, raising Her golden arms up and out in a powerful crawl stroke, and kicking a steady rhythm with Her strong legs. I tried not to stare. But at the end of these exercises, She would lift herself out of the pool, dripping wet, and make a point of asking me to toss Her a towel; once she even asked me to rub some sun lotion on the tops of the Divine shoulders.

At dinner, when no one else could hear, She'd say things like, "Really, you've turned into quite a nice-looking man, Hank." Or She'd take my hand as we bade Larry good night and made our way back to the villa.

You will think me the worst of sinners, the most irreverent of men. But as the days at Château Élan passed in a kind of blissful haze, I began to think of Her more and more in sexual terms. When we said good night and went off into our separate bedrooms, I would lie awake for a long time staring out the window at the stars and thinking about Her, wondering if She actually intended for us to have some kind of bodily relationship, if I was supposed to be assertive with Her the way I would have been with an ordinary woman, to confess my attraction, to be honest, forthright, to offer Her some physical comfort to ease Her time on a planet She did not particularly like.

This is the kind of chemistry I am talking about; this is the way the thought process gets twisted about by what I suppose can only go under the name of lust. Lust takes the shape of logic in some men, and, no doubt, in some women as well: utterly convincing, irrefutable. It begins, for example, to actually seem obvious to you that you can offer God comfort by coming on to Her.

To my credit, I must say, I denied this logic for what seemed like a very long time indeed.

TWENTY-THREE

What I could not deny was the obvious fact that I was golfing like I had never golfed before—on heaven or on earth. I feel obliged to inform you, with as much modesty as I can summon, that I shot twenty-eight one morning on the front nine of the Woodlands course at Château Élan. Larry got word of it, told the starter and the pro (grandson of the great Gene Sarazen, by the way), the landscape crew, and the dinner hostess, and, that night, had a cake brought to our table with twenty-eight candles on it. Another time, I twice missed making eagle from the fairway by a matter of an inch or two—twice, in the same eighteen holes: flew a golf ball 165 and 140 yards and nearly into a four-inch cup. On another round, from 248 yards out, I hit the flagstick on one bounce with a three wood.

Alicia played every round with me, even pretended to have the yips a couple of times and accepted my well-meaning instruction. But I had the sense that She was standing back and observing my progress, and I knew She was reporting to Larry (who was too busy to join us most of the time), giving him my scores, mentioning specific shots.

On what turned out to be our last supper together, in the Versailles Room, over fifty-year-old port, Larry said, "Hank, baby, listen. We have a situation here. I have a situation, I mean." He hemmed and hawed and tugged at his mustaches for a moment, and then said, "What it comes down to, my good young fellow, is that I have to ask you one pretty large favor."

By this time I understood that, while Larry Five Iron was certainly some kind of scout, and while he could quite possibly have been Anna Lisa's soul brother (though, mercifully, he had not mentioned her), there was another aspect to the man. It is not every day that you get to do a favor for the spirit of your late beloved father. Without a moment's hesitation, I said, "Anything."

He stalled and dawdled, glanced around as if making sure things were running smoothly in the Versailles Room, letting his gaze wander across the cloth-covered tables, the happy diners, then up to the glass ceiling high above.

"Larry, I mean it," I said. "You've been incredibly kind to me, to us. I've come to feel we're souls who've been linked for a very long time. Another few days and I'll be talking in a Brooklyn accent. Name the favor, and if I can possibly accommodate you, I will."

"Listen to this guy, will you?" he said, looking at Alicia at last. "'Accommodate you!' I mean, is he just a class act or what?" But he was obviously stalling, and obviously did not want to approach the fact of our previous relationship on earth. I worried, then, that he was going to bring up Anna Lisa, perhaps ask me to give marriage with her another try. He cleared his throat. He removed a cigar from a silver case in his inside jacket pocket, spent a moment studying it, and then, without lighting it, put it into the corner of his mouth. "All right," he said, making eye contact with me at last. "Here's my situation. We have three courses that are open to the public here, plus the par three. And then we have a private course called the Legends, in a little gated community behind the resort. I know, I know. I've been holding back on you, haven't let you play it even though I could have. I'm not sure why exactly. I'm sorry, young fellow. I was going to have you and Lishie play it with me, but I haven't been able to get the time off for that, and I won't either, but—"

"Larry," Alicia said.

"What, Lish?"

"Spit it out."

"What? The cigar? It's bothering you."

She watched him. "Larry."

"All right. Listen: Most, I would say all, really, of the people who come to this place are fine people. The members of the private course are exceptionally good souls. We do charity events here every year and you should see the kind of cashola they lay out for sick kids and so on."

"Larry."

"I'm getting there, I'm getting there." He turned to me again. "But there is one fellow who's a member there, he's kind of, well—"

"Evil," Alicia said.

"Evil is a pretty strong word. But he's kind of, well, you know, you've been around private clubs, there's always one or two of these types you can't stand, you wish you could pay them to give up their membership. You follow?"

"Of course."

"Well, this guy and I we have a sort of running banter between us. He's a better golfer than I am, I admit that, but even with strokes I can never seem to beat him, and naturally he never lets me forget it. So, this guy, he heard about you. Word has gotten around, I don't know how, but it has. And he wants a game. And he sort of embarrassed me, really, into agreeing to set it up. I should have asked you first, I know. And you can still back out if you want to, I mean—"

"I'm happy to oblige."

"I have to tell you the guy is no slouch."

"Not a problem."

"Not a problem, right. That's what I figured you'd say. I mean, the way you've been playing, who would worry, right?"

"I'm feeling good about my game."

"Good. Hah! Good would be an understatement."

Larry was trying to find his old happy carefree confident personality, I could sense that. But whereas it had come so naturally to him during all our other meetings, it now seemed forced. A filigree of worry decorated the edges of every movement he made, every syllable he uttered. I wanted, more than anything, to put him at ease.

"Listen," he said. "This guy is not just your average ordinary very good golfer, okay?"

"Not a problem."

"He's used to playing for high stakes, and you're not—that's the only thing that worries me."

"So you want me to gamble with him?"

"In a manner of speaking, well, yeah, I do. A little wager. You know how I am."

"I know how you are," I said, and almost added, "Pop."

"But, the thing is, this guy—"

"The stakes involve, among other things, the future of Larry's soul," Alicia said bluntly.

I thought She was joking until Larry squeezed the cigar too tight in his teeth and bit it in two. The long end fell into the remains of his chocolate mousse. He made an uncomfortable noise, like a laugh.

"It would be too complicated to give you all the details, Hank, honey," God went on. "But, like most of you, Larry has some unfinished business left over from one of his past lives. Nothing extraordinary, just a bit of litter he needs to sweep out of the way. Larry had the option of living one more very short, and rather difficult life, or . . . well, he decided he'd host us on this trip, and then he further decided to wager some of his soul's future on you. It's a sign of the utter faith he has in you. You should be flattered."

I knew I should have been flattered, honored even, but at that moment the solid floor beneath us in the Versailles Room had suddenly gone shaky on me. "You mean," I said, looking at them in turn. "You mean I will be playing golf against this fellow and whether I win or lose will determine whether Larry goes up to heaven for some kind of permanent stay after this life, or whether he has to come back and suffer on earth for another few dozen years?"

Alicia nodded.

Larry swallowed hard.

"If you like him so much, why can't you just grant him an amnesty or something?" I said to Her. "A special dispensation. Just say the word, and he'll be let off."

"I can't do that," She said.

"Of course You can. You can do anything."

"That I can't do. Just in offering him this option I've already set a terrible precedent that I can see is going to cause me untold trouble down the road. You aren't to tell anyone, by the way."

"Who would I tell? Who would believe such a thing?"

Larry cleared his throat. "And plus, there's sort of, you know, the test issue."

"What test issue?" I asked, but before the last word was out of my mouth I remembered.

Larry cleared his throat, made half a dozen sincere attempts to speak, then turned his eyes to God in a pleading way.

"Hank," Alicia said, "the bet actually involves more than just Larry's future. That part is true enough: If you fail, he will have to live a short life that ends with a horrible famine. Next to war, you see, famine is the thing that causes me the most sorrow. On a planet so abundant, to have people, little ones even, going hungry, it—"

God paused a moment, Her beautiful face shadowed by a sadness I had never seen there. Larry and I averted our gaze, and in a few seconds Alicia had almost gotten control of Herself again.

"And people say You don't care," Larry said, watching Her.

Alicia wiped the sides of Her eyes with a napkin. "Who says that?"

"No one, Lishie, honey. It's an expression. . . . You hear it around the pro shop. . . . It's just—" He turned to me, trying to change the subject and lighten the mood. "You know how I like to eat, Hank, right? Imagine how tough it would be if—"

But Alicia gave a small shake of Her head to signal him to stop.

A waiter came and removed our dessert plates, refilled our coffees. When the waiter went on about his business, Alicia continued: "A bit too intricate to explain in detail, Hank dear, but the stakes here are enormous. If you lose this match, then Larry has to live one last difficult life before he rises up into the next dimension, and you, well, all our talk about your soul essence, your nature as a great champion, all that goes by the boards."

"By the boards? What does *by the boards* mean, in this case, exactly?"

She paused, looking at me with such tenderness that I believed nothing too terrible could ever happen. But, as it turns out, the world is harsher than that. We like to think it's all sweetness and light: Once you perform a few admirable tasks, once you please God for a while, then all pain disappears, all risk, all possibility of failure. According to the intricate laws of sacred architecture, though, the farther up you reach in the spiritual realms, the greater the stakes, as if you are a kind of acrobat, walking a tightrope higher and higher above the circus floor. On the one hand, you have the privilege of this rare thrill, and on the other . . .

I remembered, at that moment, the story of Jesus being tempted in the desert and, later, tortured and killed. I mean, think about that. Think about Moses's childhood, the infant floating downriver in a basket, terrified. Buddha being born into a life of utter comfort and luxury and having to walk away from that and starve himself nearly to death in the fertile land of the Ganges plains in order to reach enlightenment! And we think we deserve eternal rest because we've lived a few decent lifetimes? We want comfort? We want our regular foursome at Rancho Obispo, for all eternity?

"In this case *by the boards* means . . . ," God paused. "You've heard about Muhammad Ali, yes?"

I nodded. Of course. I had been on earth when he was in his prime.

"Well, imagine if Muhammad Ali, with his miraculous talent, had never taken up boxing. Or worse, taken it up and suffered some failure of will early on. Imagine if Sam Snead or Ben Hogan had never taken up golf. Deep inside their spiritual selves they would know what they were capable of, and they'd have to live with that gnawing, secret frustration, life after life after life."

"Life after life? You mean . . ."

God nodded. "I mean, Hank honey, that it's sort of a Halley's Comet situation here. An opportunity like this, to be tested like this, to play against a particular golfer like this, comes along only once in every great while. You might get a second chance, you *are* in fact getting a second chance. And, as is the case with Muhammad and Ben and Babe Zaharias, your success will be tied to the happiness of other souls. If you succeed here, you will please them, inspire them, show them, by your example, what an individual can accomplish. But it's not like we can be offering the Great Champion title to every soul simultaneously. It's a rare honor, and it comes with a rare burden. Do you see?"

"Sort of."

"Circumstances on earth are caused by a certain exact combination of souls acting in a certain way. Think Archduke Ferdinand and Gavrilo Princip," she said. "Think Joseph and Adolf and Benito."

"Right, all right," I told her. "But You can't put me and Larry in with such buggers."

"Of course not. All I'm saying is that for the very best and very worst souls, their moment of opportunity is fleeting. Millions of things contribute to any significant event, billions of things that have to go a certain way in order for a war to start . . . or a marriage to be made, or a child to be born for that matter. If, for instance, well, let's take your father, a spirit you are very close to in the larger scheme of things."

I couldn't be sure, but I thought God winked at me.

"If your father had missed that train to London because of, say, an applecart tipping in the road when he was on his way to the station, then he'd never have met your mother in that life. You, Herman Fins-Winston, would never have been born into that particular body at that particular time. A wrong turn by an applecart driver who'd stayed up the night before for one extra drink at the roadhouse, and *pfft*—no you. Someone grabbing Princip's arm, and no assassination, no World War I, at least not then, in that way."

"So if I lose a game of golf, this particular famine will happen."

"Yes."

"And Larry will be part of it, suffer in it, I mean?"

God nodded.

"And I will miss a once-in-a-thousand-year opportunity?"

"Closer to ten thousand, actually."

"And if I win?"

"If you win, then the immense diagram you call 'history' will take a slightly different form."

"No famine."

"Right."

"No rebirth for Larry Five Iron."

"Exactly. No rebirth in this dimension. He will move on to more hospitable climates."

I hesitated. I thought of the expression *The weight of the world on his shoulders.* I could not bring myself to meet the eyes of the man who had been my father—my affectionate, roguish, golf-loving, and wager-loving Pop—in my past incarnation.

Alicia waited for perhaps the count of three, then said, "A simple yes or no will suffice, Mr. Fins-Winston."

"Yes," I said. "Yes, of course."

Larry reached out and clapped me on the back, then turned away, wiped the corner of one eye with his fist, and started signaling the waiter to bring us more port, some fruit and cheese, a cigar for me to smoke later on. The conversation swung away from famines and fates and great souls, but a sort of gloomy cloud hung over us, a sadness, perhaps, at the species Larry and I were part of, a deep existential sorrow for what human beings are capable of doing to each other and themselves.

Eventually, we emptied our glasses for the last time, sighed, wished each other good night with embraces all around. Outside, there was a terrible tension in the sweet Georgia air. Walking back to the golf villa, smoking the cigar Larry had given me, arm in arm with my beautiful Lord and companion, carrying my awful weight, I realized I hadn't asked who my opponent might be. I opened my mouth then, forming the question, and Alicia put Her fingers there, on my lips. "It's a perfect southern night, Hank honey," She said. "We've had a marvelous dinner with a good friend. Let's not spoil it with some kind of a talk that's going to upset us further. You need your rest for tomorrow. Believe me."

TWENTY-FOUR

As things turned out, knowing the identity of my opponent would not have calmed my restless sleep. The next morning, as we were driving into the gated community and toward the private Legends course (Larry said he was too nervous to accompany us, but he provided us with the code that got us through the gate), Alicia said, "His name is Victor 'Bunny' Rogan, in case you're curious."

Bunny Rogan was a name that meant nothing to me. I was nervous, naturally: Who wouldn't have been nervous, playing for a father's fate, for the chance to alleviate the suffering of thousands yet unborn, for a once-in-ten-thousand-years opportunity at greatness? But, at the same time, I knew I'd been playing fine golf, and I had the sense that the nervousness was actually going to help me this time, in this incarnation, rather than cripple me.

"Another friend of yours, this Bunny Rogan?"

"Former friend," Alicia said. "We're not on speaking terms now."

Perhaps because of those bad feelings, Alicia parted company with me at the bag drop. But before I got out of the Cadillac, She leaned over and kissed me on the lips, almost the way a wife would, and it seemed to me that there was a promise in that kiss. "Do this well," She said.

A promise. Perhaps a warning. And She seemed nervous again.

"Usually when you're gambling for big stakes," I said, "a third party comes along as a marker. I mean, there will be caddies, at least—"

"You're strong enough now. You'll be carrying your own bag," Alicia said. "It shouldn't be a problem."

"But, I mean, do we trust this Bunny Rogan fellow?"

"Oh, we know what to expect from him, let's put it that way."

God drove away. I found Mr. Rogan waiting for me on a bench not far from the practice green. When he saw me he stood up and smiled. He was in his mid- to late thirties, a tall fellow, on the thin side, dressed in shimmering black trousers and black golf shoes, a lightweight, expensive-looking red shirt with two lines of black trim on the collars, and a rather lumpy yellow hat that bore the name of the most famous club in the southern hemisphere.

He had a pointed, rather unpleasant smile, which made me distrust him immediately. But he extended his hand warmly. "Herman," he said. "Bunny Rogan. Do you have a nickname you like to go by?"

"Herman is fine," I said, to my own astonishment.

He laughed in a way that brought up a flush of old embarrassment in me, and then said, "Gee, I thought our tee time was for seven, so I've been waiting. You don't need any warm-up, do you?"

I was on the verge of apologizing when I remembered that this was a classic trick used by golf gamblers the world over. I knew our tee time was for eight. Bunny, no doubt, had been on the premises since first light, warming himself up fully, and was now trying to rush me out onto the tee.

"No," I said, firmly. "Our tee time was for eight o'clock. It's seven-fifteen. I'll take my forty-five minutes of warm-up time, thanks. You go ahead and have breakfast in the clubhouse and put it on my tab."

"You sure? The tee's open."

"And it will still be open in three quarters of an hour," I said.

"Hey, no problem. We're a little grumpy, though, this morning. Did we not sleep well?"

I ignored the remark and walked over to the practice range. I had, of course, encountered this type of trash-talking before. It was something I'd always despised. Much of the beauty of the game of golf lies in the quiet dignity with which it is played, in the fact that, for example, a competitor at the highest levels will smooth out a small imperfection on the putting surface *after* he has hit his putt, to make it fairer for a competitor who may be following him. You go silent when your opponent stands up to hit—think of professional baseball players doing that. You say "nice shot," and try to mean it. So he won't incur a penalty, you remind your opponent to replace his coin on the green after he's had to move it out of your putting line. At the lower levels, you spend some time tramping around in the poison ivy, helping someone else look for his lost tee shot. That is golf. Think of what earthly life might be like if those same rules of etiquette were applied more widely. Think of the unlikelihood of war and famine, for two examples.

But I could see, immediately, that things were not going to be quite so gentlemanly on that day. Bunny Rogan was a type. A type I disliked with every fiber of my being.

Instead of going inside for some refreshment, Bunny stayed close by and pretended to sulk as I warmed up. He stood on the practice green, watching as I hit some wedges, turning his eyes away to knock in a desultory putt or two, and then looking over at me again, expectantly. I went over to the range and hit a few dozen balls. Rogan's attitude bothered me for the first few shots, but then I fell into a quiet routine, felt my focus draw in tight around me, and by the time I had joined him on the putting green I felt ready for whatever tricks he might try. I went through a drill of draining some four-footers, moved onto some longer putts to get a feel for the speed of the green, then announced that I was ready.

What he tried next was flattery, another classic technique. The first hole at the Legends is the number one handicap hole, a 423-yard par four with no trouble in the fairway, but a tricky, elevated green with two tough traps in front. I hit a perfect tee shot, just under three hundred yards, dead center.

"Hell of a shot." Bunny shook his head in mock amazement. "Everything they said about you is true. One hell of a fine shot."

I ignored him.

He yanked his drive well left, but it cracked off a tree there and bounded out into the first cut of rough. I said nothing. There was no option but to walk beside him down the fairway. All the way he kept up a steady line of chatter, something else I hated. "So, how long are you down south for? Who was that beautiful babe I saw you drive up with? Not your wife, I hope? What do you think of the new balls, they really go, don't they? It's wonderful, isn't it? Can you stomach these types who moan and groan about the old courses becoming obsolete because of technology?" And so on. By the time we reached his ball, I was ready to knock him in the back of the knee with my pitching wedge, but there was something else nagging at me, some intuition I couldn't name.

He hit a hard ground ball that bounced up onto the green. "Topped it," he said. As if I couldn't see. Another awful golfing habit, this penchant for having to explain every mistake, aloud, to oneself and one's playing partner. I hit a wedge onto the putting surface. When we crested the hill, I saw that his ball—after two mishits—was four feet from the pin, and mine, after two good shots—was eight feet away. I missed my putt, he made his. Bunny Rogan was one up, or, perhaps I should say Larry Five Iron, thousands of other unfortunate souls, and one future great champion were one down.

The second hole, similar in length to the first, but somewhat easier, was played in a similar manner by Mr. Rogan. An awful tee shot that bounced into and out of the lone fairway bunker, followed by a clunky eight iron that hopped twice in pathetic fashion and dribbled onto the green, and a solid, two-putt par. This upset me. I had hit a perfect drive and found my ball in a sand divot—one of the few, I must say, on that beautifully groomed course. Because of the awkward lie in the divot, my approach was slightly off, and I was a bit miffed, and three-putted from twenty-five feet for bogey. Two down after two.

"Well, that's something," Rogan said. "Never thought I'd see you three putt from there. Not after everything I've been hearing."

I fumed in silence. Mr. Rogan actually hit a fair tee shot on the par-three third, and walked the length of the fairway complimenting himself on it. "Right on the screws. Right on the screws!" he was telling me. "I was a little cold there after waiting around for you to show up, but that was the way I was hitting them on the practice tee this morning."

"Congratulations," I said, but he completely missed my dry English sarcasm.

He completely missed his birdie putt, too, though so did I. Still two down after three.

On the par-four fourth, there are two bunkers that extend from the right rough into the middle of the fairway. By this point the heat of the Georgia day was upon us in earnest. It was the warmest day we'd had on our earthly adventure, and, as I may have mentioned, I am not a big fan of the warm weather, English genes and all. So I gulped down some water and doused my face and hair, prodded, still, by this persistent malaise.

Mr. Rogan laughed. "A northerner," he said. "I can always tell them. For me, the hotter the better."

"We all have our preferences," I said, but my intimation of trouble was taking clearer shape by then. I felt the hair on the back of my neck rise up.

"You have a pretty stiff way of talking, you know," he said. "You're English, aren't you?"

"I was, yes," I said, unable to meet his eyes. "I am a citizen of this country, now."

"Nah," he scoffed. "You're English. Have a beautiful swing, though, beautiful swing. Going to have to learn to putt, though, if you want to compete with Bunny Rogan."

The cruder and more arrogant Rogan became, the more I resorted to an old British politeness. He was right. I was getting stiff, which made me angry at myself, which affected my swing. I was also becoming more and more certain of who Victor "Bunny" Rogan actually was and, let me admit this honestly, it made me afraid of him. And fear—in golf as in life—summons trouble. I pushed my tee shot right, and ended up in one of the two fairway bunkers there, with a horrible lie, close up against the lip. Rogan hit a modest drive that stayed in the short grass. As we were walking toward our balls, he said, in a half-whisper that would have been appropriate for some kind of library-stacks lecher: "I know who you are!"

And *I know who you are!* I wanted to reply, but the fear had me by the intestines then, and all I could manage was a too polite "Pardon?"

He smiled, winked, walked to his ball, and hit a beautiful eight iron onto the green. My lie in the bunker was so poor that I had no option but to blast out. I then pulled my wedge shot a few yards left, and found another bunker. I blasted out again and nearly holed the shot, but Rogan sank his birdie putt and I was three down after four, a disastrous start.

We both parred the dogleg left, par-five fifth, and the dogleg right par-four sixth, so I remained three down after six and could start to hear that awful ticking clock that you feel in match play. There were twelve holes left; I had to win three of them and halve the other nine, simply to force a play-off.

On the tee of the 150-yard seventh, Rogan sidled up close to me again and whispered, "I was there at the Western Pennsylvania Open."

"What? What on earth are you talking about?"

He smiled that wicked smile of his and then held his

eight iron as if it were a putter and pantomimed a man with the yips. He even lifted his eyes heavenward and put a hand to his forehead, which was the way I'd reacted after missing that first putt. He then proceeded to announce the date, month, and year of the particular Western Pennsylvania Open that had marked the low point of my previous life on earth.

"But that was thirty years ago," I said. I had recovered some of my nerve by that point. "You must have been, what, seven or eight years old?"

"So you know the tournament I'm speaking of, sir."

"Of course I do."

"And you admit to having been there, to having failed in front of a crowd of friends and well-wishers?"

I stared at him a moment. "That was the past. This is now. It's not going to happen again."

He readjusted his yellow cap and laughed a truly horrible laugh that echoed out over the Legends course. "I'm up, I believe," he said. "Have you won a hole yet?"

I hadn't, of course. I knew that. I was shaking with anger. Hearing a rustling in the shrubbery nearby, I turned and saw the face of my good friend Larry Five-Iron. His handsome features were frozen in a mask of fear, the long tips of his mustaches trembling. And I could feel then, inside myself, the accumulated misery and pain and heartbreak, perhaps the protracted death, that he and so many others would have to endure. For an instant then, as our eyes met, I had a clear sense of the whole human condition—our penchant for strife, our awful vulnerability in the face of accident and illness, the difficult passage we referred to as old age, the even more difficult one we called death. Having been so recently in heaven, I had some perspective on it, of course. I knew the deep bonds of love that connected certain spirits through eternity. I knew that all earthly suffering passed, it all eventually passed; I knew what joy awaited the well-intentioned soul, even though that joy would be speckled with challenges of the type I now faced. At the same time, the suffering was excruciatingly real while it was being endured, I knew that, too, and I could see the awful anticipation of it painted there on my good friend's features.

Larry disappeared. Unfortunately, my moment of clarity did nothing for my golf game. Bunny Rogan hit the stick with a perfect eight iron. I played nine off the tee, and completely topped the ball. It was a shot worthy of the clumsiest weekend high-handicapper; it went all of fifty yards. I picked my ball up in the fairway and conceded the hole. Four down. Eleven to play.

I then fell apart completely. Maybe it was the embarrassment of that tee shot, or the look on Larry's face as he peered out through the shrubbery at his future being squeezed to death in my hands, or maybe it was simply Rogan's presence, his insistence that he'd been at the Western Pennsylvania Open, that he'd witnessed—perhaps caused—the missed two-foot putt that extinguished the light of my golfing soul. He seemed to know that I had given up all hope for myself at that moment, turned my back on my own beauty, my own abilities, even, perhaps, my faith in goodness and in the benevolence of God.

I double-bogeyed the eighth, bogeyed the ninth, and when we stopped for a moment's refreshment before starting the back nine I knew the match was over. You don't go to six down on the front side, against a good player, and hope to recover. My only desire at that point was to salvage some shred of self-respect and end up two or three down, a respectable loss, and then to plead with Alicia on Larry's behalf, and on my own.

But then, and this was exceedingly strange, out of the bushes to one side of the tenth tee stepped a filthy young girl, practically in rags. She was dark haired and dark complected, and might have passed for one of the Gypsy children I had encountered in Europe, a war refugee, orphaned by some politician's fear and rage and foolishness. She came straight over to Bunny with her palm up, obviously starving, and he shooed her off instinctively, raised a hand in fact, as if he might strike her. The girl shied away, cowering, then circled around and approached me. On earth, I had always kept a small supply of cash in a pocket of my golf bag, some crackers there, a candy bar. It was my little emergency stash. Out of some old habit, I reached into that pocket and, sure enough, there was my small bankroll, a candy bar that looked reasonably fresh, a package of crackers. I handed everything over to the urchin—money and food both—and she raced away, barefoot, into the steamy Georgia afternoon.

"That was stupid," Rogan chastised me. "She'll go

home and tell her friends, and the next time I play here the place will be crawling with beggars. Easy for you. You'll move on, but those of us who are members here will have to live with the consequences. You didn't help her, in any case. She ought to be in school, or out looking for paying work, the way my great-grandparents did when they first came to this country. No one gave *them* money and food. You're going to make a professional beggar out of her, you know that, don't you?"

I didn't answer. Rogan fumed and muttered. I held to my silence.

Something changed after that, something in the air, or in my hands, or in the golf ball itself. I won the tenth hole. Five down now.

I won the eleventh, as well.

We halved the par-three twelfth, but I could sense a difference in Rogan's posture. He was four up with five to play. All he had to do was halve two holes and the match was over, and yet, a thread of doubt had crept into his voice, into the way he held himself, the way he moved, the way he swung the club.

I won the thirteenth, chipped in to win the fourteenth, sank a forty-five-foot birdie par to win the fifteenth. One down with three to play. It was anyone's match, and he knew it. We both hit long irons off the tee, laying up short of the cluster of fairway bunkers on the short par four. Rogan was away and hit first, dropping a wedge four feet shy of the hole. I hit wedge, also, a foot outside his ball.

As we walked up and set our bags down near the green, he said, "The stakes of this match aren't what you were told; you know that, I hope."

"Know what?"

"It's all an enormous practical joke. You're being made a fool of. Five Iron is one of the great practical jokers around here, and I'm sure he told you he has his life savings or something riding on you, but it's all a flimflam. We're meeting him after the match for a nice lunch in the clubhouse. We'll all have a good laugh over it at your expense."

"Really?"

"Sure. What did you think?"

"I was told we were playing for your membership here. If you win, you can bring in a friend, no initiation fee. I win and you're out. Never play Château Élan again, except the public courses. They'll never let you back here. Never."

"Never is kind of a strong concept," he said. "How about a little side bet?"

I was proud of myself for having come back from so far behind. He sensed that, of course. "All right," I said, foolishly. "What's on your mind?"

He pretended to think for a moment. "Well, let's make it mean something. How about . . . how about, you lose and I go home with your pretty young wife?" His lecherous cackle echoed over the hot Georgia hills.

"If I were a younger man, that suggestion would have earned you a broken jaw."

He laughed even more loudly. "Now, now, Herman, let's keep our sense of humor, shall we? I'm not inciting you to violence or anything, am I? No offense intended, of course. How about this, then? If I win—or if we tie—you promise to go out on the town with me tonight instead of going straight home to her." He winked. "I'll be your guide to the less-than-decent pleasures of the southern night. What say you?"

I declined.

"One night. Come on. You have all the time in the world to be with her. And I could use a friend these days."

I shook my head. He kept prodding me, poking fun at my rectitude, wheedling, trying to convince me. I said, finally: "Stop it. We have our bet. Let's play out the match."

He sulked. We examined our situation on the green.

Rogan said, "This is about the length of putt you had at the Western Pennsylvania Open, isn't it?"

Those three words had the usual effect on me. I could feel them bouncing around like a barbed ball in my intestines. I could feel the echoing shame. I could see the looks on friends' faces afterward, feel the change in Anna Lisa's touch. I cleaned and reset my ball on the putting surface, then crouched down and spent a very long time looking for the line to the hole. Rogan cleared his throat. I ignored him. Not only was it the same length putt as I'd had at the Western Pennsylvania Open, it was the same putt! Precisely. Just enough left-to-right break in it so that I had to start it outside the hole and trust that the slope of the green would move it back in. I thought of the advice I had given God when He'd been having trouble with the yips those first two rounds. I thought of things I'd said to Alicia. None of it could stop the subtle shaking of my hands. Rogan mumbled something about a time limit. I looked up, past the hole, and saw a sort of shimmering light there, then I stood over my ball and just made my pendulum stroke in the direction of that light. I didn't even look, just listened, and at last heard that wonderful tapping-knocking-rattling of a golf ball falling into a plastic cup.

Just as Bunny stood over his putt, I almost said, "That's good." I could feel the charitable urge rise up in me. He would think me a good sport; I would think that of myself. I opened my mouth to speak, and then it was as if Alicia's hand were there again, as it had been the night before, fingers touching my lips. Rogan looked up at me. He said, "Did you say this was good?"

I shook my head.

He bent over the putt again, made a nice stroke. The ball rolled beautifully end over end but at the very last instant it veered left, caught the lip of the hole, dipped partway down in, and then popped up and out again. He looked up, fire in his eyes. "You didn't say that was good?" he demanded.

I shook my head again. "It's good now, though."

All square.

Both of us bogeyed the long and difficult seventeenth. On the eighteenth we each striped beautiful drives center fairway. Bunny had 140 yards in; I was slightly closer. I could feel the pulse slamming in my throat. He selected his club—nine iron, it looked like—but before he addressed the ball I was overcome by a moment of foolishness, of absolutely idiotic softheartedness. I said, "Bunny, excuse me. How would you feel about calling the match right here. We've both played fairly well—you on the front nine, me on the back. We're even. We could shake hands and walk away with no hard feelings. The wager—whatever it actually is—would be cancelled. What do you think?"

He looked at me for a long moment, then the wicked smile touched the corners of his lips. He took a step in my direction, and I thought he was getting ready to extend his hand, but instead he let out these awful words, in a hoarse, terrifying whisper: "You're afraid of losing!"

"No, not really. I've won six of the last eight holes. I'm just—"

"You're terrified of losing to someone like me. You feel superior to me. I could sense it the moment you stepped onto the practice tee. You can barely lower yourself to play against me. True, isn't it?"

"Not at all. In fact, I—"

"You have friends in high places, friends who consider themselves 'good people,' as if such a concept existed. Listen, pal, no one's a good person, okay? So you gave a few dollars to a dirty little kid, so what? The kid will give it to her mother to buy crack with. That's how it works, see."

I had no idea what "crack" might be.

"We're playing the match out as agreed because I'm not afraid of losing, and because I don't pretend to be good, and because I'm about to give you a lesson now, in what happens to people who go through life believing they're standing up on some high shimmering hill helping others, okay?"

Somehow, during that little speech of his, I should have been frightened, but, honestly, I was not. Goodness, true goodness, has an enormous power to it, and if I was not exactly the paragon of goodness, well then I had close friends who were. It seemed to me, during this angry little speech, that Bunny Rogan lost his power over me. "Certainly," I said. "Fine. The match is still on."

Rogan took a couple of breaths. He stood up to his ball and struck it well, very well, too well in fact. The anger in him, the adrenaline, added four or five yards to the shot; he flew the putting surface and ended up in the thick rough beyond. I hit a wedge to the middle of the green, fifteen feet from the pin. We went through the rest of the ritual in silence. Bunny chipped up close. I missed my putt and tapped in, leaving him with a two-and-a-half-footer for the tie. He strode up confidently to his putt, hesitated a moment, thinking, perhaps, again, that I might give it to him. I was not even tempted this time. He hesitated another moment, looked at the hole, drew the blade back, and . . . much as I had done many years before at a crucial moment, yanked the putt left.

He refused, of course, to shake my hand afterward,

and stormed off into the shimmering Georgia afternoon muttering a string of foul curses.

If our match had been written up in the eternal records, it might have looked like this: FINS-WINSTON DEF. PRINCE OF DARKNESS, I-UP.

TWENTY-FIVE

On the way north from Château Élan, through the pretty hills of north Georgia and into Tennessee, Alicia sat very still. She said little. I had pleased Her on the Legends course, lived up to Her highest expectations of me, I knew that. The strange thing was, however, that pleasing Her didn't matter so much to me then. I had saved my father spirit some trouble, conquered my own private demons, and helped remove some small measure of suffering from history. There was a deep satisfaction to that, naturally, but I was drained from the emotions of the match, and stuffed full from the gigantic celebratory lunch Larry Five Iron had presided over in the Versailles Room. I was feeling another few years younger, but tired in spite of that, and just a bit worried because the last thing Larry had said to me, through the Cadillac's open window was, "She loves you, pal. All these years and she still loves you." And I did not have to ask who he was talking about.

Alicia insisted we drive through the night without stopping, and I made no protest. It wasn't as if I had considered disobeying my Lord; it was more that I had stopped feeling I had to prove to Her how good I was, how dependable, how willing. And there was such a wonderful freedom in that. No urge to do evil, none in the slightest. Only the sense that I would do good naturally, effortlessly, without feeling observed. I knew it as surely as I knew that, on any given day, I could beat anyone on the planet at the game of golf.

We stopped for a light meal of biscuits and gravy and iced tea (God absolutely adores southern food), then drove on. "Follow signs for West Virginia," She said. "Last stop for us."

Last stop for us. I no longer even worried about that. With the defeat of Rogan, the Prince of Mockery, I had, it seemed, put to rest my past troubles and come to inhabit the present, without expectations, just as Alicia had been advising me to do all along. I enjoyed the sound of the tires against the pavement, the sight of the WELCOME TO WEST VIRGINIA sign, the names of passing towns: Whitefish, Bluefields, Crawston Notch. Alicia slept. From time to time I glanced over at Her, and it was almost enough just to gaze upon Her. Almost.

This time, I knew where we were headed. Any great tour of the luxury golf resorts of this part of America would have to culminate with a place called the Greenbrier. The great Sam Snead had been resident pro at the Greenbrier in my lifetime, and, though I'd never played there, the name was synonymous with the highest levels of American golfing luxury. From my place in heaven, I'd watched a Ryder Cup played there one year, and it had sparked a burst of envy in me. I wondered, as we pulled through the gates just at dawn and drove up a long driveway toward a huge, colonnaded hotel that looked like an architect's early version of the White House, if that envy had been part of the impulse that had brought me back to earth.

We were met by a kindly woman named Lynn Swann, another friend of God's. Lynn gave us a marvelous two-bedroom suite on the second floor of the main building, and Alicia and I collapsed in our respective beds without even unpacking. During that morning nap I dreamed another strange dream. I dreamed of the unwashed urchin who had mysteriously appeared at the turn during my match with Bunny Rogan. In the dream she was traveling from one fancy golf resort to the next, stepping through the bushes with her hand out, walking up to golfers with five-hundred-dollar drivers in their bags, and asking for something to eat. I floated nearby, watching their various responses.

I awoke in what must be one of the most luxurious, most wonderful places on earth. A warm sun beamed in through the curtained windows, basting the room with its magnificent light. The bed was high up off the carpet, the mattress thick and firm, the blanket and light quilt made of the finest material. The wallpaper showed a floral pattern, lots of yellows, oranges, and whites, and the bathroom was tiled, immaculate, the perfect combination of old-style porcelain and brass fixtures, and the colors of the modern era. I stood a long time in the shower, shaved carefully, dressed in my finest creased beige chinos and a brown and white patterned golf jersey, and saw, in the mirror, that I was the man I had always wanted to be: in better condition than I had ever been on earth, nicer looking, strong, confident without being arrogant. A person who no longer needed to check himself constantly in the mirror. I was tanned, trim, youthful, not the pale and tentative Herman Fins-Winston of old.

As we had agreed, Alicia and I met downstairs in the formal dining room. She was nursing a coffee and had obviously been there for some time, but on Her face I could see the same shine of happiness I felt. "Did you sleep well?" She inquired.

"Exquisitely."

"Look at this menu, darling."

Darling now. I had graduated from "honey" to "darling."

The menu must have had fifty different items on it. Fresh-squeezed juices, eggs in every manifestation—omelets of your choosing, Benedict, hollandaise, with corned beef hash, with homemade sausages, bacon, West Virginia honey-smoked ham. Waffles, pancakes, blueberry pancakes, strawberry pancakes, French toast. Biscuits, croissants, sweet pecan rolls, scones. Lox, finnan haddie, steak, oatmeal, yogurt, fresh fruit and berries. For a while, I just looked at it. The waitress came by twice to take my order, but I was under a kind of spell. The abundance, the glorious abundance. How did one go about sharing such wealth?

At last I settled for fresh-squeezed grapefruit juice, an onion-and-pepper omelet, pecan rolls, and coffee. Alicia had the finnan haddie.

"You've stopped asking about the future," She said.

I nodded, mouth full.

"You've stopped asking how the world is set up, and what is to become of you."

I swallowed, took a sip of the delicious coffee, and met Her blazing eyes. "I feel at peace," I told Her.

"Totally? Utterly?"

"Nearly utterly."

She laughed such a sweet laugh that the elderly couple at the next table looked over and smiled.

We didn't talk about golf during that meal, and didn't play a round afterward, or hit balls or practice putting. It was a day to be lazy. Alicia went down to the spa for some kind of treatment—I didn't inquire. And I strolled the grounds, sipping once from the awful-tasting sulfur springs, watching the children of the children of the children of American wealth romp and shout in the play area, then making my way through the gleaming tile corridors of the main building with its nooks and crannies, its side rooms for chess, checkers, and bridge, the downstairs shops. Presidents, kings, princesses had walked these floors. And now God and me.

I was, in fact, at peace. Almost utterly. Almost perfectly. The one tiny speck of confusion on my interior landscape had to do with the difficult subject I mentioned earlier. I was in my thirties by that point, and healthy as a stallion. Alicia was about that age, too, and so stunningly beautiful that both men and women stared at Her as She passed. It seemed to me that I was in favor with the Powers That Are, and then it seemed to me that, since I was in such good favor, there was nothing I could possibly do to fall out of favor. What harm could come of sharing some physical pleasure with the humanlike woman who was accompanying me? Wasn't it, in fact, a sharing, an urge toward divine union? Wasn't lovemaking the heart of the creative impulse, the source of life, of beauty?

Ah, the logic of lust.

But lust it was. I did my best to disguise it, but of course She knew. On that first evening at the Greenbrier we went out together on a horse-drawn carriage ride, at dusk, the route taking us on a gravel track that ran along the fairways of one of the resort's three fine courses. Alicia took my hand, squeezed my fingers, turned to me as if She expected to be kissed. I leaned toward Her, watching Her face, then kissed Her, kissed Our Lord. One brief, magical, heavenly kiss.

When our lips separated She seemed happy and I knew I had done the right thing. Full of confidence then, I said what I had kept myself from saying for a couple of weeks: "I want to make love with you, Lord."

"I know that."

"I've worried that it might be improper to say so. I've wanted it for a while now."

"I know that, too."

She was squeezing my hand like a fiancée might, gazing into my eyes. It is embarrassing now to admit how thoroughly I misinterpreted Her every word and gesture during these moments, but I will present it all here without the benefit of hindsight, exactly as it transpired.

"Tell me it's not impossible," I said.

The horses' hooves were clomping in a delightful rhythm, the West Virginia night settling sweetly down around us. I was sure I would remember that moment for all eternity.

She smiled a small, sad smile. "The physical act of sex can be a beautiful thing."

"Absolutely," I said. It seemed to me then, in my addled state, that She was saying She'd missed it, that being the Lord, nice as it was, didn't allow the time or privacy for a healthy and satisfying sexual life . . . for any sexual life at all. In my eagerness and ignorance I was ready, of course, to offer my assistance in this matter.

"Of all the pleasures I created to ease the difficulty of a human life, sex may very well be the most sublime."

"I think it surely must be," I agreed.

She looked at me then with such love and tenderness that I find myself unable to properly describe it. There was a kind of limitless empathy in that look, an immense patience. She said, "With one exception."

It took me a second or two before I decided—I see now how wrong I was—that She was making a joke. A lover's teasing joke. I played along. "Golf, You mean?"

Another small, sad smile. More of the immensely patient and loving eye contact. And then . . . a small shake of the head.

I became confused.

"Lovemaking is wonderful," She said. "I've set it up so that life is created from that exquisite pleasure—a good system, don't you agree?"

"Perfect," I managed. "Great. A great, perfect system."

"But at a certain stage there comes a point where the soul must turn its back on that exquisite pleasure and move on to a greater one."

"There is a greater pleasure?" I fairly squeaked. "Than lovemaking?" I felt the joy of the sweet night starting to slip through my fingers. I began to entertain the possibility that, somewhere in the course of the conversation, I had, as we used to say, misread the signals.

She did not take Her eyes off my eyes. "I think you know that now, Hank," She said.

"I do?"

God nodded.

I did know it. Of course I knew it. But I was as flustered then as any young fool at the end of his first date. It began to seem possible, just possible, that we weren't going to make love after all, and my ego received that information like a blow to the midsection.

"Take the next step with me, Hank," She went on. "You have the opportunity for something rare here. Enlightenment, some call it. Union with God. Self-transcendence. Next to that, the joy of sex is like . . . playing a perfectly nice municipal course when you could be playing St. Andrews. Do you follow?"

"I . . . I think—"

She had put Her hand on my wrist and turned Her eyes out to the fairways we were passing. "Do you see this course?"

"I haven't been focusing."

She laughed.

"This is the Old White, designed by Charles Blair Macdonald, a good friend. This is the perfect golf course. The finest course on earth."

"But how could that be?"

"It simply is. Not as flashy as some of the more famous ones. Not as long, certainly, or as difficult. If I remember correctly it is 6,652 yards from the back tees. But it is perfect. We can't see it clearly enough now, but when you play it tomorrow, if you pay attention, if you are as spiritually developed and as free of negativity as I believe you to be, then you'll sense it as you play. It moves in absolute harmony with the surrounding countryside, and it has thousands of little details that make the game more interesting—subtle breaks in the greens, slight bumps and swales in the fairways, small movements left to right and right to left. I have another good friend here, Robert Harris, director of golf. He took over from—"

"The great Sam Snead," I said.

"Yes, the great Sam Snead. Robert is going to set you up with a nice, quiet tee time so you'll have no one in front of you and no one behind."

"Not another match with the devil, I hope."

"Nothing like that. A solitary round of golf. With one important dimension: If you shoot even par or better, we'll have that experience of union we were just speaking of. Tomorrow night."

"But Lord . . . Alicia . . . I'm confused. I mean, are we actually going to—"

"If you shoot even par or better, we'll have that experience," She repeated, more sternly now.

"Why does it always have to be conditional? Why can't it just be . . ." I hesitated.

"Love?"

"Yes, love, or friendship."

"The love is there," She said. "It will always be there. Would you like me to spell it out for you?"

"Yes, spell it out for me."

"I love you, Herman Fins-Winston. With an unwavering, deep, and selfless love you cannot begin to imagine or comprehend. A love that nothing could ever sully or extinguish."

"But not only me. You love everyone that way."

"Of course. Everyone and everything. In every dimension. Every animal and insect and stone and every atom in every droplet of poison. You must know that by now."

"I do."

"You wouldn't have it any other way, would you? I

mean, you wouldn't really want God to single you out for some special love at the expense of the remainder of Her creation, would you?"

"No, of course not. Not really, no."

She smiled radiantly. "Except for tomorrow night. Tomorrow there will be no one else there with us. . . . If you master the Old White."

"Well, thank God for that," I said. But I was afraid, not quite sure what She had and had not promised. I was adrift, I see now, somewhere between the last shore of the human realm and a boundless, joyous, terrifying sea of holy possibility. But I did not see that then.

As the horses drew up to the front of the mansion, She said, through that beautiful smile, "The Old White is a par seventy."

TWENTY-SIX

I can tell you that I did not sleep very well that night, in my luxurious Greenbrier bed, after my luxurious Greenbrier dinner. I tossed and wriggled, flashes of vague dreams tugging me this way and that, into and out of the various mind realms of creation. I woke very early, parted the curtains, and looked out at a bright West Virginia day. I showered and shaved, dressed in my lucky black-striped white golf jersey and chocolate brown trousers, tapped on the door to Alicia's bedroom. There was no answer.

I made my way down the carpeted stairs and through the grand ballrooms to the dining room, but She was not there either, so I took a table and worked my way through a huge breakfast of pancakes with real maple syrup, a bowl of fresh fruit, two pecan rolls, two cups of decaffeinated coffee, two glasses of water. I waited for God to come and sit beside me.

While I waited I looked around at the families there. All of them, I knew, were affluent, perhaps even tremendously wealthy, and each was surrounded by a sort of balloon of quiet poise. You could see fine breeding printed on their gestures, you could read it in the casual sparkle of the jewelry on the women, in the bearing and tailoring of the men, the way the children were rambunctious, but only within certain boundaries, as if they knew that a life of privilege and high duty awaited them. Probably, many of these families had been coming here for generations. Probably there were family legends about a particular week, anniversary, or birthday celebration at the Greenbrier. Perhaps they had a nickname for the place, favorite rooms, favorite golf or tennis partners who traveled in the same circles as they did.

In the interest of full disclosure, I probably should confess that, during my most recent life on earth, I'd had a sort of disdain for the very wealthy. I'd rubbed shoulders with enough of them at my club to be put off by their sense of superiority, their fussiness, their lack of simple appreciation for things others can merely dream of. But on that morning, basking in my newfound peace, I saw how wrong I had been. Strangely, the Greenbrier did not have a snobby feel to it—maybe it was the abundance of children that made such an atmosphere possible; maybe it was the fact that the waiters and waitresses were treated respectfully; maybe the people on vacation there had nothing left to prove in the wealth and status department, and that took some of the edge off. I don't know. But I saw, at last, that in the grand scheme of things, the very wealthy are very wealthy only for a very short period of time. They grow old, suffer from family problems, anxieties, illness, and death, just like anyone else. It sounds trite, perhaps. But on that morning I felt I more fully understood the vast complexity of creation, and seeing my terrible old prejudices in the clear light of that, I vowed to abandon them.

After my enormous morning meal, and after I'd lingered over my third cup of coffee in the vain hope that Alicia would join me, I went out onto the Greenbrier's manicured grounds and strolled around, watching the children at play, watching an elderly couple, arm in arm, as they crossed the main lawn toward their cabin. The man was wearing a sport coat and tie, the woman had her hair held up neatly in a bun at the back of her head, and there was something marvelous in the way they walked with each other. I believed I could actually see that the barrier between them had broken down, after decades of honest arguing perhaps, and that they were almost one soul.

That feeling was exactly what I longed for with God.

Half an hour of this kind of musing and wandering and I walked down past the tennis courts to the golf shop, stood at the counter there, waiting my turn, then asked for Robert Harris. I was soon greeted by a trim, good-looking man who took me into his small back office and offered a chair. Not surprisingly, the walls were covered with Sam Snead memorabilia — pictures, old scorecards, autographed programs. "Alicia is a great friend of ours, and a great friend of Mr. Snead's," Robert said. "He's visiting today, you know."

I said I hadn't heard.

"I'll arrange for you and Alicia to say hello to him. But, in the meantime, she tells me you'd like to play a quiet round on the Old White."

"If it's not a lot of trouble."

"No trouble at all," he said. "But she tells me you're quite the golfer, and I was wondering if you'd like to play the Greenbrier course instead. We had a Ryder Cup there recently. It's about the same length, but much tougher. Might be more suitable for someone of your skills."

"I'd really like to play Old White, thanks."

He smiled some kind of a smile I could not read, called in his assistant, and set me up with a tee time, shook my hand, wished me well. As we were heading back out to the shop, I had the sudden urge to ask him for advice, I didn't know why. Chances are that I was a much better golfer than Mr. Harris, but I was overcome by a moment of humility.

Well-known teacher that he was, he seemed pleased to be consulted. "Let's go down to the range and I'll watch you stroke a few," he said.

The Greenbrier's practice range is a beautiful one, with

greens and flags and bunkers at various distances and pyramids of perfectly clean practice balls set up on every tee. Under Robert Harris's watchful gaze, I loosened up with some wedges, then worked my way through the bag until I was blasting drivers that sailed over the far end of the range and into the trees there. Robert stood by quietly until I was finished. "Not much I can say," he told me, as we were strolling back toward the golf shop. "You have an almost perfect swing. If anything, you stand a little bit long over the ball. Almost looks like you still doubt yourself from the days when you might not have been this good. Just have faith. Just stand up there, know how proficient you are, make your swing, and you'll be fine."

I thanked him. He escorted me personally to the Old White's first tee, a raised tee looking out over a creek to the fairway of a 449-yard par four. We shook hands. He went back to work, and I stood there, alone except for the starter, staring out at the folded green mountains and the just mowed fairway, diamonds of darker and lighter grass there. Heaven.

It was then that a fit of nervousness descended on me like a sudden thunderstorm in the middle of a hot Pennsylvania afternoon. I believed I was about to enter the last stage of my "great test." I wasn't quite sure, but it seemed I was about to play a round of golf for the chance of making love with a spectacularly beautiful woman, God Herself. There was something exciting about it, in the way that sin can be exciting, as if I were transgressing some mysterious moral boundary. I wondered, as I put my tee into the ground, if Adam and Eve might have felt this way when they disobeyed God. Oh, the power of it, the pleasure, the thought of actually being, if only for a while, God's equal.

I smashed a heavenly drive so far down the middle of the fairway that the starter, a heavyset fellow with a yellow golf hat pushed back on his balding head, let out a gasp.

When I walked to my ball I saw that it was sitting perfectly on a perfect fairway, dead center, 111 yards from the green. I hit my sand wedge to six feet and made the putt.

On the second, a straightforward par four, I made birdie again. On the long, par-three third I made par.

As is the case at Augusta National, all the holes on the Old White have names. First. Creekside. Dip. Racetrack, and so on. The sixth, Lookout, offers a picturesque view down a long West Virginia valley, and I could see then why Alicia said it was the most perfect golf course on earth. There was something about the way the holes made a sort of echo against the surrounding Allegheny Mountains, a kind of song being played back and forth between them, as if the architect of this dream had been imbued with some larger-than-human perspective.

By the time I finished playing the ninth, Punchbowl, I was three under par, and the pulse was slamming in my chest and hands as if I were playing for the green jacket. I was marking my scorecard in careful numbers. I envisioned myself presenting it to Alicia at dinner that evening, saw us finishing our expensive bottle of wine and walking arm in arm up to the room, even imagined Her loosening the straps of Her expensive dress. . . . and then I was remindeed of our conversation in the horse-drawn carriage. I took several deep breaths. I struggled to do what every spiritual apprentice tries to do: push out beyond the constraints and habits of an old, imperfect self.

I tried to keep my mind in the present, on golf, but these selfish visions kept crowding in.

And so I bogeyed the tenth and eleventh. One under par now with seven to play. I parred Long, Alps, and Cape without too much trouble, and stood on the tee of the fifteenth hole shaking with anticipation. You may choose not to believe this, but the fact is that the fifteenth hole of the Old White course at the Greenbrier resort is called Eden. It is a 220-yard par three cut by a wide river, with a fine iron bridge and gorgeous stonework in the retaining walls on the riverbanks. I hit a four iron high and straight; it bounced to the back edge, thirty feet from the pin. From there, I ran my lag putt to three feet, but then I must have let the nervousness get the better of me, or been distracted by more thoughts of Alicia's beautiful body. I pushed the ball just slightly, it caught the edge of the cup, made one circumnavigation of the hole, and popped back out onto the grass. Bogey. Even par. No room for error now.

To complicate matters, I had by that point caught up to a pair of golfers in front of me, two women. They weren't playing badly from what I could tell, but I was a single,

and playing even par golf, so I'd closed the distance between us quite easily. Usually, it wouldn't have been a
problem. I don't mind being held up a bit now and again;
that's just part of the game. But on that day I was in a
good rhythm, and my margin of error had become razor
thin, and I'd been promised, by God Herself, that this
kind of thing wouldn't happen.

The sixteenth is a 417-yard par four called Narrows
with a tee shot over a pond to a narrow fairway. The
women were off their forward tee by the time I arrived at
mine, one of them just beyond the water, walking toward
an errant drive in the right rough. I assumed I'd have to
wait for her to reach her ball and hit, but she and her
partner seemed to sense I was there, and before reaching
their balls, they turned and waved me on.

I took an extra breath and swung, and my drive split
the fairway. Two and a half holes to play now, and all I
had to do was par my way in.

In order to reach my ball, I had to walk past the
women. One of them was on the fairway, so I thanked her
as I went by and she smiled and said, "Enjoy the day."
The second woman was over in the right rough by that
point, probably forty yards from me. When I turned to
thank her I saw, with a sense of shock, that she bore a
striking resemblance to my former wife, Anna Lisa. The
resemblance was in her posture, in the way she turned her
face to me, lifting a lock of hair aside with the backs of
her fingers. It couldn't be, I thought at first. My dear
friend Juanita had assured me that Anna Lisa was up in

heaven. But then I remembered that I had been up in heaven, too, and here I was, walking the sixteenth hole of the Old White, human again.

For a moment I stood there, paralyzed by memories of our marriage, the strong physical attraction we'd always had, the pleasure of the early years when it seemed we would have done anything to make the other happy, and then the slow souring, the nasty fights, the final, agonizing decision to part. All this came over me like a cold ocean wave, and for a moment I stood there just trying to hold my ground in the thunder and rush. No one, I think, goes through the trauma of divorce without a deep feeling of sadness. There might be relief mixed in. There might be a sense of freedom, of erasing a terrible mistake. But there is often a lasting anger, and almost always sadness, and Anna Lisa and I were no exceptions to that rule.

When the first shock passed, I was acutely aware of having this thought: She's going to spoil it for me again, and just as I'm about to be happy, really happy. Just as I'm about to become the man I know I can be. But then the woman who looked so much like Anna Lisa raised an arm. It was just a little wave, held, perhaps, for a second more than would have been expected, but in some old, secret language of our marriage it said: Forgive me, Hank. I'm sorry. Good luck.

I hesitated only an instant, then waved back. Sorry here, too, my raised arm said. I'll see you.

I felt a sense of peace. So much peace, in fact, that I pulled my approach shot five yards right of the greenside bunker, then chipped on and three-putted for a double bogey.

I could feel a sort of smoke blowing across in front of me as I walked to the next tee, an acrid, wispy despair. But I am proud to say that, on the 514-yard Oaks, like a real champion, I made birdie.

So I stood on the tee of the eighteenth, 162 yards, straight over two bunkers and a stream, needing a birdie to shoot even par. An odd sense of déjà vu assailed me as I planted my tee in the earth. Hadn't I had this very shot before? No, couldn't be. But hadn't I been here, or near here, once before, and hadn't I made some kind of subtle interior choice? Anger over forgiveness. Bitterness over success? Despair over hope? Hadn't Alicia told me that something had happened in West Virginia, a few weeks before my grand Pennsylvania failure. I saw Anna Lisa waving at me. I remembered Robert Harris's advice. I seemed to flash back across all the time I'd spent with God, all the advice I'd heard, all the stern encouragement. It seemed then as though the shell of all my old assumptions split open. I felt some larger, better self breaking out into the air. I set my ball on the tee, addressed it, made my swing, without doubt, without hesitation, and the round white creature flew off my seven iron and up, up, arcing into the sunlight, pausing there, and then dropping like a hawk to its prey, just missing the top of the flagstick and stopping near the back edge of the green, leaving me an eleven-foot downhill putt for birdie, even par, and the fulfillment of my deepest dream.

What a long walk that was! It seemed to me, as I carried my bag along the fairway and across the small bridge, that I was replaying all of my lives—the passions and errors, the fears and dreams, the stupidities and kindnesses. All of this seemed to flash past in a sort of new silent language. I understood then that each soul has an energy pattern governing it. Some people are drawn to people, life after life. They take their spiritual nourishment from the social realm—from friends and family, public service, the allure of the crowd. Some are drawn to evil, or to the repeated seeking of solace in bursts of illicit pleasure: drink, drugs, sexual adventures. Some labor in the artistic arena—painters, dancers, sculptors, poets—and, life after life, work out their particular interior dramas via their art.

I saw then, very clearly, that the center of my energy pattern was golf. On some level I had always known this, but my time with Alicia had scraped off the last layers of delusion. There was a tremendous sense of freedom in this understanding, because I had always been slightly guilty about playing golf, had always wondered if I should have been doing something, well, more essential. But as I approached my ball on the eighteenth hole of that perfect course, I saw that golf was as essential as anything else. It was my purpose, my destiny, my route to salvation. I also knew, somehow, by some magnificent intuition, that it was my route to an ecstatic union with the Lord.

Upon reaching the green, I did a very strange and risky

thing: I did not even pick my ball up and clean it. I fixed the ballmark, then just took out the flagstick and laid it carefully on the apron. I glanced once at the line of the putt, and then stood over my ball and knocked it firmly into the center of the hole. Seventy strokes. Even par on the Old White. I marked the two on my scorecard with a shaking hand, signed it, dated it, carried my bag calmly back to the pro shop, tipped the attendant there with a twenty-dollar bill . . . and then walked at top speed back toward the main building.

I entered on the lower level, where the fancy shops are, and made my way hurriedly to the staircase. Outside one of the shops, I saw a man standing with two women. One quick glance and I realized it was Sam Snead, past his prime, of course, close to the age I'd been when Alicia first took me to earth. He was standing in that relaxed, confident way he stood, with a certain bemused look on his face. Almost nothing else could have slowed me down on my way to Alicia, but I stopped, introduced myself, shook the great man's large, spotted hand. And then I said: "I just want to thank you for everything you've done," because the man had, in fact, found out who he was supposed to be in this life, and had, in fact, inspired others—myself included—to do the same.

He was kind enough to accept the remark without making me feel like an idiot. "Oh, I just stand back now and watch," he said, and then someone else came up to him, and I smiled and nodded, and turned away.

By the time I reached the bottom of the staircase, Sam

Snead was a distant memory. Hot blood was coursing through my young body. I held the scorecard tightly in my right hand. Instead of walking up the carpeted steps, which was the proper way to behave in a place like the Greenbrier, I sprinted. By then, however, I felt—you will please believe me—that I was merely acting an old and outdated role. Part of me knew perfectly well what was about to happen; part of us always knows. Part of me understood that the golfing test had been used by God in a metaphorical way. I had done what one always has to do to move closer to the Creator: I had shed an old, stale self with all its assumptions and reflexes, broken free of a used-up identity, and was leaping into the abyss that separates us from our truer self.

I sprinted up the first flight, made the corner holding tight to the bend in the railing. Sprinted up the second, all full of my pride and my urges. Just at the top of the steps, just as I reached our floor, I felt a stab of pain near my left shoulder. A little out of shape, I supposed. Or perhaps there were parts of my body that had not yet made the transition into my thirties, the lungs not quite keeping up with the legs, or something like that. I turned down the long, carpeted hallway and saw a porter there, a handsome man with dark skin, wise eyes, and a beautiful smile. He smiled at me warmly, almost as if he knew why I was in such a hurry, and there was a kind of magic and dignity in that smile. Move on, now, he seemed to be saying. Move out into that wider realm. I could see the door of our suite. I was on the point of offering the porter a friendly greeting when the sharp pain struck again, so powerfully this time that it knocked me to my knees. I clutched tight to the scorecard, I remember that. I felt then—how can I phrase this?—I felt the physical touch of God, an ecstatic sense of intimacy that simply cannot be measured against any human experience. I remember the look on the porter's face as he rushed toward me, and then I remember starting to fall forward onto the floor. And then, nothing.

TWENTY-SEVEN

When I regained consciousness—if that is the correct term for the state one is in after the passage from human life into the afterlife—I realized immediately where I was. Heaven smells like lilacs. And I understood immediately, as though I had been splashed with a warm glassful of humility, that there are various layers to paradise—precincts, compartments, realms. How foolish it had been to think otherwise, to believe that my little condo on the thirteenth fairway of El Rancho Obispo somehow included all heavenly possibilities, all of God's majesty, all the facets and foldings of eternal peace.

How can I describe this part of heaven to you? Well,

this is only an approximation, of course, but the place had the feeling of one of those great eighteenth- or nineteenth-century buildings—the lobby of a famous European resort hotel perhaps, or the interior of some Russian palace or Italian courthouse from a glamorous era.

We were somehow indoors and outdoors at the same moment. I say "we" because there was no sense of solitariness here, after my solitary passage through death. The floors around me were made of exquisite marble, some of it pure white and some of it pink, black, brown, or banded with streaks of gold. Enormous columns rose up to either side, though the walls were far away. Here and there were bouquets of flowers, vases as large as an automobile filled with six-foot-tall lilies, tulips, gladioli. Chandeliers hung everywhere, though there was no ceiling for them to hang from, and they were made of brilliant clusters of diamonds, sapphires, and rubies, lit by an invisible source. Then, above this fantastic scene, spread a radiant sky of wide, shimmering rainbows, as if the entire spectrum of light were on display. There were dozens of shades of silver and gold and blue and green and red and scarlet and pumpkin and lemon, and blacks and browns in abundance. There were colors I have no words for. There was a sense of vastness. There was the sense that time was not passing. There was, in the background, beyond the colonnaded walls and the chandeliers and the rainbow sky, an understanding of worlds and worlds, each of them peopled by billions of souls, and filled with plant life, insects, stones, a million different ores, a billion inventions, hundreds of thousands of languages.

Had my brain not been in a particularly calm state, I believe all of this would have overwhelmed me. But there, for those moments, it was all somehow graspable, an impossibly complex symphony of whirling color and form. Life.

And then, as if we were, in fact, in some rococo courtroom, the God of Gods appeared. If my above descriptions of the physical setting were approximations, then probably I should not even try to describe the Being who came upon the scene then. If you have seen the ceiling of the Sistine Chapel, you might use that as a starting point. If you have heard the phrase "God of power and might," that will help. In fact, in that moment, one of the strangest experiences for me was the realization that all the terrible clichés usually applied to God are true: all loving, all powerful, mysterious, terrifying, glorious, wrathful, merciful. All true, all of them.

Imagine my terror then, my awe, my excitement, when I understood that this Being's attention was focused on me. I saw Julian Ever, handsome, elfin, dressed in robes of gold and blood red, approach the God of Gods like some kind of court clerk respectfully approaching a stern but fair judge. I thought I heard him say, "Lord, this is the golfer we spoke about."

I saw, playing within the diaphanous figure of God, images that reminded me of Alicia (I understood by then how impossible it would have been ever to have made love with Her), of the Einstein-God I had first seen on the practice range of Eden Hills, of the Zoe-God I'd seen on the driving range, of Jesus, Mary, Buddha, Moses, Abraham, Muhammad, Krishna's various manifestations, all the Holy Ones. He, or She, or It encompassed them all.

And then this stern face was looking up from the materials Julian Ever had presented, staring at me. At me. I felt tiny as a speck of sand in a huge fairway bunker. I felt divinely addressed.

What happened next was that the magnificent surroundings began to fall apart. The light from the chandeliers dimmed, and the precious stones there seemed to shrink, and then disappeared altogether. From the columns to the marble floors to the vases of lilies and gladioli, it was as if the color and form were slowly leaking out of everything, as if this magnificent hall were undergoing its decay at the rate of a century a second. But *decay* is the wrong word. There was no sense of decay, of rotting. The petals of the lilies did not wither and drop; the chandeliers did not sag; the marble floors did not scuff away to dust. It was more that everything seemed to be composed of molecules of light, and the molecules had temporarily arranged themselves in certain shapes, and now those shapes were swirling back into a pure, shapeless energy.

At the center of this was no longer a figure but what I can only call a Presence. It had, at first, been in the form of a powerful Old Testament God, but now that too had whirled and spun apart and I was facing something awesome and unnameable, without boundaries in terms of size or wisdom or power. No one else was there, only this enormous Presence and my little self, and even my little self was no longer encased in a body. I, too, was some sort of presence, as if what I thought of as "I" was nothing more than material of this Material, light of this Light, a much reduced version of what swirled and glowed in front of me.

There was a definite sense of kinship, and of being addressed, and it was at once soothing and terrifying. I will use words here, as if there were a voice speaking to me, but there was no voice, just a sense that this Presence and I were able to communicate. I felt tiny and helpless, and at the same time a sure part of something grander, perhaps the way a small child feels in its family. Just as the child does within that family, I had a place in the universe, but it was not, I understood at that moment, limited to a man's body in a condominium on the fairways of El Rancho Obispo.

Heaven was very big, God was immense, and He or She or It was addressing me. Lovingly, and yet, there was the sense of being seen through completely with a kind of merciless honesty.

"Fins-Winston," the "voice" said, "what have you to say for yourself?"

I muttered and stuttered and skittered left and right for a few seconds, then managed, "Teach me, Lord."

This seemed somehow to have been a good start. I had the feeling that the Presence was amused, generally pleased with me. There was a pause, something like a sigh, almost a sense of weariness being overcome at the end of a very long labor.

"You understand," God said, "that everything has been a teaching."

"Yes I do, Lord." God remained silent, so I blundered on: "I learned a great deal in the trip to earth, I wanted to thank you, I—"

"Not this one trip to earth, Fins-Winston. Everything. Everything that has happened to you up to this point has been a teaching of one kind or another. Your billions of lives as various insects, your millions of lives in one animal form or another, your thousands of human lives. They have given you a full sense of the earth, all its peoples and species and climates, its immense capacity for death and creation, for mayhem and distraction, for benevolence and courage."

I was a speck in space. All I could bring myself to say was: "Yes, Lord."

"You've had a great curiosity—an enviable and rather rare curiosity—as to the nature of the workings of the universes, and that curiosity, along with your mistakes, your foolishness, your good deeds, has ultimately carried you here, into my presence. Now."

"Yes, Lord."

"We won't get into the millions of years you wasted. We won't get into your selfishness, your envy, your fear and foolishness, your various excesses, and, last but not least, your lust. Suffice it to say that all of that has now finally been left behind; you have lived through all that, and its consequences."

"Thank You, Lord."

"As you no doubt now understand, all your various appetites and drives have led you to Me. Not in a straight route, of course, but ultimately they have led you to Me. This is always the way. From single-cell organism to the most advanced human and beyond, all creatures chase pleasure and flee pain. That chasing after pleasure leads them down one blind road after another, into murder and theft and covetousness and apparently hopeless addiction. Life upon life is used up in such things, and in the pain they bring."

The Lord paused, and it seemed to me a sorrowful pause, brim full of empathy.

"And then," the Presence went on, "then, finally, something shifts. The pain is too great. Understanding dawns, and in the depth of the soul there is the realization that a more profound pleasure is available. One then moves naturally, if very slowly, in the direction of work, generosity, selflessness, love."

"Golf," I said, without knowing I would say it. All censoring mechanisms in me, it appeared, had ceased to function.

The Great Creator laughed, then sighed, rested. I felt the object of an intense contemplation. "Yes, golf," came the sweet words.

So I had been right!

"In your case, at least. And it is your case we are dealing with here. Before we go on, do you have any more questions? Any more of your unquenchable curiosity?"

"No, Lord."

"Any more selfish desires?" the Presence asked, and at that instant it was as if I could feel the shadow of my lust for Alicia there, hovering at the edges of my mind. I felt drawn to it as if to a magnetic field. I saw that I could embrace it, chase after it again, spend another entire life ogling and sleeping with beautiful women. Or let it pass on. I felt Zoe urging me toward something larger than that. I felt an invisible orchestra of angels singing me on toward the next dimension of myself.

I said: "I want to be of service, Lord."

"Excellent!" the Presence thundered, and a feeling of divine approval washed over me like a warm scented bath. "Just right, Fins-Winston! Just right!"

"I love golf," I said, trying to stick with what had worked. "I want to be of service."

"And you shall be. There are still more lessons to learn, a continuous expansion that has to take place through you. You have one more life to live on earth before moving onto another realm where subtler pleasures will draw you farther and farther into your true self, closer and closer to I AM. One more, fine, earthly life."

"Yes, Lord."

"Any objection?"

"No, Lord."

"Any requests?"

"None, Lord."

"Good. You shall now be named."

"Yes, Lord."

Named. I had the clear sense that this naming meant a great deal indeed. And then, that the Lord was shifting and sorting, as if through a billion possibilities.

"I am choosing your parents now," the Presence intoned. "Patience."

"No hurry, Lord."

"Your parents, your time, your place. Your purpose is already written within you in the language of the soul and need not be described. You can act in concert with it and be liberated from the trials of earth, or you can falter, become distracted, fail to do the work, cause suffering to yourself and others, fall back again, and so on. . . . Clear?"

"Clear, Lord."

"Very well, then." The Lord pronounced my new name, and a difficult, unusual name it was.

I couldn't contain myself. "No, Lord!" I shouted. Of all the colors, impressions, and sensations that remained from my millions of earthly incarnations, it seemed that the pain of being Herman Fins-Winston still stuck to me. Even in the presence of God I couldn't pretend otherwise.

"What?"

"Nothing, Lord. Herman Fins-Winston was a fine name, it's just that, in that particular place and time, it . . . well . . . there was some discomfort. And I feel that way about this new name, too. It's unusual. It's. . . . Forgive me. I recant."

Then, strangely, it was as if there was an invisible consultation going on there before me, as if some old friend, my wonderful grandmother, Juanita, Zoe, Anna Lisa, or Larry Five Iron was making an appeal to the great Presence. After a strained silence, I heard this: "There has been an intercession. You shall be allowed a nickname to soften the difficulty. Anything further?"

"No, Lord. Thank You, Lord."

"A marvelous life awaits you then, the life you were designed for eons ago. You will inspire, you will serve, and you will golf. Enough?"

"More than enough, Lord." I thought about the course-designing job that had been promised to me, but decided not to mention it.

"Fine then. I'll say what I say to every soul: Go forth with my blessing, and do the work for which you and only you were created."

There was some type of impossibly wonderful embrace then, a flood of love through me. It was as if the lovemaking with Alicia was finally taking place, but it was something so much larger and more pleasurable than human lovemaking that I'm loathe to compare the two. And then I was drawn past the re-established chandeliers and columns and vases of flowers and down, down, into some faint echo or copy of that divine embrace, two souls uniting on earth, and then deep into the center of the woman who was half of that embrace, another familiar spirit.

And then all consciousness of heaven was reduced to some seedling in the center of me, a buried sweet memory. As the months passed, as I grew out of the happy innocence of childhood, life on earth once again began to seem like the only reality, a reality measured in years and minutes, a linear stream of time; everything else was vague and unlikely, just twinges of awareness amid the busy adventure of life. I took up golf, of course, and began to play very well, but there seemed nothing mystical about that choice and that success. And then, on the night before my twenty-second birthday, I experienced a dream that caused me to remember all that had happened in my previous life and in heaven, all that is written here, from Julian Ever's first visit at Rancho Obispo, to my final Greenbrier round. I awoke from that dream and began to write this story.

I suppose I should tell you, as a sort of epilogue to my tale, that I am not yet quite the great champion Alicia groomed me to be. But the possibility is still alive. I am not allowed to tell you my name, or provide many identifying details, but I can say that I am, in fact, a young star on the PGA tour, and that there are, in fact, people who predict great things for my career. If you follow golf you surely have heard my name. I have some of the grace of Els, the joie de vivre of Michelson, the work ethic of Singh, the courage and determination of Sorenstam, the charitable instincts and will to win of Tiger Woods. And perhaps, just perhaps, some of the skill of Nicklaus and a piece of Arnold Palmer's charisma.

This is most important, though: I don't aspire to be any of them. Great champion or no, what I want now is to be fully and unabashedly myself. I want only to claim my birthright and my destiny as a full human soul who has attained—I say this in all humility—some degree of intimacy with the divine intelligence we refer to as God.

There are, of course, many other people who have been on similar trips with God, men and women in various professions in various parts of the earth—political and business leaders, athletes, musicians, artists—all of them sent to earth on a similar mission. Throughout history there have been souls like this, some famous, some unknown. If you look closely, you can recognize us by our patience and empathy. We work hard, but in good humor. We suffer and enjoy like everyone else, though a part of us stays separate from those highs and lows. We inhabit all sorts of bodies and personalities, but we never lose sight of our secret purpose, and in greater and smaller ways we make our mark on human society, preparing the way for the great champions who are to come.

Read on for a special preview of the first
chapter of Roland Merullo's forthcoming novel,
due in stores in fall 2007.

My name is Otto Ringling (no circus jokes, please), and I have a strange story to tell. On the surface, it is the story of a road trip I took, at the suggestion of my wonderful wife, from our home in the suburbs of New York City to the territory of my youth—Stark County, North Dakota. In fact, it is an account of an interior voyage, the kind of excursion that's hard to talk about without sounding flaky or annoyingly serene, or like someone who thinks the Great Spirit has singled him out to be the mouthpiece of Ultimate Truth. If you knew me you'd know that I am none of the above. I think of myself as Mister Ordinary—pretty good husband, good father, average looking, average height, middle-of-the-road politics, upper half of the middle class. Friends think I'm funny, a little on the wiseass side, a decent, thoughtful, middle-aged man who is not religious in the usual sense of that word. My story here will strike them as strange—I guess I've said that already—but there's nothing I can do about that. I promised myself that I would just tell the truth about the whole trip, right down to the color of the wallpaper in the hotels where I slept and the quality of the food in the restaurants where I ate, and let people believe it or not believe it according to their own convictions.

So, in the spirit of full disclosure let me say this: Before the trip, like a lot of people I know, middle-aged and otherwise, I suffered now and then from a nagging puzzlement about the deeper meaning of things. I functioned well, as the saying goes. My wife and children and I had a comfortable life, really a superbly satisfying life—beautiful house, two new cars, restaurant meals, love, peace, mutual support. And yet, from time to time a gust of puzzlement would blow through the back room of my mind, as if someone had opened a window there and my neatly stacked pages of notes on being human had blown off the desk and out into Long Island Sound.

After returning to New York from the wilds of North Dakota, that changed. I did not start to levitate when my wife wasn't looking. I did not shave my head and turn vegetarian. I did not quit my job and take the family to live in a restored monastery in the Sicilian countryside, or leave Jeannie and the kids and move in with a twenty-two-year-old editorial assistant from the office. But, inside me, something had changed. And so, even though I am a private man, I made the decision—again, at Jeannie's suggestion—to write down what had happened to me during those days on the American road. If nothing else, I thought the story might drop a few laughs into someone's life, which is not a bad thing.

So let me begin here: I am an ordinary, sane American man. Forty-four years young. Senior editor at a well-respected Manhattan publishing house called Stanley and Byrnes, which specializes in books on food. I've been married to the same good woman for almost half my life. We have two teenage children—Natasha is sixteen and a half, Anthony fourteen—an affectionate mixed-breed dog named Jasper, and a house in one of the nicer New York suburbs. Jeannie works, very part-time, as a freelance museum photographer, and very full-time as an attentive mother. It's not a perfect life, needless to say. We have had our share of worry and disappointment, illness and hurt, and, with two teenagers in the house, we sometimes experience a degree of domestic turbulence that sounds, to my ear, like a boiling teakettle of hormones shrieking on a stove. But it is a life Jeannie and I made from scratch, without a lot of money at first, or a lot of help, and we are proud of it, and grateful.

Six months before my trip, a sour new ingredient was dropped into the stew of that good life, into the swirl of dinner parties, arguments over homework, and two-week rentals at the shore in August. My parents, Ronald and Matilda, seventy-two and seventy, were killed in a car crash on a two-lane North Dakota highway called State Route 22. Modest, decent, slightly mixed-up Midwesterners in full possession of their mental faculties and in good health, they were familiar voices on the end of the phone line one day and unavailable the next. Gone. Silent. Untouchable. Hardy farm people with forceful and distinct personalities that were turned to ash and memories by a drunk just my age in a careening blue pickup.

We all went out for the memorial service. (My sister Cecelia, who also lives near New York, took the train; she inherited my mother's fear of air travel.) Tears were shed. There was talk of the old times, good and bad. There was anger at the man—soon to be imprisoned—who killed them. I expected all that. What I did not expect was the persistent feeling of emptiness that came over me in the weeks following my parents' burial.

It was more than bereavement. It was a kind of sawing dissatisfaction that cut back and forth against the fibers of who I believed myself to be. Sometimes even in the sunniest moods I'd be aware of it. Turn your eyes away from the good life for just a second and there it was, not depression as much as an ugly little doubt about everything you had ever done; not confusion as much as a question.

Is this all there is? would be putting the question too crudely, but it was something along those lines. All this striving and aggravation, all these joys and sorrows, all this busy-ness, all this stuff—a hundred thousand headlines, a million conversations, e-mails, meetings, tax returns, warranties, bills, privacy notices, ads for Viagra, calls for donations, election cycles, war in the news every day, trips to the dump with empty wine bottles, fillings and physicals, braces and recitals, Jeannie's moods, my moods, the kids' moods, soccer tournaments, plumber's bills, sitcoms, oil changes, wakes, weddings, watering the flowerbeds—all of this, I started to ask myself, leads exactly where? To a smashed-up Oldsmobile on a country highway? . . . And then what? Paradise?

All right, I'm a fan of the old idea that if you live a decent life you rise up to heaven afterward. I'm not opposed. But sometimes, riding the commuter train home past the tenements of Harlem, or calling Natasha and Anthony away from their IM-ing long enough for the frenzied ritual of a family meal, or just standing around at a friend's birthday party with a glass of pinot noir in one hand, I'd feel this profound ache, as if I were suffering from a strain of existential flu. Just a moment, just a flash, but it would pierce the shiny shell of my life like a sword through a seam in armor.

I'd had similar moments even before my parents' deaths. But after that day — February 3, a frigid North Dakota Tuesday — it was as if a curtain had been lifted and the ordinary chores and pleasures of life were now set against a background of wondering. The purpose, the plan, the deeper meaning — who could I trust to tell me? A therapist? The local minister? A tennis partner who'd lived ten years longer and seen more of the world? Who could I trust to answer the kinds of questions that now had begun to haunt me? I thought about it at night before I went to sleep, and riding the train to work, and watching TV, and talking with my kids, and even, sometimes, just after Jeannie and I had finished making love.

And so, I suppose, such a state of mind left me perfectly primed for my extraordinary adventure. All chopped up on the cutting board, ready to be tossed into the skillet. If I can risk a sweeping observation, it seems to me now that life often works that way: you ask a certain question again and again, in a sincere fashion, and the answer eventually appears. But, in my experience at least, the answer arrives according to its own mysterious celestial timing, and it comes in disguise, and it comes in a way you are not prepared for, or don't want, or don't like, or can't, at first, accept.

Amanda S. Merullo

Roland Merullo, a critically acclaimed novelist and golfing aficionado, is the author of six books, including *Passion for Golf: In Pursuit of the Innermost Game* and the recently published novel *A Little Love Story*. He lives with his wife and daughters in Massachusetts.

Other Titles of Interest from Algonquin Books

Dream Golf: The Making of Bandon Dunes, by Stephen Goodwin

"This is much more than a golf book; it's the story of one man's unshakable vision and the extraordinary people who helped him bring it to life."

— George Peper, former editor in chief of *Golf Magazine*

SPORTS
ISBN-13 978-1-56512-530-8 • ISBN-10 1-56512-530-4

The Beggar King and the Secret of Happiness: A True Story, by Joel ben Izzy

"[*The Beggar King and the Secret of Happiness*] invites readers to see their own lives as stories, overflowing with meaning and never predictable." — *San Francisco Chronicle*

MEMOIR
ISBN-13 978-1-56512-512-4 • ISBN-10 1-56512-512-6

Water for Elephants, a novel by Sara Gruen

"Gritty, sensual and charged with dark secrets involving love, murder and a majestic, mute heroine (Rosie the Elephant)."

— *Parade*

FICTION
ISBN-13 978-1-56512-560-5 • ISBN-10 1-56512-560-6

Responsible Men, a novel by Edward Schwarzschild

"Think Arthur Miller's *Death of a Salesman* or David Mamet's *Glengarry Glen Ross*. Now add to that brief list *Responsible Men*. . . . Eminently readable, frequently hilarious, and always deeply moving." — *Pages* magazine

FICTION
ISBN-13 978-1-56512-543-8 • ISBN-10 1-56512-543-6